A TRIUMPH OF MY SOUL ANTHOLOGY

The Soul of a Man

EDITED BY ELISSA GABRIELLE

ISBN-13: 978-0-9819631-3-6
Library of Congress Control Number: 2009922530

Peace In The Storm Publishing, LLC.
P.O. Box 1152
Pocono Summit, PA 18346

Visit our Web site at www.PeaceInTheStormPublishing.com

PRAISE FOR

THE SOUL OF A MAN

"*The Soul of a Man* is a timely piece of literature that speaks to the very essence of men. Readers are given an insightful and honest look into the soul of some of today's brightest and gifted writers. Over a dozen writers who above all remain men of faith, conviction and substance. A powerful and reflective compilation that is sure to talk to you while inspiration fills your souls. Sure to be a best seller."

~James Michael Lisbon, Publisher,
Awareness Magazine & The Queens Light

"Revelations of His-story, His-trials, His-fears and His-triumphs sums up the essence of this magnificent literary work. Through this candid compilation, *The Soul of A Man,* allows readers a rare insight as to what lurks in the hearts of men of great literary prowess and purpose."

~Dr. Linda F. Beed, author of *Business Unusual*

"*The Soul of A Man* presents an admirable collection of inspirational stories that share the innermost thoughts of real men. These are sincere, candid, and engaging stories about men who dealt with the challenges of life by placing their complete faith in God. Their stories reveal how they used faith to handle the day-to-day struggles, pains, and temptations to show what real manhood is all about."

~Memphis Vaughn, editor *TimBookTu*

"Elissa Gabrielle has done it again! Ms. Gabrielle has put together a collection of short stories that will ignite your soul and this time, they are all written by some very talented men! From the social and political stance of Mr. Alvin C. Romer who takes us to another level with his story "What Lies in the Souls of Men?" To Mr. William Fredrick Cooper who dares to bare his soul as he talks about love and heartbreak with his story "No Regrets." A collection of this magnitude would not be complete without looking at the spiritual journey through the eyes of a man and that man is Mr. Brian Ganges who teaches us about "Manning Up with God." There is something for everyone within these pages. Well done Ms. Gabrielle."

~Jacqueline D. Moore, author of *Serving Justice*

FOREWORD

The soul of a man arrives precisely at the same time as his muscular substance. It is not likely he will have real knowledge of its existence at time of arrival. He will see the food he eats, the water he drinks, and take notice of the sea, sky, and land all about him. He will not see the one thing that he cannot exist without; his soul. He may know that something of great power abides within him. He is cognizant that his very existence totally relies on that something, and in time he becomes very conscious of his soul. He realizes that it will serve as his guide through life and by his belief in God, it will live on long after his mortal self has been returned from which it came, the Earth. Therefore, he must continue to search his soul, to keep it as pure and as clean as possible, knowing it is far more valuable to lose a world, but a man should never lose his soul.

Take a journey into his soul, his mind and his heart. Learn from him and accept his words as only he can deliver them, with truth and vigor, honesty and vitality. Experience his pain, joy, his plight, his deliverance through his story of triumph over adversity. Discover what's really on his mind as he bares his soul.

So, the question remains; What lies in the soul of a man? Love, laughter, heartache and sorrow? Pride, fear, rage and contentment? The true measure of a man lies in his heart and in his soul.

Trials are measured and grounded by inner feelings and the expectations placed on them and they persevere. The weights of the world sometimes are carried on their shoulders.

From socio-economic barriers, to racial tensions, broken hearts, to new found faith-experience the plight of man, as only he can explain it, told from his perspective and from his heart. Through expressions of the history of his past, the reality of his present, and the optimism of his future, these gifted men relate what stirs a man's soul and ignites his actions and his thinking.

Men the world over have always been much maligned and strident in how life portrays and prefaces their successes and failures. This collection of enlightening stories personifies the sentiment, faith, resilience and love embodied in the creation

God made in His own image. *The Soul of a Man* is a Divine truth and an affirmation of the passion running through the minds of men where hearts and souls are bared.

I am very pleased to present to you, *The Soul of a Man*.

Peace and Blessings,

Elissa Gabrielle, Publisher
The Soul of a Man: A Triumph of My Soul Anthology

CONTENTS

What Lies in the Souls of Men?

Alvin C. Romer

Does anyone really care about what men think nowadays, or what really lies deep within our souls? In this day and age, most men that have lived a bit should be at the crossroads of their lives. Living the life and being able to transcend to levels of expectancy may not have been what we lived, give or take a few triumphs here and there. Of course there were the pitfalls, and we talk about them in bedrooms and boardrooms. We've had time to look deep within ourselves to exact some modicum of responsibility for the things that have been at our grasps to control…and if change is indeed indicative of wanting to do what is right, there are quite a few who wouldn't complain. As husbands, fathers, sons, brothers, uncles, nephews, and mentors there are varying degrees of angst still lurking on the periphery that have not proven to be harbingers of good for men in general and Black men specifically, and we have a lot to say about them. Some would argue that the scales have not been equal, and parity is nothing more than a dream. Our conversations continue where voices are open and the volume much too high where truths are not arguable to good intent. Thus, the identification and definition of outward manifestations of inner soulfulness are portrayed in the minds of those that want to make a difference. Is it far-fetched to believe then that accountability should be first and foremost a prerequisite for first impressions? This is uppermost in my mind, and holds the glue to anything cohesive in this essay. Psychologists have analyzed the minds and souls of men for the longest and still there are doubts and intrigue to the psyche of what makes us tick, and why do we do the things we do. Undoubtedly there are collective reports that may be subjective to theories of thought, but what about individuals coming full circle to ask some of the same queries to gauge truth for better understanding, and to dispel any notions of negativism? What we think is important, and I feel that people DO and want to know what we are all about.

So here I am ready to solve a piece of a puzzle that is missing coherence and clarity to some to shed light on this dark passage – understanding men! My good friend and editor of the book you're reading approached me with the query, "what is in the soul of men?" If you think nobody gives a hoot what Black men are thinking, think again. I often wonder myself! Nonetheless, some people would rather open us up and see why we do what we do, especially when there are those that fear us, and would do anything to keep us second class. We are a force – I know this because I'm aware that the corporate world loves us because they can coerce us to buy their products. Politicians have exploited us for years with promises and more promises. Banks coddle us because they want the deposits that fuel their institutional worth. The media, including TV, radio, and now the internet, want you to redefine what role models they want you to emulate…they want you to pay attention to more stereotypical crap. The point is, all of them want something from us. And when someone has a demand, and it's us that they are after, we got power over them. Yes we, do! Anytime a collective group of people can earn more than 400 million dollars a year – that's clout, baby! As a man of color, there are a plethora of things I'm always thinking about that have the propensity to make the grade for reflective thought. The depth of my soul is like a bottomless pit that cannot define volume. I've thought long and hard on how to answer this question and have come up with a few caveats that I'd like to share.

But first, hear me out. There's just too much on the minds of men, where our souls are retched with pangs of how to do the right thing. It's not far-fetched that men should be scrutinized for any meaningful intent in times like these. I welcome the chance to talk about my thoughts personally, and generically what other men SHOULD be thinking about. Every now and then the Black man's long odyssey in America demands that we be heard. People want to know what lies beneath the shroud of anger and foreboding that has dogged us in time...and we haven't been quiet, mind you. When the whispers get louder, the voices cry out in despair, rail against injustice, defy oppression, and have spoken truth with power and eloquence. For every man like me who will not be stifled by passivity, hundreds more are rising to occasions to be viable in communities struggling to be held accountable to legitimate concern. Other variables and paradoxes are at play, too. I think about the homeless and the predicament that dog the jobless. I'm at wit's end with how to cope with the reality of stereotypical angst that propels the former and the latter. Success runs in our race for sure. At times we are embraced, sometimes we're ignored, but mostly we are not understood by many who only see what's on the surface. We endeavor to soar in triumphant unison where demand for respect is par for any course of acceptance. It's when nostalgia reign supreme and my mind revert to thinking about the injustices and ill-will that we've had to endure that causes the hackles on my neck to stand on end. I feel that it's always a moment to lament and wish that the pendulum swung yet the other way. I believe that time and circumstance has ways of affording the most astute among us chances to be the progenitors of good things despite all of the above. Moreover, we've always had our voices for self-affirmation and a sense of legitimacy. Each generation brings about change and new hope for better understanding as we talk among ourselves, and bring a sense of honor to our thoughts. It inspires us anew, and our souls and minds are full of the aforementioned 'voices'. Thus, the real machismo insists that we are heard – our souls cry out to be taken seriously.

My idea of what lies in the soul of a man has many elements. Black men are much too complex for only surface matter to suffice, without myriads of other situations floating subconscious in mind. We're not without reproach for things that we should be doing. I feel that men should first look in the mirror and see intrusively the need for concern dealing with self-esteem, lack of integrity and no accomplished value to have a better meaning to life in positive ways. What lies in the soul of a man? I can answer the question easily from a personal vantage point. It starts with me by being true to myself and maintaining an innate sense of relevance. Alas, I know that God made me in the image of Him, and had great plans for me, but along the way I stumbled... The African-American male, much maligned as he is, cannot be stereotyped any more justifying damages already incurred. What lies beneath the hubris is enough to begin the process for challenge and change as I regained my balance. With a new lease on life I picked up the gauntlet and ran with it! The intent is to posit frames of references to illustrate what black Americans should expect out of their men as opposed to what has been shown thus far on the surface. Interestingly enough, the first man of creation, Adam was given a blueprint and a set of directives and he failed miserably…so much so that the Divine plan originally entrusted to him didn't exactly go awry to the point where we couldn't eventually get it right. The souls of men should first emanate with a strong presence for spirituality where integrity can define a sense of worth for any progressive success. I feel that we could do a better job of stepping up, exerting ourselves and demanding respect on all levels of achieved reckoning.

What are we thinking about when we sit passively watching our communities fall in disrepair, see our families grow apart from apathy and lack of spiritual resolve, and most importantly, allow our progeny to fall prey to icons that are detrimental to their growth? I won't say that my past is not checkered like so many of my peers, but having been there and done that, maturity served its purpose when my attention became centered on blueprints to construct a better role model. It is for the roles I'm destined to play in communities of thought and action. The wrongness that existed in my former life demanded that I make this change, and it took away the momentum of a nagging nemesis for intangibles to become much more than reality. You see, I once begged, borrowed, and stole anything that would allow me to be at the top of my egotistical game. I dressed the part, and allowed material things to define the fabric of my being. I was insecure at a time when I didn't want to make mistakes that would have subsequent bearing on my career. I was a slave to sex, and at times disrespected women, myself, and distorted the truth enough to render me a mere caricature of the natural talent I had. Yes, I recall the times – 'The 'sensational seventies' where the music was live and my imaginations ran away from me!

Time in its proper place will always be the barometer for change. I was able to triumph over adversity and iniquity by professing to elicit a better way of being respected, as there was something in it for me. I learned that in order to respect, one must intrusively pay homage in humble ways to see empathy in those with whom they endeavor to respect. Self-esteem became my focus, and it was not easy loving yourself in order to love others. I learned this by studying the Word. I began to think personally about how I could stop the degradation of women that I readily exploited in various segments of my carnal spirit. Instead of being the hunter after the game, I allowed the game to capture me…and in doing so I was forced to give them something to be respected of. Moreover, I thought about how equal parity could be afforded to women who were heading households while I was laying in the cut, or being cut down by society's injustices. I sought to stop feeling sorry for myself and thinking that someone of another persuasion was the reason for my angst. I needed to think about what I can do to loosen the strings of racist attitudes and not allow it to hold me back

I can't speak for all men, but I'm sure enough will agree that our dreams will often be imprisoned and relegated to the mockery and amusement of an unbelieving and unforgiving public. At times, life's struggles, external and internal, will test the very souls for challenging resolve to go within. This is where self-esteem and integrity play the better part for us to get right. Social ills render us helpless, and we harbor thoughts, and sometimes do detrimental things to exacerbate the problems. Change allowed me to get completely naked; and as I stood before the mirror and saw myself for whom I really was, I stripped myself of all of the shame, guilt, and temptation of that which was not good for my soul. It forced me to get to know Him better as I looked deeper and saw the wonders of God's penchant for putting everything where it should be at this point in my life. I had to find myself and the gift of discernment to let options be definitive of my actions – those where common sense would give good meaning to deductive reasoning. I couldn't ignore that still small voice that roared so vociferously in my soul in the dead of night whenever He visited. It's often at this hour that God prodded me to continue beyond sunrise to give more light at sunset!

The career I've carved learning to be a respected as a journalist and freelance writer is best exemplified in my writing. That's my voice. I endeavor to write with clarity hoping that my peers see my worth. Along the way I got spiritual and spirited. I no longer worry about the friends I may have lost in my quest to be the best I can be. Words, wit, and new-found wisdom are my bosom buddies and my creativity will always flow. As I wrote, my thoughts gave new meaning to humbleness, and an ego that was lessened and lengthened for my journey subsided. It is my hope that my brothers and my many peers join me on this trip in making our race a good one to challenge what is needed for acceptance, be it from and to ourselves, or from different persuasions. The road we travel is not an easy one. What are we thinking about then? Our minds are not idle, and my mind is full and reverberating. I'm a conversationalist at heart and will talk to anyone willing to debate realism vs. ambiguity. There are some like myself who will run as fast as we can for the finish line of life, where God would be there to shake hands and say, "well done my faithful servants!" I want to be deserving of this, because I do not want to see women continuing to be the head of households, and where my community is not run by matriarchy. I want my young folk to take inventory of their lives so that self, family and community are interwoven for sustained awareness. I want black-on-black crime to cease for Agape Love to permeated using a sense of connectivity, commitment and the commission of good intent.

Lastly and certainly not lease of my thoughts were of those where I could be looked at with respect in any setting and excel because of, and not despite my race. Nowadays, it's all about living vertically and continually seeking space to keep my thoughts just as reverent. The triumph of my soul is complete as I strive to make my achievements accountable. I've done some serious re-evaluation of my life while thinking back on my past. I do not lament for that which should have been, or what should be! I looked intrusively in that mirror I spoke of earlier, and didn't allow laxity to dispel the truth that stared back at me. I lay bare my soul, and as black men with so many wrongs to right and for accountability to have value, we must challenge and be challenged. Of course I pray more now as I seek a greater audience with Him. I did it by using a triumvirate sense of awareness putting self, family, and community at the forefront of my initiatives. There's a lot I will uphold to justify my covenant with God, with the changes I made in my life. I want to continue on an even plain. The applications that I'm adhering to, and the solutions thereof, are about a simple plan: I will live a code of honor where ethics and just doing the right thing will give much more to meaningful intent; I will live, learn, and listen more. Live for the moment that is, and allow a free spirit to guide me in my liberal leanings; and I will learn through the knowledge afforded me in my natural advantage it gives for discernable options, the importance of deductive reasoning, having common sense and good logic to define how I conduct behavior patterns. There's more -- I endeavor to gravitate around those that propel me higher as I will choose wisely my new friends. I will unclutter my mind, shore up my surroundings for a neater disposition. I will not hesitate to initiate and follow through on those things that need dumping, and will abandon what doesn't work, and not dwell on things I'm unwilling to commit to fully.

What lies in my soul is everything that can and should fix what is wrong with the world according to man's agenda to challenge and change the society in which he lives. My soul is my temple and my spiritual being is alive bubbling to the top waiting to explode! Asking me what's on my mind is opportunity waiting to vociferate anew. I think about how we need to mobilize and support the election of that Black man running for President. The litmus test of loyal is upon us. We need to circle the wagons and support him, and in doing so change would start souls to solidify race to a new dimension. I'm sure there are those that DO believe in his progressive campaign for change, and in the minds of the men I talked to there are hopes, dreams, and accomplished verve that are ours to claim. We shall continue to talk, voice our opinionated views, and be on the mind of others who are wondering what we are thinking. The triumphs of our souls are the victories we claim over adversaries and how we can let others know what we are thinking in our souls. I think about loving the right way, and being loved in return. I think about doing my part to build the Kingdom and make sure that the Joshua generation has the role models to see what needs to be seen for measurable self-esteem. If we can dare to dream, let us have those great expectations and speak volumes for our victories. Check out my smile and measure my heart for the things I say and what I do. I will tell my constituents that there are peaks and valleys to life and that success will require opening up and being accountable. But by no means should they stop the flow of words between them. Continue talking, my brothers, and let your voices and actions be instruments for change. Perhaps the most important regimen for us to grasp is the need to reassert collective genius which has always empowered us in the past to survive. We can do this by loving each other more –but we'll shout if we have to, and it should be okay!

No Regrets

William Fredrick Cooper

It's been a long time...

As this missive arrives to caramel fingers, I remember oh so well, I hope it finds you and your family in pleasant health and spirits. Evoking a vivid memory of your son, he must be doing his thing in college now. Recalling his father's handsome beige countenance and gangly, yet athletic build, how many sticks he has gone through beating off hordes of adolescent female admirers? My guess is plenty. Your sibling--is life treating them well at this juncture? If not too presumptuous, can you send warm regards on my behalf, as well as to your mother? Have the years been good to my fellow Gemini? Please give her a heartfelt embrace for me.

Do you still maintain communication with our mutual friend Miki? Our contact lines were disconnected years ago, however periodically my mind drifts to Joey, her offspring. There was a special connection between us, and for a brief period he was the son that I always wanted. Lord knows, I loved that little guy (Well, at last report he wasn't *that little* anymore.). In retrospect, confidence surges through me, knowing he felt our bond as well. Holding him very dear in a special place, he'll stay in my heart eternally, as I hope life brings him all he deserves.

My daughter is a teenager now, planted firmly in those crazy high school years. Thus far, she's been a blessing from God. Reared as a Christian, she took swimming and piano lessons. She was an advanced member of her dance academy, not to mention a co-captain of her cheerleading team. Possessing everything a father could ever want from a child, she also has my sense of humor, heart, giving spirit, as well as a confidence and maturity that belies her tender age. My only concern is that her endless cupboard of benevolence will be exploited by someone undeserving. Through my actions, I only hope to show her what she is to look for in a potential soul mate.

My former spouse has done a wonderful job with her; for that I am eternally appreciative. She and I parted company years ago, but with each passing day my admiration and respect for her grows leaps and bounds. Grateful that we share a free and easy rapport, maturity helped us avoid the acrimony that often accompanies the unfortunate circumstances of relationships gone awry. She is one of my closest friends; that said--there isn't a better feeling in the world than knowing that the security of one's daughter is in trusted hands.

My job as law clerk at the firm can be inundating at times as a lot is required of me, but petty gripes and grievances are minimal. In light of the catastrophic occurrences that hammered our city since the turn of the century, how can one complain about arduous responsibilities when thousands have perished and many more remain homeless, unemployed and emotionally devastated? Having witnessed the 9/11 tragedy and ensuing bedlam first-hand, I am fortunate to be:

1) alive today, and

2) working.

Resiliency has settled in, for I am a resident in this tough town.

Gotta keep moving, you know.

Funny, but my knowledge of that credo was learned years ago.

Simultaneously, I ask your forgiveness for this sudden, and I'm certain, unexpected intrusion into your life after quite some time and now turn my focus on the reason for this letter. If you're wondering why the memory of you resurfaces on occasion, the answer lies in the response to a question recently posed.

When asked to contribute a story to *The Soul Of A Man* Anthology, I thought of a defining period of my life that forged resiliency, resolve, and character-building fortitude. In spite of all the drama, emotional catastrophes, and tragic events transpiring throughout the world; despite joyful and wondrous events like watching my daughter grow and where my present endeavors reside, my mind kept wandering back to you.

Why, you ask? It's because your entrance into my world on February 6, 1987 had such a profound impact on me that continues to affect me to the very day. Don't worry though, I bear no ill feelings, have no regrets, harbor no resentment, nor do I still feel pangs of unrequited love. My friend and first love, you assisted greatly in transforming me into the man I am today, a man I'm very proud to be.

My evolution started with a chance meeting that mid-winter Friday evening. When our eyes first connected at the Copacobana nightclub, my soul--down to the marrow of my bones- thought you were the one for me, my eternal soul mate. Upon closer inspection, however, I found that you had a different agenda, one contrary to mine.

You see, your heart belonged to another.

So why didn't I take off running in the opposite direction? Often times when low self-esteem works in union with falling in love, the intelligence and reasoning of a young man can be non-existent. My heart--tender, foolish, and desperate to escape a world of weird dating practices and painful outcomes, nevertheless urged me to follow it. A curious look in your eyes encouraged the same.

Venturing into murky waters of emotional vulnerability and insecurity, where was I going with this? Secret rendezvous, long talks on the phone, passionate love letters sealed with heartfelt kisses. Where would it all end? Would it end?

Once all lessons of self-worth were understood and embraced, only then would the process be complete. That revelation came years later. How, then could I see the finish line when my heart was shattering every time you appeared late for dates, or sometimes not at all? How could I recognize the value of that message while battling insomnia whenever thoughts of another inside a secret garden I fantasized about tormented my nights? How could I see through the pain while enduring accusations of crack addiction by my mother because of sudden weight loss; while being called a homosexual by co-workers because of my loyalty to you; while warring with feelings of despondency when attempting to remove myself from this increasingly unhealthy situation? Frustration found a brewing place in my soul as I drowned in nocturnal sorrows, pining, craving for something just beyond my reach -YOU.

I later realized He was teaching me *perseverance.*

That desire to love you kept me moving forward, never giving up hope that one day you would realize singular feelings within and reciprocate my affections in kind. So I sat, and I waited... and waited. Hearing you utter, *"There's something about you..."* stirred bleak thoughts, cleared away gray clouds and uplifted fading spirits. Unconditionally giving my all to you--my heart, my soul--I just knew tolerance would prevail and I would end up the winner, my prize being you.

Such was not the case.

But in the end, the futile exercise established another virtue needed later: ***strength.***

Was there pain in knowing I was unappreciated while you were with your former beau, then subsequently bypassed for an eventual husband a few years later? I can only say that there were scars so deeply embedded into my heart, even the most skilled surgeons could not have removed them. Damage was inflicted upon the innocent because of this. My wife deserved a better husband, one free of emotional baggage. After the painful detachment, the minute I captured a glimpse of apathy--a woman in my life. Destructive tendencies emerged from a broken heart and self-preservation became my theme.

The law of averages eventually caught up with me on numerous occasions. One instance while attempting to salvage one of the relationships, I found my belongings soaked with bleach, then, placed outside of a townhouse that was shared. Another example came in the form of having to take a three hour train ride one New Years morning to apologize to a woman that I had made plans with. The reason for the apology was because I had arrangements with another.

I became masterful at pushing people away that genuinely cared about my feelings. In a little over a decade, the negative transformation from the most benevolent male a woman could have met, to a man no woman could trust with her heart, was complete.

A renewal of faith in the man once thought of as special was needed in the worst way. So one day in the summer of 1996, a decision was made to open myself up and lay emotions bear by way of the written word.

With that, phase two of this defining process was launched.

I've always found it amazing that a person's nadir can often bring out the very best in them. Feeling as if the wheels of my life had fallen off, confidence, of which I was already lacking, was at an all-time low. Rows of perspiration running down my neck while sitting at they desk of my old law firm, I read the only letter you ever wrote me. "Everything happens for a reason," and "negative things preparing you for something greater in life that will happen on a later date," were quotes that stood out when I began typing.

Or shall I say tapping. Never blessed with clerical abilities, my odyssey began after working longs hours at the job. Laboring hard from dusk until dawn, I can honestly say I poured my heart and soul into my initial composition.

What did I hope to accomplish from this? The core of me yearned to eradicate the demon that was driving me to foil my personal relationships, which all fell apart around me. Attempting to purge myself of guilt that plagued me for breaking the hearts and spirits of innocent women, I searched desperately for the reasons why I had changed so drastically. The end result of this introspection was my first novel, an unconventional work of African-American male literature filled with sensitivity and emotional pain.

Unable to afford a home computer or laptop, a steely determination took over as I pecked away for answers. This process lasted until sunrise, leaving me just enough time to rush home to my mother's apartment on Staten Island for a quick shower. Soon, the harried jaunts turned to nights in hotel rooms, ceasing the disturbance of others with my mission. As that luxury became too exorbitant for meager earnings, the last resort was my office floor. Cold industrial carpet beneath me, I shivered through many nights with only a coat as support and a box top emulating a pillow. Weekends consisted of this compulsive ritual, then the painstakingly frustrating task of typing with one hand until my fingers cramped from exhaustion. Slowly creeping through each word, I found the answers to the questions that had tortured my existence for years.

Had I built a barrier around my heart to protect myself from the pain that came from losing at love? Had I purposely used unsuspecting victims as sounding boards to release my heartache, inflicting pain before they could hurt me? I'm ashamed to admit that this was the realization I had to face before healing my fractured psyche.

I'm sure it's hard for you to believe this was the man I had become. No, it was not the same person who pined for you endlessly. This individual was a by-product of loving ... NO... of being obsessed with acquiring affection from a woman who did not love me. You. But for that, I have only myself to blame.

This newfound tenacity to find emotional closure was not without adversity. Enduring a major dose of cynicism and skepticism from immediate family members, most of the initial support was received from people who read excerpts of my catharsis during rush hour trips along the Staten Island Ferry. An education was needed in WordPerfect- first in DOS format, then subsequently,

Windows and Microsoft - as I was unfamiliar with even the basic computer elements.

Another obstacle was my inability to let go of sordid memories. To combat that affliction, I relied on the legacy of Phyllis Hyman.

For many nights, the late singer's spirit lived vicariously through me. Identifying with her need for love and appreciation through song, hearing her desperate pleas for help through gut-wrenching, vocal improvisations, I knew what it was like to be "always goin' through changes," as described in "Living In Confusion." My "Old Friend" was a comforting lover during troubled, tear-filled nights, and my inspiration through lyrics that allowed me to be reflective of my own life.

One night that stands out in memory was the evening of January 3, 1998. With "When I Give My Love (This Time)" flowing through me while writing the last page of my manuscript, a strange chill escaped me as I felt the exodus of her spirit leaving my soul. Having served her purpose in my life, it was time for her departure, and my ensuing two-hour watershed of emotions was a fitting tribute to the spiritual connection shared. Relating to her battles with internal torment, perhaps Phyllis wanted success from me where she had failed. Perhaps she chose me to emerge victorious for both of us with regards to conquering internal demons and insecurities.

That triumph, however, was still years away.

Considering the circumstances that surrounded this journey, the completion of a manuscript would have been sufficient cause for exoneration of the agonizing memories. My friends had taken notice, and expressed heartfelt praises. Further buoyed by the support from co-workers, I could actually feel the mending of my broken heart. However something deep inside, an unspoken drive, screamed the mission remained incomplete. In order to take the final steps on my climb to the mountaintop of closure, to completely unburden my soul and realize the tantalizing prospect of opening my heart once more, the initial manuscript had to become a novel.

So, for two long years, the work was shopped to agents and publishing houses. In all, seventy-three rejection letters were received, some of which brought me to the brink of tears. The last one, which was received in February of 2000, was blunt and brutal, as it stated the following:

"Mr. Cooper, while your prose is well-written, your story is not an Eric Jerome Dickey or Omar Tyree type novel. It's too emotionally sensitive for a black man, and we don't have a market for it."

Though clearly in recovery, each refusal seemed to eat away at the momentum built. Coupled with the literary setbacks was another series of failed relationships. Wondering if I truly deserved peace and happiness, frustrating questions of vulnerability resurfaced, whittling away at a fragile confidence and returning me to the depths of a dark world once removed. My emotional state had not matched the requisite mental toughness and strength needed to complete this journey. In order to crush the psychological hold this emotional turmoil held over me, I called upon the greatest basketball player of all-time.

When mired in a traumatic quandary, sometimes that last ounce of strength needed to prevail comes from the most unlikely source. Rummaging through sports tapes one spring morning in May of 2000, I stumbled across "Learning To Fly," a 1991 sports documentary about Michael Jordan and the Chicago Bulls first championship season. The brilliance of Jordan's career is so illuminating that parts of it, like this poignant portion of his first shining moment, gets lost in the glare.

That day, it provided sorely craved inspiration.

The middle of this captivating film contained the seeds of motivation needed to put the specter of personal failures of my heart behind me. The nine-minute segment spoke of Jordan and his teammate's three straight Eastern Conference playoff losses to the Detroit Pistons, backbone-building trials of fire that shaped a championship mentality that lasted well into the 1990's. In those three demoralizing losses, in 1988, 1989 and 1990 respectively, his Chicago Bulls endured grinding times, narrowing the competitive gap between the two teams yet always coming up short. The last loss left Jordan so devastated, at game seven's end he rode on a bus alone, in tears.

Feeling his frustration as I reviewed the video, the ironic connection was inescapable. My disappointments in love were the Pistons, and I was Michael Jordan, heroically seeking vindication, desperately trying to hurdle the years of emotional turbulence wrecking my soul. A failed attempt at marriage; hurting others because of unhealed wounds, the lonely nights of tears, and the debacle that started the negative spiral, the futile pursuit of your heart.

The breakthrough for the Chicago Bull's franchise came in 1991. Sensing how close they were to exorcizing their tormentors in their last defeat, they simply learned the mental aspect of playing through all adversities, and that bitter failure, when acknowledged and channeled correctly, can produce positive results. An emphatic triumph followed these lessons. In vanquishing their three-year Piston nightmare with an emphatic four game sweep, the narrative summary of the segment told it all. "For the first time, the Bulls were moving on..." Yearning to dismiss the burden of failure I had carried for over a decade, I would follow suit with the completion of this journey. Unknowingly, Air Jordan and the Chicago Bulls showed me that I was on the right path; the course charted by successful at turning all negatives into positives. And with this video, the necessary mettle was provided to finish the task at hand.

From that point forward, I was a man on a mission. Fortified with renewed intensity and refueled confidence, a stare down with the ache that gnawed at my battered soul followed. Succumbing to an unwavering laser-like focus, the anguish of yesteryear -most notably, the pain of losing you - blinked first. Again my heart gave praise to the dual inspiration of Phyllis Hyman and Michael Jordan. With those forces guiding me, the finish line of a heart-rending cleansing was in view.

My willpower now in overdrive, whatever was needed to be done to carry this quest to its gratifying conclusion was done. If it meant exploring the expensive cost of Print-On-Demand publishing, then that was the road to travel. If it meant my fourteen hour work days were extended to sixteen, then I would do what needed to be done. If it meant more nights were spent on that cold office floor during the editing and galley revision process, then I packed a pillow this time. There was no stopping the one-man freight train to fulfillment.

Except, of course, the triumphant destination. It seemed fitting the emotional trek would end on February 6, 2001, fourteen years to the day I met you. The work day was an arduous one, and as I clicked on the Print-On-Demand web site to survey the production process, a simple word "BUY" appearing next to the paperback edition of *"Six Days In January ...",* brought to close a fight with a beast that changed my soul into something I did not recognize. Tears of joy connecting at my chin, I looked at the smiling angels above. Comprehending the road traveled and the lessons learned along the way, my quivering lips could only muster a simple, yet heartfelt "thank you."

As a new year goes into full swing, I think of the journey of writing from my soul, and where it has led me. That initial self-published book evolved into a writing career that has spawned two novels, several anthology contributions, feature articles in national periodicals, and major literary award nominations and awards. Picking up the mantle of Timothy McCann, one of my writing mentors, the compositions have challenged the typical novels that shape our community. Showing the insecurities, emotional vulnerability and the journey of African-American men on the road to personal triumph while delivering deep messages, some of my peers have compared my stories to contemporary writers of yesteryear; scribes that paved the way for today's influx of creativity.

While humbled by the blessings God has bestowed upon me, they have not come without more adversity, things I never would have imagined would reconstruct my life. In

2004, while basking in triumph of my first novel being released by a major literary imprint, I became jobless for almost two years. Living off of royalty checks, I staved off several eviction notices and somehow saw through the turbulence to produce a second novel. *There's Always A Reason,* an inspirational story of love and hope that many have called an emotional masterpiece, is something that came from deep within.

Even with the release of this story came more drama. Petty jealousies that infect the crazy world of African-American literature and ferocious character assaults had me questioning my visions. Under siege because of certain associations, the viciousness of these attacks was unceasingly brutal. Taking full responsibility for my actions while enduring another storm, my mental psyche was as calm as a still ocean.

Do you want to know why?

Whenever my strength wavers while dealing with dilemmas that shape this crazy thing called life, I simply recall the initial journey, and know that God will provide guidance and discipline whenever I slip with a poor choice, and the strength to resume this incredible ride to reach the destination of His glorious sun.

I long to hear Him say "Job Well Done, Son."

Love still, proves to be an interesting journey. Relationships come and go, and yes, as a human I still make mistakes in my decision making. Rather than dwelling on the negativity that shapes the world's cynicism, I have learned to enjoy each experience, and, if forever is not in plan, take only the good away. Lessons concerning this uncontrollable emotion have told me to be patient, and to enjoy the completeness of the journey. The tests within the confines of love are to produce testimonials that serve as inspirations to others.

Besides, God has taken me on a journey once before, so I know that there's more to be learned, right?

After reading my first novel *Six Days In January*, many felt that I should harbor deep resentment for you, unearth buried hostilities, and exact revenge in some fashion. Not a single iota of anger runs through me. I have no regrets in knowing you, for to me, you were one of the most important ingredients in this evolution to manhood, as well as the angel that guided the way to my success as an award-winning, national best-selling author. Treasuring what once was, I smile when savoring the wonderful moments we shared, and wonder sometimes what could have been. Finding happiness in the fact that you have succeeded in your endeavors, and I in mine, I have no regrets in the love I possessed for you, or the pain it often caused. I only express appreciation for the time shared in your presence, and express gratitude for the defining period in my life that you provided.

Thank you for the lessons you taught me about life, love, and internal peace. And thank you for being the impetus behind a dream come true.

Sincerely,

William Fredrick Cooper

MANNING UP WITH GOD

Brian Ganges

Responsibility is the thing people dread most of all.
Yet it is the one thing in the world that develops
us and gives us manhood.

~ Frank Crane

In a quaint suburban New Jersey township, lived an energetic, well meaning but unfocused and out of balanced young man. Yours truly was that young man. I wasn't out of balanced because I was causing trouble, or being a nuisance in the community; but I (like many of our youth) acted without thinking about the consequences of my actions or my future. I was raised as an only child in a good home with my dad and mom for most of my childhood. We weren't churchgoers or Christians, but we were good people that believed that God was real. My dad exposed me to many positive things, such as African American events, literature and history. He stressed to me that God didn't create us (African Americans) as junk, but he wanted to familiarize me with the great African American heroes that instilled in me a sense of pride for our race. We had some of my grandmother's paintings of people like: Dr. M.L. King, Jackie Robinson, Joe Louis, Thurgood Marshall and others in our home. So I always had the example of my dad and other positive African American men to watch and to emulate. This is how I differed from a lot of my friends, and started to get a glimpse of what it was to "Man Up."

We lived in a comfortable home and I had everything I needed and most of what I wanted. I was a very personable, and fun young man who was more commonly known as the class clown. My teachers and other people who knew me would tell me that I was very bright and that I could be anything I wanted to be, if I applied myself. But what did I want to be, and how can I apply myself to something that I don't know? I was a decent looking and a very athletic guy: All-Star Baseball and Soccer player, and All-County Track runner who got invited to the State Finals in my junior year of High School; and as I remember back to my High School yearbook, one of my old teammates wrote: "…I *just hope that you stick with either baseball or track. You have a great deal of talent and something like that shouldn't be waste…you were the best athlete in all of my high school days*." Many people had confidence in me and thought highly of me, but I was still very unsure of myself to a great degree. It seemed as though everyone wanted to see what I was going to do with all of my ability, intelligence, and personality. If I failed, people would've viewed me as the "once a clown, always a clown;" but if I succeeded, then people would've gleefully smiled and said, "yeah, I remember him." This is my story; a story that shows the struggle of where I was, to where God wanted to take me; the ultimate struggle for the soul of a man who didn't realize that there was a purpose and a destiny; a purpose beyond what I knew and could articulate. But before God formed me in my mother's womb He already ordained me for a Divine purpose (**Jeremiah 1:5**); God's thoughts and plans for me were always for peace and not for evil, to give me hope in my final outcome (**Jeremiah 29:11 Amplified**).

So off to college I went with all of those wonderful words of encouragement and a vote of confidence from all of my friends and family. My plan was to get away from home, have fun at college and one day I would become a rich lawyer. Well, I certainly got away from home, and I had a lot of fun at college; I had so much fun that I forgot about being a lawyer. During my sophomore and junior years of college everyone started to finish most of the electives and general classes, and started taking the major courses for graduation. I was still having a good time just hanging out, enjoying my freedom, and doing some homework every now and then. Life was just a joke to me, and I always had the sentiment that my current situation was always going to take care of itself. I was like a person that was high on "weed"—walking around like a zombie with no cares, worries, or adverse thoughts. I had been the class clown since elementary school, and that escalated into being the party guy, getting drunk, and sleeping around during my college years. My new found freedom was exciting to me: alcohol and having different women hang around were my new drugs, and I was getting my "fix" as often as I could. Besides, that's what all of my role model rappers were talking about all of the time.

My biggest concerns in life were having fun and not obeying any rules. In my mind, I was legally grown and my parents weren't around to hassle me. I called all the shots, and I was taking advantage of an opportunity of a lifetime: living in a college town, going to a historically black university where the ratio of women to men was approximately 15:1 and alcohol was flowing like water. I loved the attention that I was getting from the ladies, and I couldn't remember ever seeing that many beautiful women in one location: tall, short, brown-skinned, light-skinned, big breasts, big butts, pretty feet, sweet smells and everything else in between was there for the taking. I got so caught up in this aspect of my life that I began to forget the true objective of why I was in college. In my youthful ignorance, I didn't realize that rules and laws are not meant to enslave or control, but to produce order, structure, and discipline (something I didn't have).

All the while, I knew that God was calling me to repentance. Ever so gently, since my sophomore year of college, I knew that God was dealing with me about committing my life to Him. I felt "the pull" to make that decision many times. But I was having so much fun, and I just wanted God to leave me alone for a little while and let me explore this new freedom. But as time progressed, the desire to know more about God and the Bible got stronger; and at that point, I really began to examine my life and my future. In those quiet times in my room, I always wondered about God and what this life was really all about. I would read my old, dusty Bible but had very little understanding of what I was reading. So I decided to join social organizations like the Masonic Lodge and the Eastern Stars that claimed to teach about God. One of my college professors was a minister of the Gospel who told me about salvation, as well as my aunt and many others.

But there were two final episodes that I encountered that truly made me want to reconsider my ways. The first episode was when I paid for my first and last prostitute. I needed to feed my sexual addiction, so I found a woman who was up "for whatever." It was a horrible experience, I didn't enjoy it and I was ready for it to be over. When we finished, I gave her my last $3.00 and felt really disgusted with her and myself. I started telling her that she needs to consider some life changes. It was a somewhat awkward situation since the two of us just got finished "gettin' busy," and there I was telling her to get her life right with God. Well, God was giving us both a wake up call in the midst of that rendezvous. The second episode that was truly the final straw for me. It occurred while I was in a college English Literature class. As my female professor was instructing the class, I began to undress her with my eyes and I was having sex with her in the class. She was a nice looking older lady, and my mind started to wonder if she was a freak that needed a young man to get that pressure off of her. By now this sex thing, started to consume me more than I wanted. I was enjoying all the female attention that I was receiving, but I started to be honest with myself while I was fantasizing that I was increasingly becoming more of a lonely, empty and unfulfilled young man. But I just wanted to think about her and finish this session with an older lady. I tried to shake the thoughts while I was in class with my professor, but I couldn't; every time I opened my eyes it got more passionate and became more and more exciting to me. I was going back and forth like a tennis match: I wanted to try her out, but I wanted to be free. I was really getting caught up in the idea of a more mature. I wanted to leave class, but I couldn't. Since I was fantasizing about her for so long, I started to get an erection, and if I got up during class she probably would've called me out, and brought more attention to me. So I remained in my seat and thought about baseball or something else of a non-sexual nature, and I eventually ended up leaving early without disturbing the class. The battle that was going on in my mind was so strong, I thought that I was going crazy. Sex was starting to take over my life and I started making life decisions based upon my strong sexual prowess, such as: Do the ladies like short hair? Will the ladies notice my green eyes in this outfit? Do I look appealing to the ladies in a sleeveless shirt?

Like the prodigal son, the inevitable finally happened on the evening of January 25, 1993. I stopped running from God and decided to run to God. With a Gospel tract in my hand, I knelt down beside my bed, repented to God and asked Jesus Christ to be my personal Savior. A spiritual weight seemed to be lifted off of me and something was definitely evident to me: on the inside, I was instantly changed. I couldn't explain it, but I knew that I finally found that for which my spirit was yearning.

Finding Myself in Christ

I finally achieved what I was looking for—a true sense of acceptance, love and peace. I was full of zeal and eager to walk my "new walk," so I put away many of my vices "cold turkey," and I was determined to please God. The Bible was my new instruction manual and I was determined to read it as much as possible; and even though I couldn't intelligently articulate my own salvation yet, I was a happily loaded gun bouncing around and trying to save the world. I quickly realized that a lot of the teachings and viewpoints that I held were diametrically opposed to the Word of God. It was a battle within me, because most of my friends and family didn't necessarily ascribe to my Biblical views, at least not as dogmatically or literally. At times, I felt as though I was in the "Twilight Zone" and Rod Serling was spinning my head like I was in a state of vertigo. Questions and thoughts bombarded my mind continually. Am I the only one who feels this way? Am I reading too much into these Scriptures? Am I crazy? Am I in a cult? Or do I just need some guidance? When I came off of my spiritual highs I felt like I was the only person on the planet, and I felt so alone in the midst of a crowd of people. Something was seriously wrong, but I didn't know what it could be. I was saved, because I asked Christ into my heart. But how could I feel so lost after making such a positive decision for my life? Isn't my life supposed to be better now? As a newborn babe in Christ, I wobbled around trying to learn how to walk out my soul's salvation with fear and trembling (**Philippians 2:12**).

Like many Christians, I was a blindly obedient Christian with a good heart and a genuine desire to serve God at all costs. In the early stages of my walk with God, I was trying so hard to separate myself from sin and worldliness, that I alienated my friends and family away from me in the process. I wasn't building bridges to win them to Christ through my new life; rather, in ignorance I was building religious walls. I was transitioning from a life with little to no substance to a life that meant everything to me, and I was having trouble finding my way. I was in desperate need of Godly guidance.

Later that year, at a very immature and unstable 21 years of age, I decided to leave my dad's house, drop out of my senior year of college, get married and start my own family; and shortly thereafter a child was conceived. I was happy, but I was also worried. I was totally saturated in this ocean called "life" that was full of sharks with no boat in sight to rescue me. The only thing that I knew for certain was that I accepted Christ as my Savior, and if I died I was going to Heaven. But I didn't know what to do with a wife and a child. My family support system was over 500 miles away; I had very little money, and a pregnant wife. My church family consoled me and basically said "just have faith, believe and keep your hope in God." That was very spiritual advice, but I had a family to maintain, and the landlord, and the electric company didn't want to hear anything about "God's going to send a blessing my way." Besides, my name was on the bills, not God's. They wanted money, and not any excuses, sob stories or prayer requests. The weight of the world seemed like it was on my shoulders, and I couldn't lift it off. I gravely needed the Lord to send someone to help me.

I was in the Church, being encouraged, but I still felt lost. Even with God in my wife's and my life, there was something truly wrong. The only way that I can explain it is: you know how your physical body or your car normally performs, and when it acts differently than normal, then you know something is wrong. Even if everything seems and looks fine, you know there's a problem even without a professional to articulate a diagnosis. Well that's how I felt at this stage in my life. I knew I was on the right path, but something was still missing and wrong.

The Struggle

I struggled, was ridiculed and was broke; but my family and I were going to Heaven one day. I was ashamed to be a Christian sometimes, because in some regards I became like some of the people whose lives discouraged me from wanting to become a Christian years before. All I had was a hope of Heaven. How sad was that? I could quote Scriptures, but I wasn't happy. In my heart, I knew that I was a good person, but I wondered why someone would want to live like me. How could I win anyone to Christ living like this? All of my old friends and contemporaries were apparently surpassing me in achieving levels of success, and all I to had to show for myself was that I'm living right in the eyes of God. Well, living the right life sure didn't manifest any material blessings into my life, at that point. I tried so very hard to be a good Christian, father and husband. But it seemed as though everywhere I turned, I would get knocked down. I finally came to the point where the smart-alec, know-it-all façade couldn't stand the pressure of constant failure, no direction and no sign of hope in this life. My only release was to cry a lot. I was the tough guy with a family to support, and my wife and daughter had no idea that I was feeling my way through the dark.

During these moments, I began feeling sorry for my wife and daughter, because I couldn't do more for these good people. I was totally broken down, and sometimes I wished I wasn't even alive. To me, I was a disgrace to God; and my dad told me that I set the family name back decades by some of the decisions that I had made after becoming a Christian. I always thought that, but to hear him say that really crushed me, and I cried like a baby. At that point, I was totally lost and really had no clue of what to do. I remember my wife and dog consoling me during that down time, because the devil really knows how to use people to kick a man when he's down. I contemplated suicide many times, and I started having long stares at myself in the mirror. I would go into the bathroom to do nothing but ask the image in the mirror "Who are you and what are you doing?" I was an empty shell of a man in private, but in public, I was a mature and aspiring man in the Word of God. I would stand in faith and believe God's Word on one hand, but I would hate what I saw in the mirror. My confidence and self-esteem were both running on fumes, and I was making it day-to-day on pure will power because I wanted Heaven. For a while, I asked myself "What is the purpose of going to church anyway?"

While I was taking my bumps and bruises, and going through my Christian growing pangs, God truly began to reveal some insightful principles to me. Could this be my breakthrough? I began to see visions and dreams, and I started to see that my life had a meaning and a purpose: being a Christian wasn't just about going to Church and one day going to Heaven. He began to show me that being a Christian is about being an influence (salt and light) to those around me and to bring forth fruit (**John 15:16**). I soon realized that God had something special for me to do in the earth. This new revelation made me feel like a kid in the candy store. The sun's rays even seemed to shine brighter to me. I was finally alive and happy, and God started showing me the gifts, talents and abilities that I could use for His purpose. People began to sense a gift and a calling of God on my life. How fulfilling and refreshing it was to know that my life had a reason for existing. I was so full of joy that the God of Heaven was using me for great things and that my church family bore witness to it. I began to preach, to teach, to do radio shows, and I even had a local television program (in Spanish), and everywhere I went in the city people recognized me and encouraged me to continue to reach out to people with the Gospel.

I was truly excited about God and the ministry, and things seemed as though they were finally coming together, but my marriage was not doing too well. We had our church faces on outside of the house, but we came home to be miserable with each other. We were born-again, filled with the Holy Ghost, loved God and our daughter, and we all desired to serve God with our whole heart. But why was my marriage in shambles, God? I was somewhat shell-shocked concerning God during these marital spats, because the more it seemed that I wanted to press in and get closer to Him, I would enjoy a level of blessing, and then the bottom would fall out from under me. For some time this cycle hindered me from fully placing my trust in God, because I didn't want to get my hopes up and fail. We were singing church songs about God's goodness, but I wondered why they didn't add a verse about the pain of picking up that cross and following Him. As the bickering and disagreements continued in my marriage, my wife and I realized that the quick and not too well thought out marriage decision may have been a mistake for us, but we decided to stay in faith and believe God to manifest the victory in our household. So I continued to study and to minister the Word, and my wife continued to sing and be a blessing to the choir and praise team. As we continued on in our Christian walk, we sensed that there was more teaching that we needed but weren't getting from our church. So we decided to search for other Biblical ministry teachings. We found several television ministries and another church in our area that was a blessing to us, and we continued to grow in God's grace. Sometime later, I was awakened by a very vivid dream: My wife and I were at Kenneth Copeland's ministry as members of the church and God specifically told me to move to Texas. I told my wife about the dream and sometime later He confirmed it to her, and a few years later we moved to the Dallas/Ft. Worth metroplex.

I know that God guided and directed our steps to Texas, but in the natural, everyone was looking to me for strength, provision and direction. To them, I'm the one that was moving us away from our family and friends to a strange place with no one there that we knew. So we prayed, packed up and traveled half way across the country with all of our earthly possessions. Three days later, we arrived in Arlington, Texas. I assumed that coming to a land God showed me meant that all of my problems and struggles were going to disappear; needless to say they increased. My wife and I had our usual marital ups and downs, but as time progressed, the ups got fewer and far between, and the downs became more frequent. Prayer, talking, hoping, and believing couldn't salvage what we had. My wife didn't want to pray with me about the situation, and she didn't want to see a counselor. So I prayed alone and with some other solid Christians around the country. I also cried and prayed with my young daughter a few times. Nevertheless, a few years later we eventually split up, and got a divorce.

So now I'm even further away from my family support system, and now my immediate family is gone. What is going on, God? My heart felt as though it was ripped out of my chest and thrown into the middle of a busy highway. My sense of leadership, direction and authority was truly suspect to me, at this point. I'm a more seasoned Christian now, but I'm still failing. Why, Lord? My self-esteem was really taking a beating, and I hit a very low point in my life.

Surprisingly, I never blamed God or became bitter with Him. But I questioned and blamed myself for the things that I possibly could've prevented. Sure, we all have 20/20 vision in hindsight. But the marriage was over and there was nothing that I could do about it, but suck it up, and move on. But I always said, "No matter what happens, I'm going to be apart of my daughter's life: physically, spiritually, emotionally and financially." I produced her because I am a male, but I care for her because I am a man.

But the pain, the emptiness and the disgust that I felt needed to be eliminated; instead I just covered it up. I was desperate and my head was thinking of anything that I could possibly do to be free from the anxiety of depression, rejection and loss. I didn't want to pray, confess the Word, or stand fast in faith. I did all of that and look where it got me. I'm alone! I thought that I was mad at God, but I wasn't. I was mad at myself for listening to some of the unsound teachings and bad advice that I received earlier in my Christian walk. So I just decided to find an outlet in order to forget about my problems, so I started dating women outside of God's will. This is the part of my life of which I was ashamed, because the very thing that I was adamantly preaching against was what I found myself ultimately doing. I always tried to shield this away from my daughter and some of my friends because my façade was on the line. My integrity and self-esteem was already gone, so all that I had left was a phony Christian walk to espouse in public. But it felt good to the flesh to be desired, wanted, sought after and pleased by women. They catered to me and my ego, and all of the things I didn't get during my marriage; I was finally getting the payoff. My college days were back, and I was being bombarded by women young and old. Meanwhile, I was constantly being reminded of the Words of Jesus in the midst of it all: *When a spirit is cast out, it goes out and after time it returns to see if its house is clean and swept. When it finds its former house in this condition it returns to it with seven more spirits and the latter condition of that house is worse than the first.*

I was newly separated, but still legally married and frustrated. My sexual prowess was actually my insecurity and my ego desiring attention, because I got dumped but my wife. So I decided to go out and see if I could get "my groove back." This is precisely why men need to be first complete in Christ before finding a wife. My separation and divorce shook me to my very foundation, and at the time I was weak and vulnerable. I was looking to please my wife and make sure that our relationship would last. But I couldn't control that relationship because it was a two-person commitment. The most important relationship that I should've been nurturing was my relationship with Christ. Then when I got weak, He would've made me strong. But I decided to handle things my own way for a while. So I continued acting out my frustrations and insecurities, and covering up my hurts in a destructive lifestyle.

All the while, God was dealing with me about making things right, and getting ready for a new chapter my life. In my promiscuity, I learned many things about people, our society, and myself. We all have issues, even Christians, but if we continue to sweep the issues under the rug, and never address them with sound, reasonable and principled solutions, then we will continue to be defeated. I also learned that people are willing to go outside of the church to find solutions or ways to cope with their issues, if the church doesn't realistically address their concerns. I started to see how God was going to bring good out of a bad situation for me. It seemed like I was troubled on every side, yet not distressed; perplexed but not in despair; persecuted, but not forsaken; and cast down but not destroyed **(2 Corinthians 4:8-9)**.

I remembered the vision that God showed me and confirmed through a strong sister in the Lord that I would be preaching to multitudes of men in seminars and going forth in the name of the Lord. But I was stuck in a hog pen. No! I came to myself and decided to go back to my Father's house. I got cleaned up, re-focused and I have picked up where I left off. I thought to myself: "the life that I am living isn't about me; it's about the lost souls who need to receive the anointing of God that is on my life. Those people don't need me to be sidetracked, and they don't need my excuses." So I dusted myself off, stumbled some more after that, but I got back on track to serve God from my heart. I felt a brand new exhilaration. My life was restored, and I was back in the race. Time didn't heal me, God did. I was finally satisfied with God and tired of the mess in the world. It was always a lie, but God had to heal me and reveal some things to me about the situation, the "big picture" and myself. God's goodness and mercy is what brought me back into focus. While I was "creepin" and satisfying my flesh, God was setting the table for me to come back home. When I thought about that, I just thanked God, because I didn't earn it or deserve it. Pain, trials and tribulations came, but God never left me stranded. We are the ones who leave and forsake God.

Reflections: The More Balanced Man of God

The spiritual man with many natural experiences has now led to a more balanced life. No more am I so Heavenly minded that I am no earthly good; nor am I seeking only to gratify the flesh. I had to go through some things and grow in God's grace to understand the life that I am living. This doesn't mean that one has to smoke crack to relate to a drug user. But my experiences and my relationship with the Word have allowed me to get a deeper understand and another aspect of this life first hand: the struggles, commitments and the victories.

We are all a product of our environment: a little piece of this and that experience, and a little bit influenced from this person and that person. But more importantly, I see myself as a reflection from a myriad of some great Bible men who stood for truth and overcame adversity through faith in the Word of God. This is the part of my life that was broken into stages: the John the Baptist stage; the Apostle Paul stage; the Abraham stage; and the King Solomon stage.

John the Baptist

He was a young man (Jesus' cousin), dogmatic and bold for the Gospel's sake. God used John to inspire me to be humble and to not desire to be in the limelight. John was a very modest man, to say the least. His clothing was camel's hair, he ate locusts, and he preached in the woods. Yet Jesus said that he was the greatest prophet of all (**Luke 7:28**). God also used John to inspire me to take principled stances on matters, especially when it pertains to the Word of God. Although his principled stance against King Herod cost him his life, he will always be remembered as one of God's true standard bearers. The world and even the Church might believe a certain way, but I truly believed that Christians should stand firm in the Word of God, and be salt and light at all times.

Through various experiences I did learn some very valuable lessons. One thing that I learned is that you can still be a principled person without alienating people away from you. In recent years, I have made amends with some people that I know and love who didn't initially understand my God-given mission; in retrospect, nor did I understand it. But it was a learning curve and I was humble enough to repent and to build a bridge with my family and friends rather than continue to build religious walls. Everyone in my life was/is not a Bible believing Christian, but God does strategically place people in our lives in order to reach them with the Gospel in Word and/or deed. I had to learn that, because I received a lot of unsound teaching from some well-meaning ministries. Jesus began to teach me about Zachias, Mary Magdalene, and the fact that He wants us to be salt and light to the world. So in order for the world to see Christ in us, we have to be around them, so that we can let our light shine. Goodness is contagious; the world calls it "Pollyanna." But Christians, especially men (who are the crown of creation) are anointed and commissioned to be victors and standard bearers. People are looking for solutions; all we have to do is make ourselves available, because the Wisdom of the Ages is on the inside of us. We need to let the effervescence of the

Spirit of God on the inside of us come out and permeate our communities for positive change.

Apostle Paul

He was the religious persecutor of the Church of God, who had a life altering experience. His experience and life inspired me to go forward in the midst of persecution and ridicule. I, like Paul (formerly Saul of Tarsus), mocked the Church. I respected religion, went to Church sometimes, but I had no true, personal relationship with Christ. On the road to Damascus, Saul was confronted with a choice to serve Jesus or not. Similarly, I had a college experience that made me seriously reconsider my ways and follow Christ. When I finally gave a 100% heart-felt commitment to Christ, I was dedicated to find out all about Christ according to His Word.

When Saul became Paul, he wrote in **Galatians 1:12** that no man taught him what he learned about God. Rather, he received personal revelation from Jesus Christ. I am a witness to this type of instruction coming directly from the Lord in my own personal life. I'm not saying that Jesus appeared before me physically, but many of the insights that I have received over the years have been from my own personal study time and devotion with the Lord. God is real, and people will know if you truly know God. Often times, people are amazed at what I know and I have people calling me from all over the country who ask me for my opinions, advice, and principled input on a myriad of topics. God is good!

Abraham

A man that was willing to surrender, and forsake all for the sake of following God. He inspired me to put everything on the line, to be a conduit for God to use to bless the inhabitants of the earth. I have learned and have walked in the example of Abraham to follow God's leading when prompted. I left all of my familiar surroundings, friends and family in order to go to a strange land and to fulfill and to accomplish His assignment for me. In the natural, this was very hard to do; but I made a covenant promise with God years ago that I would do anything He asked, in order to fulfill my destiny in God.

Moving from North Carolina to Texas with my wife, child, mother-in-law and dog may not seem like such a big deal, but when there's very little money, no support system at the destination, a family that was looking to me (as the man) for strength, leadership and provision, that was a big load to carry. In North Carolina, I was already 500 miles away from my family, and then I went another 1,200 miles away. But I knew that God told me to do this, so I obeyed. In the spirit I was calm and at peace, but in the natural I was shaking like a leaf. I must say that following God is never without a challenge, but He always knows best and sees us through.

King Solomon

He was a man of much wisdom and insight, yet he fell into the trap he warned other people to avoid: desiring and falling for strange women. I was once a type of King Solomon who let the fleshly desires and pretty women get me off focus from the purpose and assignment that God created me to fulfill. My divorce took a real toll on me, even though many people couldn't believe how well I was handling it. Nevertheless, I was becoming another divorce statistic and there was nothing that I could do about it. The divorce had good and bad implications associated with it. First, it was good in that it set me free from a situation that was stunting my spiritual growth and keeping me bound to a situation that God didn't originally ordain; and second, it was bad because I wasn't going to see my daughter everyday; and third, the lust and immoral sexual activity that I once experienced in my teenage years and covered up with a quick wedding, was now coming back to revisit me to see if its old home was willing to receive it again.

We live in a world where everything is sexualized: car commercials, athletic events and even a popular hot wings restaurant will arouse the sexual beast in all of us if we let them. We were taught to be "alienated" from wholesomeness and to seek fulfillment in romance. I fell into that trap and I gravitated towards what society and the advertisers teach is the cool and accepted desire: sex. It's a game and a trap, because I came to realize that even though sex is a wonderful act created by God to be enjoyed in marriage, it is also highly over-rated and blown out of proportion by the secular world. But sex sells. Right? I liken its importance in a healthy relationship to the spark plugs of a car. It's the spark in the car, but it's a very small part of the entire structure. King Solomon called it all vanity.

Unlike so many stories, this one isn't over. I am still living it out. I have learned and am learning a lot from the Word, from my experiences and from other people. Many people don't know this story, they only know what I show and tell them. But everyone has a story to tell. Maybe not the same story, but we all have to overcome something and are still overcoming things. That's what is so inspiring about life and living for God; there's always a new challenge; there's always a "ram in the bush;" there's always, faith, hope and victory. It's in all of us! But are we going to just let it remain dormant in us? Have pity parties? Complain? Or are we going to rise up and be righteous victors in Christ? How will we know if we have victory in us if we never encounter defeat? How will we know that we can win if a Goliath never shows up? How will we know if miracles are real if we never arrive at the Red Sea or step out of the boat? Even if we are faithless and fall seven times, we are supposed to get back up again. I've learned that although we may desire to follow God in all of our ways, the unfortunate reality is that we may fall short. Even if we have a stubborn mind, if our hearts are towards God, then He can reach us. God planted a seed in me, and God didn't plan on aborting that seed. So God extended me grace, mercy and favor during my hardship. Today, I am back on track for God and picking up where I left off in the ministry for God. I have a website that teaches about many of life's critical issues from a Christian perspective. I counsel many people from across the country who are looking for perspective and insight on spiritual and secular matters. I do public speaking and God is getting me into position so that I can be a more effective influence that He needs in order to bless people; more specifically teaching men about "Manning Up With God." What is a Man? A Man is responsible and acts responsibly. What is a Man of God? A Man of God is a Man who chooses God to be his anchor and guide. This is my life's mission: to birth men, spiritually, in the earth. God has need of us, men. Let's rise up and Live well!

LONG TERM

Maurice M. Gray, Jr.

I hate hospitals. Almost every time I'm in one, somebody dies.

Three years ago, my mother went to the hospital for minor surgery and never came out. A few months later, a drunk driver who should've been off the road three crashes ago, broadsided my brother; he died instantly. We hadn't finished the food from his funeral when the doctor diagnosed my favorite aunt with pancreatic cancer. Auntie Shane was gone within three months of her diagnosis. Now I'm heading to the hospital again. The odds of me getting out without grieving another loss are slim and none- and Slim already left town.

A flash of red light brings me into a scary reality.

A cop car. Great.

I can stop and risk not getting there in time or keep going and risk having that cop force me over and legally change my name to Rodney King.

I'm stepping on it. If Officer Unfriendly wants to beat the crap out of me, he'll have to do it in front of the hospital. At least I'd be able to get medical care quickly. And, if by some miracle he- or she- doesn't wail on me, I can still get there in time to do what I have to.

Three minutes later, the ambulance and I pull up at the hospital. As soon as I stop, a voice loud enough to startle a deaf man booms from behind me.

"STEP OUT OF THE CAR SLOWLY WITH YOUR HANDS RAISED!"

I'm out the car before he finishes the sentence. I keep my hands where he can see them so I won't wind up on the front page of tomorrow's News Journal.

"Nate Carter?"

"Symon?"

He steps into the light, and I nearly faint with relief. Not only does Officer Symon Donovan go to my church, but I see him in Men's Bible Study every week.

"If I didn't know you, I'd have you in cuffs right now. Keep your hands where I can see them, but I'm giving you a chance to explain yourself."

All I can do is start from the beginning.

I get to work fifteen minutes early to lock myself in my office and pray. I thank God for all the things that didn't happen while I was ravaging the female population of Delaware (and the rest of the tri-state area). Despite having slept around to a ridiculous degree, I never caught any diseases or became anybody's baby daddy. Nobody ever stalked me, keyed my car, threw hot grits on me, or anything like that. Folks might laugh about the grits, but a guy I went to high school with is in the hospital right now with third degree burns. Apparently his wife caught him with her former best friend. The next morning, she served him breakfast in an unexpected fashion. I hear he'll be all right once the skin grafts heal.

Anyway, after I thank Him for all the bullets I dodged, I pray for the women from my past. I've encountered two since I got saved last year, and both were pleasantly surprised when I apologized. I know God has forgiven me, but I need to deal with the damage I did. They were all willing participants, but that doesn't excuse me from using them.

The sound of high heels causes me to end my prayer and prepare to work. I'm Transitional Employee Coordinator for Statebank's credit card operation. I oversee all of the temporary employees in Customer Service (Correspondence and Phones) and Credit Analysis. My assistant Susan Lassiter is in my office every day promptly at nine A.M. to review the day's work. I tell her all the time how much I appreciate her. She made my transition from temp to HNIC easy, despite the fact that she was also in line for this position. It would be easy for her to sabotage me so she could get my position, but she's not like that.

"""Nate, this is Medina Holloway. Medina, Nate Carter."

I'm used to Susan introducing me to temps on their first day, but this is a huge surprise.

"He's the guy who approves your hours, so be nice to him," she adds jokingly.

We laugh, but two of us have to force it. Medina looks about as happy to be working under me as I am to have her here.

Most men in my position would try to holler at Susan. Besides being such a great person, she is FINE. She's five seven (which puts her about at my chest), and her figure is provocative. But I decided that dating coworkers isn't a good idea when you're the boss. I can tell Medina's gonna test my resolve.

Medina is shorter and not as physically gifted as Susan, but she has this intangible something that drives men crazy. Her tangible isn't bad either; she's five feet five inches of brown skin and killer curves, and those brown eyes of hers can charm cash from a miser.

Help me, Jesus.

I shake her hand while I fight to free my tongue from its temporary paralysis.

"Welcome back to Statebank, Medina."

Susan raises an eyebrow. "I didn't know you'd worked here before."

Medina doesn't blink. "It was two years ago. Nathan and I were on the same long-term assignment."

I ignore the frosty attitude in her voice and the anger in my gut. The five minutes it took to get through my standard new temp spiel seemed like five hours, but Susan finally takes the heifer out of my office. When the door closed behind them, I prayed again.

"God, I asked to find women I slept with, and You sent me the one that did ***me*** wrong! What am I supposed to do with her?"

I remember something Pastor Nathan said in his sermon yesterday. "Prayer isn't just us telling God what to do and asking for stuff; prayer also involves listening.

"Okay God, I'm gonna keep listening, but I better get to work before I get fired. I hope I hear the answer when You give it."

Medina

Medina quickly learned the ropes and was left alone with a folder of letters to work on.

Ain't this nothing? Medina thought. *Bad enough I had to leave North Carolina, but now I have to work for Nate and Susan. God clearly hates me. I hope neither of them is vindictive, or this job will last all of today before I'm looking again. ..*

Medina chuckled and kept working.

Susan

Susan made the rest of her rounds, and mentally prepared a report for Nate.

Nothing out of the ordinary, she thought. *Everybody's working and nobody seems off kilter.*

"Susan! Can I talk to you right quick?"

Check that- - -.

Susan sighed. Kelvin Grant was a good worker, but aggravating.

If he hits on me one more time, I swear I'll have him released from this assignment.

"What can I do for you, Kelvin?"

"I was just wondering if you needed any help training the new temps. I got some free time if you do."

Susan concealed a smile. "Thanks, but we're fine. Only one started today, and she's doing well."

Susan finished her rounds and headed for Nate's office, suppressing laughter all the way.

Nate

I'm still laughing at Susan's report as I head for the cafeteria. If Susan is right, Kelvin's got someone new on his mind.

That could be a good thing. He's asked Susan out so many times I had to put him on report for harassment. I'd better keep an eye on him. He was on that assignment with Medina and me, and I think she slept with him too. If she encourages him, there will be drama and it will be loud.

"Mind if I join you?"

Medina's expression suggests she'd rather be the visual aid at a Klan meeting, but she fixed her face and gestured for me to sit.

"Relax, you're still on the job."

She chuckles in spite of herself.

"I like to have lunch with new folks during their first week and find out how they're doing. It helps me get to know everybody in the department that much faster."

She focuses on her sandwich instead of looking me in the eye. I figure I've wasted enough of her time.

"Okay Medina, cards on the table. You don't look any more comfortable than I feel right now."

Her head snaps up, and those gorgeous brown eyes of hers reflect surprise.

"Don't look so shocked. I meant what I said last time we *saw* each other."

She chuckles. Clearly she remembers like I do that the last time I saw her was when she slid out of my bed and my life. I can't help but blush; nowadays I try not to think about naked women.

"I know we didn't part on good terms, but in the interest of us working together, I won't treat you any different than how I treat anyone else around here. You'll stay or move on depending on how well you work. And from what I hear, you're doing great."

"Thank you."

Her response stuns me. The Medina I remember boldly stepped to me on the first day of our assignment and initiated a conversation that led to us becoming "friends with benefits." This Medina sounds more humble.

"If you don't mind me asking, what brings you back here? I assumed you'd moved down south permanently."

Medina sighs. "My mom needs both knees replaced. She had the first knee done and she's doing well, but she needs someone with her all the time."

I nod. "I suppose hiring a nurse or a home health aide is out."

"I could probably afford one, but this is my mother. I'm the only child and it's my responsibility."

The little devil on one shoulder is screaming at me to stop thinking she's so great when she did me wrong, but the angel on the other telling me to get over it. The angel's winning when she grabs the conversational steering wheel and hangs a sharp left.

"Okay Nate, I appreciate your honesty. Now I want you to appreciate mine."

She locks her gaze on mine. I feel like a mouse being eyed up by a snake.

"I know you got religion while I was gone. I also know you still want me. Religion or not, I will break… you… down."

"Hope I'm not interrupting anything."

I nearly jump out of my skin. Susan materializes out of nowhere, lunch bag in hand and pleasant smile on her face.

"I hope you don't mind, Medina-- Nate and I usually evaluate new employees together."

I could kiss Susan right now.

Medina

Medina smiled as she entered her mother's house. She paid the neighbor who stayed with her mother during the day and said good night. Thoughts of Nate, Kelvin, and all the other interesting men on the job took a back seat as she cooked dinner, helped her mother bathe, and enjoyed pleasant conversation. After she got her mother settled, Medina changed out of her work clothes to relax.

Not much has changed in Delaware since I left, she thought. *The women are still haters and the men are still predictable. Since I'm going to be here a minute, I'll have to see what I can do to stay entertained. Since Nate's not interested, I'll definitely need to have a word with Kelvin. If he's still pissed about what happened, I'll have to put it on him good enough to give the brother amnesia.*

Medina laughed as she put *Waiting To Exhale* in her DVD player.

Nate

I come to work a half-hour early this time. I have no choice--I'm responsible for three divisions worth of temps, and I can't let one woman in Correspondence distract me from Phones and Credit Analysis. All three deserve my best.

Yeah, but neither of the other departments has a ticking time bomb in it.

I put my head down and plow through paperwork. Before I know it, Susan's at my door wearing a frown. That means I have to deal with an issue right away.

"Dress code violation."

"Male or female?"

Susan rolls her eyes. "Female. Short skirt and excessive cleavage. Want to guess who?"

One day and Medina's starting her mess already. I should have seen this coming. After all, she can't entice any coworkers if she covers everything up.

"Did you address it?"

"I did. I got an insincere apology and a comment under her breath implying that I'm just hating because I'm too "skurred" to dress like her."

We both get a laugh out of that. If body-by-Serena Williams Susan ever came in dressed like Medina, productivity among the men (and a few questionable women) would drop like a stone. I thank God every day Susan's wardrobe is appropriate.

"Okay, I'll handle it. Anything else?"

"I'm scheduled to monitor calls in Phones, but I can stay while you talk to Medina if you need me."

"Thanks, but I need to address this alone or else more women will think they can get away with it. Can you send her in before you head over?"

Susan barely clears my office before I start praying.

I can do all things through Christ who strengthens me. That means I won't stare at her cleavage when she comes in or her behind when she leaves.

I think I hear Jesus chuckling.

Medina arrives within two minutes. I get right to the point.

“Your outfit doesn't conform to the written dress code.”

She glares at me as if to say, “That's the idea, fool!”

“I have a division full of men who need to focus on their work instead of your body.”

She locks eyes with me like she did in the cafeteria yesterday. “I dressed like this when we worked together two years ago. I didn't hear any complaints from you then.”

“Two years ago I wasn't your boss. I was a trifling fellow temp who used his assignments to get women.”

I have surprised her--her eyebrows go up so high they almost hit her hairline.

“I try to keep personal stuff out of work, but it seems appropriate to do this now. Medina, when we worked together before, I used you. I said and did whatever I had to in order to get you in bed. I'm sorry for using you like that.”

I have no clue how Medina will react. Each of the other two times, the women I apologized to were shocked and accepted my apology. I suspect Medina won't be like the others.

She maintains her unnerving eye contact. “Nate, unlike Kelvin, you have nothing to apologize for. I hooked up with you for a reason, and you didn't disappoint me.”

Okay, that I didn't see coming.

“You didn't use me sweetie--we used each other. I enjoyed every minute of it, and I'm sure you haven't lost your touch.”

She crosses her legs just high enough to give me a hint of what I was missing without completely revealing Victoria's Secret.

I put on my best poker face. “Medina, I'm flattered you think so highly of me, but I don't roll like that any more. I gave my life to Jesus Christ about a year ago. As part of my walk, I choose to abstain from further sex until marriage."

Medina uncrosses her legs and smirks at me. "Mmm-hmm. I've got your salvation right here. If I wanted to, I could knock that Bible on the floor and make you *marry* me on your desk."

I'm not speechless often. This is one of those rare moments. As my larynx locks up, I grab an incident form and fill it out. We both sign it, and I give her a copy.

"We're done here, Medina. You've had a verbal warning from Susan and this is your written one. If you come to work inappropriately dressed again, I will release you from this assignment. Is that clear?"

She does the hypnotic eyes again, but backs down without making it a contest of wills.

"Clear as day. I hope you enjoyed the view--you won't see it again."

I dismiss her back to her work. As she leaves, she makes sure I can look down her blouse and then to admire her behind if I choose. I don't choose.

Medina turns back as she clears my door. "Being HNIC suits you. You handled this well."

A nearly imperceptible shimmy and she's gone, with only the residue of her perfume to remind me how close I came to backsliding just then.

I go to Susan's office for our next meeting for a change of pace. Hers is in between Phones and Credit Analysis, while mine is in Correspondence. How appropriate--my office is closest to my biggest headache.

I always enjoy looking around Susan's office. Family pictures, pictures from her drum major days (high school and college), graduation pictures--she's made this like home.

"All of our phone reps are on point--everybody's logged into their phones and taking calls like they're supposed to. And considering the fact that nobody warned them I was monitoring today, that's exceptional," Susan beams with pride.

"Good! All's well in Credit Analysis except for Mary, who's been fifteen minutes late every day the past two weeks."

"You warned her again?"

"No, she's already had three warnings. I'm releasing her. There are too many other temps lined up to work here for us to put up with that."

We both sign off on her release. "And last but not least, Correspondence. Susan, we officially have drama."

I tell her about my talk with Medina and show her the paperwork. Susan shakes her head in disbelief.

"Nate, she's lost her mind. I've known her for awhile now, but she's never been this bad."

My eyebrows rise. "I didn't know you knew her before she started here."

Susan shrugs. "Guess it never came up. We grew up across the street from each other. We were tight as little kids, but when we got to be teens, we drifted. She felt like she had to compete with me for everything, including boys."

Susan looks like she swallowed a lemon. I have to smile. "She lost this time. You're her boss--if that ain't losing the competition, I don't know what is."

Susan stays solemn. "We have another situation, and it's related."

She tells me about Kelvin's desire to train Medina.

"On my way back from Phones, I noticed three folks paying more attention to each other than their letters. Medina was flirting with Felipe Santos, and Kelvin had so much steam coming out his ears I thought he'd burst into flame."

I roll my eyes. "Susan, you need to know this. Kelvin slept with Medina during a previous assignment. I did too."

I give her the short version. Susan doesn't blink or flinch; she just listens.

"It looks like she's playing her games again. I'm not letting her take me there, but Kelvin may be a different story."

Susan nods. "Thanks for telling me that--I hate surprises."

We laugh and make a pact to keep a closer eye on Correspondence until further notice.

Day three of the Week from Sheol started off full

throttle. Kelvin and Medina walk in at the same time; Medina's outfit is conservative, and Kelvin is wearing a huge smile. Math isn't my strong subject, but I can add one and one and get two.

When Susan comes in, I don't waste any time.

"Medina and Kelvin look rather chummy today. She's dressed code compliant, but that big Kool-Aid smile on Kelvin has to violate some code or the other."

Susan's face drops. "They didn't!"

"That "I got some" grin on his grill suggests they did."

I push a folder towards her. "There's more. Kelvin was dismissed from a previous assignment after nearly getting in a fight with a coworker."

Susan groans. "Great! We definitely need to keep an eye on this situation."

We put the Correspondence department head on alert, Security on speed dial and decide to alternate walking the floor once an hour.

Susan goes first, and has no issues. When my turn comes, I have a feeling I won't be so blessed. Unfortunately, I'm right.

I'd had walked the length of Correspondence and circled back towards my office when the department head flags me down. I look where she points. One of the men is standing behind a seated woman, kneading her shoulders like bread dough.

"I got it, Zeena--just keep an eye on the other inmates so they don't try to go off too."

Zeena's giggle echoes in my ears as I head towards my nonworking temps. Neither of them sees or hears me coming. Medina's expression is blissful as Kelvin works her neck like a professional. I tap him on the shoulder.

"While I appreciate your concern for your coworker's well-being, this is neither the time nor the place for a chair massage. I need the two of you to get back to work."

I turn to walk away, only to find an angry Negro in my face.

"Don't be hatin' because I got what you ain't man enough

to handle."

I give him my patented "Negro, please!" death glare. To his credit, he didn't flinch.

I keep my voice low and ignore Medina's satisfied smile. "Kelvin, I don't care what you handle on your own time. Right now, you're on *my* time, and I need you working."

Kelvin raises up like a teenager and officially gets loud on me.

"Oh, I see. She ain't give you none and now you tryin' to punk me 'front of everybody."

I maintain my poker face and manage not to break his jaw.

"In my office. Right--Now!"

Kelvin doesn't budge. He swells up even further, and gives the distinct impression he wants to fight.

"Think you better than me? Punk, you ain't nobody!"

I don't budge either.

"Kelvin, you're not making sense. When did I--or anyone--say I was better than you are?"

He cuts his eyes to the side, and it all falls into place. Medina's smirk reminds me of how I used to look after I successfully charmed a woman into bed.

"You might have got there first, but I'm with her now! And you ain't gettin' her back, so don't even think about it!"

He hits me with the N-word and a few creative curses. Back in the day, that would've earned him a fat lip and a black eye--*before* he hit the floor.

"Kelvin, you have officially lost your mind--and your job. Grab your things and get out!"

We shoot eye lasers at each other until Kelvin decides that getting his butt kicked by his former boss wouldn't look good on his resume. He grabs his jacket and storms out just as a security guard responds to Zeena's call. Susan is right behind them, eyes wide.

"Okay folks, show's over. Anyone who's ready to go to lunch now--can go--otherwise, back to work. Medina, can I see you in my office?"

I nod to Susan to follow me. As I pass Zeena, I ask her to check with security--to both make sure Kelvin left the building and to not allow him back unless I say different.

Medina takes the chair right in front of my desk. Susan pulls the extra chair beside mine so we could convene our miniature tribunal. I nod to her to go first.

"Medina, you and Kelvin came in together this morning. Did he seem out of sorts to you?"

Medina gives her that same irritating smirk she wore during the confrontation. "Not that I noticed. He was in a great mood."

"Did you ask him to give you a massage?"

Medina smirks on. "No, that was his idea. I couldn't get comfortable, and Kelvin said that since it was his fault I'm stiff and sore, he'd try to get the crick out of my neck."

"Did it occur to you that maybe it wasn't a good idea to do that during work hours?"

"I told him to stop, but he kept massaging. After a few seconds, it felt so good I forgot where I *was*!"

She laughs alone.

"Medina, would you happen to know how he got the idea in his head that I think I'm better then he is?"

She giggles. "We spent time together last night and your name came up."

"I really hate to ask, but in what context did my name come up while you two were socializing?"

Medina looks as innocent as a baby. "I accidentally said your name instead of his."

Susan and I both keep our poker faces, but I know her well enough to know that, if it were just us in the office, she'd be rolling on the floor laughing.

"I assume that put a damper on the evening."

"He asked why I was thinking about you, and then he demanded to know if you were a better---socializer. I didn't say you were, but he considered the fact that I still remembered your "socializing" skills two years later, and decided that you are."

I shake my head in disbelief. "Medina, like I told Kelvin, what you do on *your* time is *your* business. When your personal stuff affects your work, then it's *my* business."

She gives us the innocent look again. “Why are you on me? *Kelvin's* the one who went ballistic.”

Susan stares holes in her. “And *you* were the one who instigated. You might not have said anything, but your expression spoke volumes.”

Medina wisely says nothing; our Bad Cop--Bad Cop routine told her she's skating on thin ice and we just turned on the heater.

“Medina, your work performance is impeccable. That's the only reason we don't release you right now. Make no mistakes though--one more incident involving you, directly or peripherally, and you're gone.”

Medina nods. “Anything else or can I get back to work now?”

Susan's glare chills me on its way to Medina. “No. Just remember what Nate and I said. Despite the drama, you're a good worker. We'd hate to lose you.”

Medina leaves without another word. Susan turns to me.

“Ever wish you'd gone into a different line of work?”

We laugh ourselves to tears.

Medina

Medina was glad to see 6:00. She wasted no time clocking out and caught the elevator to the lobby. She fumbled for her car keys as she cleared the door, and reminisced about the chaos she caused earlier.

Why I had to call Nate's name instead of Kelvin's, I don't know. That'll teach me to drink more than one glass of wine at a time. But I couldn't be with Kelvin sober.

As she started laughing, a hard blow nearly knocked Medina unconscious. She threw her hand up to ward off the next, and screamed as the impact of a hard object reverberated all the way to her shoulder.

The beating was swift, brutal, and replete with repetitions of the b-word; in less than a minute, Medina lay bleeding on the asphalt.

“Who's better now?”

Her assailant spit in her general direction and strolled away.

Nate

Susan and I get ready to write the mother of all incident reports. This report has to be tight and I have to be ready for a Guantanamo-style grilling from my superiors once they get it.

Since I've got a ton of other paperwork, Susan volunteers to write the initial report. I'll edit, add my input, and review it with Susan before submitting it. Looks like we're both working late tonight.

I stay in my seat for hours before getting up. Susan's engrossed in typing when I pass her door, and I don't disturb her.

The floor's empty--all three departments left for the day about ten minutes ago. Unless I lost track of an equally-overloaded-with-work department head, Susan and I are the only ones still here.

Amazing how drama bonds people. There was a moment after we finished debriefing when Susan and I did the meaningful eye contact thing. I can't speak for her, but I'm surprised. I mean, she's a great assistant and attractive, but I don't date on the job anymore. I figure I did enough damage before and including Medina--no sense inviting Armageddon ever again.

I'm still wondering if I should revisit that hard line stance when I trip over something and nearly do a face-plant into the asphalt. Once I recover my balance, I look down to see what it was.

Oh… my… God.

Officer Donovan nods as I finish the story.

"We're here to see the same person. My partner's at your job interviewing your assistant, and I'm here to see the victim and the man who found her. That would be you."

We go inside and head for Medina's room. I'm feeling better about the situation when Kelvin comes at me out of nowhere, cussing and fussing about fake Christians trying to steal women. When he shoves me, I interrupt his profane tirade by slamming him against the wall.

"Kelvin, I have unfinished business with Medina that involves me, her, and God. You and your drama aren't part of it. I *am* a Christian, but if you don't get out my face, I'll beat you like a tambourine at a revival service!"

Kelvin reads the truth of that statement in my eyes. When I let go of his shirt, he backs away slowly. Officer Donavan looks amused--I had forgotten he was there until now.

"Are you Kelvin Grant?"

Kelvin nods. Officer Donovan asks a few quick questions, and when Kelvin can't account for his whereabouts for the past two hours, he finds himself in handcuffs.

"I didn't do nothing! Ask this bougie Negro where his butt was!"

Officer Donovan's partner enters the waiting room just in time to take possession of Kelvin. Susan comes in right behind him, eyes wet with tears.

"Did Kelvin do this?"

"He's their prime suspect. I'm sure they'll find out for sure soon enough."

It takes us nearly half an hour to learn what we already knew; somebody beat the snot out of Medina with a blunt object and left her for dead. The doctor adds that she was critical when they brought her in, but she's improving.

God, I know I messed up. I should have done what you told me sooner, but it's not too late. Help me say what You need me to say, Lord.

Except for the bruises and bandages, Medina looks like she's simply in bed asleep. Awake or not, I need to do this.

I don't know how long I spend sitting beside her bed holding her hand. I apologize again, and this time I tell her about Jesus.

"Nate," she whisper in a barely audible voice.

I almost fall out my chair.

"Medina? You're awake?"

Real smooth, genius. Of course she's awake--she just talked to you, moron!

"Hurts," she pushes through her lips with a struggle.

"I guess so. You were beaten pretty badly. Want me to call a nurse?"

I reach for the call button, but she weakly puts up a hand to stop me.

"Who--did--?"

I take a deep breath. "They arrested Kelvin Grant about an hour ago, when he came here. Is he the one who beat you?"

She mumbles something I barely understand and falls back asleep.

I jerk awake, and had a "where the heck am I?" moment. A whispering sound woke me, and the shadow that slid by put me on full alert. I'm still in Medina's room, and I'm not alone.

My eyes adjust to the darkness just in time. Someone is standing over Medina and holding something where her head should be. Fear catapults me out of the chair. I yank the shadow person away, and see a pillow hit the floor. Whoever it is fights like a wildcat on crack, but I'm not letting them get a second chance to smother Medina.

I take a shot to the mouth, and grab the fist that sucker-punched me. I pin the person's arms to their sides, and get the shock of my life when my hands graze breasts.

The light hit like a physical object. Apparently Medina hit the nurse call button, because the duty nurse is staring at me like I'm crazy. Small wonder--I'm in a patient's room after hours and I've got an attractive woman in a half-nelson.

"Nurse, can you call the police?"

Susan wilts in my grasp like a flower during a sudden frost.

"Susan, why?"

Cold and Calculating Susan must have replaced Scared Susan when I wasn't looking. "You weren't going to release her, Nate--I heard it in your voice. If we kept her, she'd have every man in Correspondence fighting over her inside a month."

I heard Medina gasp.

"Sleeping with her was a mistake. You repented, but she was going to make you pay for the rest of your life. You deserve better, Nate."

"I can't believe you did this just for me. What do you get out of it?"

Her smile scares the devil out of me.

"The satisfaction of beating the smirk off that heifer's face. Payback for all the boyfriends she stole from me over the years--and now you."

I know my eyes bugged out this time.

"Don't pretend you don't feel anything for me, Nate. If she hadn't burned you, you wouldn't be afraid to date now. You and I could have had something, but she ruined it again!"

A burly Hispanic constable runs into the room. After a quick explanation, he takes Susan to hold her for the police. Her expression never changes as Officer Donovan takes her away.

Epilogue

Medina slides into the wheelchair the nurse offered. "Is my ride here yet?"

"Yes I am."

Medina's eyebrows raised. "I'm kinda surprised to see you here."

"I needed to be here. And I thought you might need to talk."

She stays quiet until I transfer her from the wheelchair to my car and pull out of the parking lot.

"I didn't realize she hated me."

Help me to listen, God. Not dwell on things she's said or done to me--listen.

"I can't blame her. I've done a lot to her. I stole every boyfriend she ever had when we were kids. I suppose it didn't take much for her to think I stole you from her too."

Touch her heart, Lord.

She surprises me by chuckling. "Clearly she hasn't lost her drum major skills. She hit me with a mop handle, and I swear I saw her twirl it while she was beating me."

I laugh in spite of myself. "Can't fault her skills."

"If that had been Kelvin, I'd be dead."

Medina blots a few tears and composes herself. For the rest of the ride, she talks, I listen and I pray. I help her out of the car and escort her to the door. She surprises me with a kiss me on the cheek.

"I just wanted to thank you. For everything--You've given me a lot to think about."

She starts to go inside and hesitates.

"I'm still not sure what to think about God, and whether or not he wants anything to do with me, but when you get your butt kicked and there's a list of suspects the size of a phone book, something has to change."

She hesitates again. "Susan was right about one thing--you don't deserve all the drama I brought you. I'm sorry I put you through all that."

She kisses me on the cheek; for the first time, I see past the front Medina usually keeps.

"Pray for me sometime---I think I need it."

She goes inside, leaving me standing there stunned.

As I start my car, something occurs to me.

I visited a hospital and nobody died.

Letters to Caged Kings on Lockdown

Jihad

What up Nephew,

Right now, you're walking through the Valley of the Shadow of Death. Not many come up out of the Valley, but a real soldier finds a way to rise. And if I don't know anything else, I know my nephew is a soldier--a no-limit, by any means necessary, non-compromising soldier. I say this because look at all the mess you've had to face your whole life by yourself, and just you keep rising. How many headz you left seven plus years ago when you first went down, and how many of those headz were still in the same place as they was when you first left the streets. Marinate on how you came up, how fast you did it. Now I ain't talking about how you grew, cause everybody know a rose can't grow out of concrete, but a weed can find a way to rise, and that's what you were, a weed, but now nephew, you a rose. You rose from the concrete jungle cause the savages of the streets listened to you, not cause you had the best game, the best dope, or was the baddest, but they listened to you because of your character. Young-bloods from Baltimore projects to Haulville revered you, because everyone who knew you, knew that you say what you mean and mean what you say.

They respect you. And RESPECT is the most powerful thing you can ever have. You can't buy that. I know you messed up, and ain't nothing I can do to stop the pain you feel, but I can show you that you ain't alone, been there done that, and YOU GOT ME. I thank God as I write this letter that I have you for a nephew. Keitz, I love you man. Regardless of me not being there while you grew up, I was a kid myself, but I am now a grown FREE Black Man, and I won't let LIFE, and the SYSTEM take your mind. I've often blamed myself for the life you led. I do that because I could have done more, and you saw what I was and that crap looked good when you was nine-- ten years old. You remember when you came to the ATL, back in the summer of 1990, before I got shot and had that car accident. I gave you a grocery bag of one dollar bills. That was jacked up and I'm sorry. I can't help but to think, that you saw how your uncle was living and you wanted that life, so when you was thirteen, you started slingin' and in no time you became me. And for the first couple years I watched your life my life from my prison cell.

I don't blame my sister, because she ain't never had a clue, I don't blame the sperm donor that helped create you, cause he ain't never had one either. But me, Keitz, once I started to read on the inside I knew, and I didn't do enough to try and stop you. I probably couldn't have, but I didn't do enough to try. That's why I want you with me, in GA. Cause I know how hard it is. I use to smoke laced joints in private, and I went back to it once I hit the bricks, but no one knows. I been clean for five years now, but once you start messing with that stuff, it's close to impossible to stop. ALL THAT GOOD I TALK, AND I WAS JACKED UP MY DAMN SELF. I ain't perfect, nowhere near, but I have a reason to live, a reason to fight and I have an enemy, IGNORANCE. That brotha got my family blowed. That brotha got black people blowed, and at times I can't see why they can't see it, but it's clear as the sky to me. So I write and speak out against those who perpetuate ignorance in the Black community.

But check this out nephew, Jesus was the same type dude as we are. He was a soldier, straight no-limit. He wasn't the milk toast sissy, the church puts out there. He didn't ball out off the people, he stood with them, he fed they them, and he smiled when the gov't came after him, he knew they was gone take his life, but he never once sold out, or sold in, and he never once compromised, and he was mad respected, NOW WHO DOES THAT SOUND LIKE. **YOU.**

From Moses, to Marcus, to Malcolm, to Geronimo Pratt, to the Minister Farrakhan, they all came from dirt and they made sugar. And none of them sold out, or sold in. They had to walk through the Valley, and they had to dance with the devil and they all smoked from his pipe, but at the end of the day, they figured out that Satan wasn't they friend and they knew him well, so knowing him, they were able to fight him, and they did until they left this Earth Plantation.

Nephew, this thing is so much bigger than us, your momma, and your immediate family, this is a cycle of self-perpetuated ignorance, slavery. Ever since they beat Kunta Kinte into submission cutting off his foot, we been naming our kids Toby and cow--towing to a government that never meant for us to be FREE, INFORMED. But it is soldiers--generals, like you and me that have to fight for those who don't even know they in a fight. Yeah, you had to be busted in the head on more than one occasion, but that was because you was half sleep and half wake, now you are waking up and when you fully awake, there's going to be major problems for the HATERS and Government Makers. I've already recognized and told you about your voice, now it's up to you to find it, and I'm gon' keep sending you books, if I can't send you money I will arm you with what you need to find your voice.

And when you do you will help change the system responsible for your condition, your mommas, grand mommas, and my condition. I'm strong, but you are stronger than me, you are a younger version of me, a more creative version of me. And you will do what I won't be able to do. I realize, recognize, and respect that. So for these reasons, I have to get you away from NAP and Chicago, I'm gone take you back, so you can be the KING you were born to be. But while you in a Hotel Hell prison cell, I'm gon' feed you with food that will make you want to get out of the desert of ignorance in NAP and Shy. And as far as your boy Shaun, is concerned, he's the SLAVE that society made him, no disrespect but it is what it is. He chose running women over Friendship, and his greed for money is why he back on the inside. His ignorance of self makes him what he is.

Everybody ain't built for this task. Everybody ain't built for war, but WE are. Now we, not you, but we got eighteen months to build and prepare for tomorrow. Now, I need you to man up, suck that crap up and start preparing. Read what I send you, keep writing, and the FEDS can can keep disconnecting us when you call cause of how I bring it, but I'm gon' bring it the only way I can, and that's real.

Now as far as the public is concerned, I'll water things down, so I can begin to get through to them, but I won't sell in, or sell out.

Please believe that I will not let them take you without a fight. You are my blood, and I love you more than you possibly know. So, smile in them pilgrims faces, while you prepare to rise up out of they hell and change the way they keep us down. The difference between a thug and a soldier, is a thug does things with no rhyme or reason, and a soldier has a plan.

Love and Life,
Jihad

King Antwain,

I wanna thank you for your words. You are why I do what I do. In the 80's and for the better part of the 90's I was Antwain Chapman. Different face but all the same, I was you King. It took not prison, but the brilliant minds behind the walls of Amerikkka's new slave plantation to make me want to wake up. On the streets in the so called free world, I wasn't really trying to hear that we shall overcome, work hard and get a good job crap. I'm a hustler, was born to be a hustler, came from a long line of men who hustled. So how could I listen to a suit or a do gooder trying to tell me how to succeed when they may have looked like me but didn't seem to be like me, or they didn't seem to be from the ghetto unforgiving streets that raised me and so many like me.

But once I started reading while serving 7 years in the feds, books about me, my ancestors, my brothers who came from even rougher streets that I had been spawned from and how they lived my life and how they overcame the impediments and the genocidal stereotypes that the media and society places on Black men, it was a rap. King I started seeing obvious stuff that I had never saw before, I began to analyze my condition, why I was in my condition and why our people where in the condition that we were in. And I saw history repeat itself over and over again. I began to understand the mind games that the media, had played to keep us ignorant and divided. I saw that 1808 wasn't a whole lot different than 2008, with the exception of how then we knew we were slaves.

It's when you close your eyes, and use your mind that you will begin to really see. What rights do we have, the rights that our oppressor gives us. We weren't allowed to read then, now we only read what they spoon feed us and what is deemed socially and scholastically acceptable to the slave master. We were enslaved because of our own abject ignorance. We sold one another out in Africa, as we are doing today, but it's all because of what we don't understand. But King it's not going to be the suits, and the Harvard and Howard grads that will spark revolution.

Jesus didn't have a degree from the University of Rome. Harriet Tubman didn't graduate from Princeton, Malcolm, didn't attend Harvard, Marcus didn't get his degree from Brown, and yes Martin went to Morehouse, but he was an exception. What all these folks had in common was they began to read, and their conditions created revolutionary thought and as they read and began to understand, they grew into being revolutionaries who spoke truth to power and showed the (ignorant-the oppressed) how not to be scared, and to fight for knowledge, because that is the only thing that will free you. And as you grow as they grew you will never go back to being a slave, and then you will be driven to go back and try and rescue the slaves.

I don't know you. Never met you, but from your letter, I know you want to be free. You wouldn't have written the words you did if you didn't realize that those bars you behind don't make you a prisoner.

I'm saying all this because you are about to hit the bricks and I can't afford for the SYSTEM to take any other Black King from his people. Hell no. And I need help, raising Black Kings out of slavery. I don't have to tell you how hard this is, hell you been captured and caged three times. But you have to keep reading, you have to keep fighting the temptation. You have to fight the urge to go back to working for THEM, murdering your people with the perpetuation of ignorance. Stop being the prey and become the hunter. It's so easy to sell dope, freak queens left and right, put a gun to your brothers head, but that only destroys US and makes the unjust SYSTEM even stronger. You wanna kill something, Kill Ignorance, put a gun to a system of oppression, Freak and trick the media into exposing injustice. FIGHT FOR YOUR FREEDOM AND YOUR LIFE.

Love and Life,
Jihad

LIKE FATHER, LIKE SON

Joey Pinkney

I wake up every morning five to ten seconds before the Amtrak rushes through the woods behind my neighborhood. This is my regular routine set in stone between 5:37 and 5:42 a.m. I don't how it worked out that way. It just did...

It wasn't unusual for this morning ritual to make my heart race, but this time it was different. I couldn't relax through this adrenaline rush. I paced the bedroom sweaty and nervous. The dark sky started to part for the sun as it made its switch to a swarthy purple. I swear I didn't want my jitters to be justified, but my wife Mary and I had really let loose the night before over our son, Andre.

I slowed my pace down and plopped face-down on the bed and placed my hand on the empty spot where Mary normally slept. The reality of the cold sheets cut deep because her space had been deserted for some time. When we bickered, Mary normally turned her back to me and stayed on her side of the bed. If it got really bad, she slept in the guest bedroom because I had a rule that I would never go to the "dog house" and sleep on the couch. So she would do the honors on her own principles.

When I first met Mary, everything was cool between her and I. Andre made it obvious from the very beginning that he wanted his mother to have no parts of me. But what little man did? I wasn't offended. In fact, I gave a silent ovation to his desire to protect the only person that had protected him. I never felt provoked to challenge his bond to his mother. Simply put, I was a stranger invading his space.

I went from courting Mary to actually marrying Mary. I proposed to Mary after church one hot Sunday afternoon in July. All of her family and friends present in the parking lot praising the King of Kings and appraising the engagement ring. Six months later, we married with those same family and friends in that same sanctified church. Hands down, it was one of the best days of my life even though Andre practically ignored me.

I remember hugging him and praying that God help him come to accept me as the man I was. In time, I wanted him to realize that I seriously loved his mother and had the same love for him. He showed no signs of appreciation. Instead, he pushed the buttons on his new Game Boy Pocket that he successfully begged Mary for.

I understood that position when he was a little boy. I gave him room to figure things out. He had to get used to having a father-figure after eight years of just having a mother. I took the lead and remained the adult. I didn't embarrass him in front of his friends, I never laid a hand on him that wasn't warranted and I never talked down to his mother during our disputes.

Over the years, the tension continued to build. At sixteen, Andre was where he was at day one: I was still a stranger invading his space. Despite all that resistance from Andre, I continued loving Mary like there was no turbulence, by the name of Andre, interrupting our relationship. I struggled against the strain of juggling life with an enamored wife and an egocentric son.

My patience with Andre dwindled when he started committing petty crimes around the neighborhood. This was the same neighborhood Mary and I had to show our faces in. It was no secret that Andre and his "gang" were the culprits. We even had neighbors show up at our doorstep demanding their stolen property back. Here I was, busting my knuckles at my uncle's body shop so we could eat and live comfortably, and he was disappearing for days, smoking weed and doing illegal things with that fake gang. All of his life, Mary had been Andre's protector, guardian, and excuse-maker. I knew it was hard for her to see people whispering about her baby boy as she walked down the street. This was the same child, as she told me, who had started speaking in full sentences before he could walk. He was very smart and could read while his friends could barely say their ABCs. I witnessed his straight As in elementary school, so I knew he had above-average intelligence.

Unfortunately, intelligence and common sense don't always live in the same person. Andre's ciminal behavior defied reason. He was loved, clothed, and fed. He was definitely fed because we couldn't keep food in the house with his appetite. We weren't filthy rich, but we were far from filthy, so his misadventures made us muddled. Why did the devil choose to destroy our child?

My brittle heart was broken every time I saw Mary on the verge of having a nervous breakdown because of a missing Andre. My blood would boil to the point of producing a migraine-like headache when Andre would show up days later high, nonchalant, and completely oblivious to his mother's deteriorating state of mind. I knew that something bad was going to have to happen before reality knocked him upside his head. I was guilty of praying for that bad thing to hurry up and happen.

It didn't surprise me when the cops knocked on our door early one Sunday morning searching for Andre to ask him about a robbery he may have witnessed. We knew he was in his room, but we didn't like the idea of our neighbors seeing the police at our house. We asked for a warrant to counter their question to look in Andre's room. One of the officers threatened to make Andre's life as hard as humanly possible if we continued to be uncooperative. That was all Mary needed to hear. She led the officers through the hall and knocked on Andre's door. Hearing no answer, she opened the door and slowly peeked in.

We all shuffled into Andre's room only to find his window wide open. The screen was cut neatly on the left side and the bottom. The curtains were gently waving in the chilly breeze. I wasn't shivering because I was cold; I was shaking because of an anger induced by shame. I should've been surprised, but I wasn't. This was just a sure sign that Andre's was up to no good. When the cops saw the scene, they laughed and commented to each other that I was afraid of Andre. Afraid! Me afraid? No way.

After we showed the cops out, I calmly sat Mary down in the living room and told her exactly how it was going to be. I had finally reached my breaking point. There wasn't a hint of hesitation when I said that Andre could no longer live in the house. It was embarrassing enough that the entire neighborhood knew that we were sheltering a criminal, but it went to another point when the cops mentioned that I lived in fear of our child.

Mary was furious with me. I expected her to be. I told Mary that I couldn't allow Andre to drag us into his mess. That was that. Mary screamed that she had Andre's back no matter what. I tried to calm her down while explaining to her that this Sunday morning visit by the cops was a sign of worse things to come. Obviously, Andre had gotten mixed up in something that placed him under investigation.

Mary lashed out at me like I was the one that was slipping out the window to do destructive things. It hurt like hell to tell my wife that our son was no longer welcomed where we dwell. But it cut like a knife and bruised my soul to know that Mary would take Andre's side no matter what. Could she not see all the destructive things he had done and said over the years? Needless to say, she didn't go to church, and I used her as an excuse to miss church myself.

Slowly a rigid rift rose between the two of us. I wasn't sure how, or even if it was even worth it, to break down the barrier. Sadly, I was starting to feel that it was time to call it quits after almost eight years of marriage. The air was so thick, I could barely inhale. I felt like I compromised on everything for this marriage. I had stopped pursuing my MBA to work as a mechanic in my uncle's body shop to make a steady paycheck for the household. I started to go to church on more than just Sunday in order to stay consistent with the way that Mary wanted Andre to be raised. I ate those scrambled eggs almost every morning even though I told her I didn't like scrambled eggs when we first got married.

Speaking of scrambled eggs, there was something that I always heard after the trains came through: a mixture of clanking, sloshing, and scraping. Like clockwork, the sound of the eggs scrambling was one that would await me on the far end of the house, each and every morning. It got to the point where I could tell which fork and which bowl Mary was using. On this particular morning, she was furiously fusing the yolk with the white using the plastic fork with the three prongs one of our porcelain bowls. I guessed that it was the white bowl with the brown trim around the edge.

I paused and thanked God for waking me up that morning. I relieved myself, washed my face and mentally prepared for battle. This gave the cliche 'I hate Mondays' a new significance.

"Good morning." I figured I would enter the room and break the ice. I slid my chair out, sat down and accidentally shifted the table.

"Morning..." Mary barely said. She sounded like she was asking me a question. I silently watched. Mary solemnly turned from the stove, looked at the table, squinted at me, and paused to look back to the table. She stared at the table for only a split second, but it felt like a whole minute. She turned back around to finish scrambling my eggs. "You hurt my feelings last night..." I could barely hear her over the sizzling grease. She pulled out a spatula from the squeaky drawer.

And there it was...the beginning all over again.

"I hurt your feelings? By wanting to protect the safety of this household?" I figured that if I'm going to go in, I'm going to go all in. Her body stiffened as she turned around and pointed that old, melted spatula at me.

"No! You don't love Andre, and it shows!" I could see a mist of spittle spray the message out of her mouth like a shotgun blast.

"Calm down. And stop pointing that spatula at me. You know that ain't cool." I hated being pointed at. It always reminded me of the time a cop pointed his gun in my face for nothing more than chuckles and to impress his partner. I was eleven and vowed to never be in that situation again. I told her that story a million times, but she never stopped pointing things at me.

"You hate him... Don't you..." She wasn't asking me. Mary was telling me. My world stopped spinning. My face felt flushed with anger as her question forced its way into my mind.

"Yeah, I hate him," I said with anger lacing my every word. She gasped like a roach had jumped out from my mouth. Before she could jump in and say anything, I finished my statement. "I hate him so much that I call him my son, even though he has always refused to call me anything but Terrence in the eight years we've been a family."

Mary triggered a strange spirit within me. I couldn't stop talking. "I hate him so much that I sit down with him after I get home from work. Even though I'm tired, I make sure he does all of his homework. Even though I'm tired, I make sure he understands the lessons he should have learned in class since the teachers have him all day."

Mary tried to jump in the argument, but I rambled on. "I hate him so much that I take time off of work during the day...to run up to the school with you...to plead with the principal...to not expel him for smoking weed in the girl's bathroom! The! Girl's! Bathroom!"

At this point Mary was screaming at the top of her lungs, but I couldn't hear her. I only heard my own words. "I hate him so much that I make it a point to talk to him about being a Black man in America even though he strives to be a low-life nobody."

With that last statement, Mary dropped the burnt spatula on

the floor in utter shock. Chunks of scrambled eggs splattered on her feet and her eyes welled up bitter tears. When I saw her lips trembling, I tried to tell her I was sorry, but I couldn't get the words out. She ran out of the kitchen shrieking, "Why God?!!" After she slammed the bedroom door shut, she cried at the top of her lungs and from the bottom of her soul.

I wasn't sorrowful. I was satiated. My soul was serene. I felt like I just had superb sex, and I was spent.

I sighed as I scooped the spatula off of the floor and rinsed it in the sink. I cleaned the mess off of the floor that I had caused. I rinsed out the bowl she used to prepare the eggs. That's when I noticed that she had used the white porcelain bowl with the brown border. I dumped some eggs on a plate and sat down at the table with my hot sauce. I clutched the fork with the plastic handle and the three big prongs and bowed my head to pray over my food. I was in peace as the storm caused by Hurricane Andre surrounded me.

I hated when she Mary backed me into corners like that. It was never good. We had been married for almost eight years, and in that time she could never grasp the slant of my sarcasm. All she could hear me saying was "I hate him" and nothing else. But I'm equally at fault for being slow to figure out how to communicate with her. She backed me in the corner, and I always lashed out at her knowing good and well she couldn't handle it.

At this point, I wondered who would be the first to break. When we got a phone call at two in the morning, the first thing I thought was that somebody had died. I mean, seriously, who calls at two in the morning unless someone is dead, a house is burned down or, more than likely in our case, someone is in jail. Mary picked it up before the first ring could end.

That's when it came back to me that Andre had been missing for the past two days. I grew so numb of his antics that I forgot he was gone. I knew I loved Andre because I was passionate about him getting his life together. But something inside of me was giving up on him actually

having a good life. I begged God to forgive me.
All I could hear Mary saying was yeahs and uh huhs to a guy who had a loud baritone drawl. She hung up the phone and jumped out of the bed faster than I've ever seen her run. I hopped up, too. She rushed past me through the darkness into the bathroom.

"Oh. You can stay here. Officer Griffin wants me to pick Andre up at the police station." She clicked the lights on and started brushing her hair down real hard. It's bad when you know the police by their first name.

"Oh, they got him?" I tried to sound concerned.

"Yeah!," she shouted. I could tell she thought that I could have cared less and wanted to go get him by herself.

"Cool." I started grabbing my jeans out of the closet.

She stopped scraping at her hair. "What you mean cool? What's cool about this?"

I could feel that spirit of argument slowly gaining strength. "I just meant…never mind. Just get your clothes on, and let's go!" I quickly slid my shoes on without socks. I always wore socks, but I had to get out of that room in my truck before I ended up in jail sitting next to Andre.

I rushed out of the house out shaking my head. Why is she getting on me? Last I checked, I came home after work every night. I don't lie, cheat, or steal. I stopped smoking weed and cigarettes long before we met. I never drank alcohol, not even socially. Last I checked, I was at the breakfast table every morning eating those scrambled eggs smothered in hot sauce.

"What's cool about this...", I mumbled as I started up my Ford Explorer. "This is crazy," I continued to whisper to myself. "And this is really happening... It's really happening?" I started laughing, and it startled me. This was not funny, but I was tickled in a dark kind of way. I had prayed that something would happen that would make or break Andre so that he could get his life together. As I sat there replaying my spat with Mary, I wondered if this was playing out exactly how I'd prayed it would.

I looked down at the clock on the radio and noticed it was 2:06 a.m. As soon as it turned flickered 2:07, Mary rushed past my truck and hopped in her Probe. Thank God she had to dig in her purse for the keys. That gave me just enough time to cut my truck off and get into her car before she put it in reverse.

"What's up with that?" I barked as I leaned forward to look her dead in the eyes. The gears whined as we rocketed down the driveway. We jolted back into our seats as she put it in drive, and we sped to our next destination. "You know what? Don't even try it. This is not your issue." She never took her eyes off of what she was doing. She never looked over at me. It felt like she was talking to me like I was on speaker phone – loud and distant. "Until he's eighteen, Andre's got a momma who got his back. It's not your fault that you aren't his real dad and weren't there when he was born. It's not his either. Maybe then you two could have got along."

"First of all---" I got cut off before I could start up good.

"I am his mother. Yeah, I was a baby who had a baby. But that's my baby! My baby!" She was talking to me like we were sworn enemies. "Whatever he's going through, only God can judge him." I couldn't believe that I was witnessing my wife going crazy. "Not me! And not you!" Instead of anger, I felt sorry for her. I looked out of the window as the city passed me by. Something in me wanted to stare Mary down, but I focused my eyes on the pitch black sky with speckles of bright stars shining back at me. She kept going on and on about Andre's problems. She blamed everything but him. I waited until she was finished before I started talking.

"But---" She cut me off again.

"But nothing! There ain't no buts. Andre is far from being right, but he deserves the best I can give. He deserves a mother and a father at least until he becomes an adult. Just like I deserve a husband. Just like you deserve---"

"A wife!" We said those two words at the same time. It was like a baton passed between two Olympic athletes.

"I need love and respect, too! I'm not some little boy. I'm your husband. I work hard. Not for me, not for you, not for him – but for us. All of us! I deserve the best you can give just like he deserves it. But you know what? You deserve the best from him, too. Just because he's sixteen doesn't mean he doesn't have responsibilities to honor thy father and thy mother. Is this how he honors us?"

I finally glanced over at her and raised my eyebrows as a facial challenge. I was ready for her answer, but she never took her eyes off of the road. The tears slowly streamed down her cheeks and reflected red, green and yellow of the traffic lights. When Mary didn't respond, I knew I had said something that had resonated with her. I had more to say. "I could halfway see if he was doing all of this criminal stuff to survive. But he has a house to live in. Better yet, a home. He has a mother. He has a father, maybe not the one he wants, but since I came into his life, I have been a father to him. He has clothes, maybe not the clothes he wants, but he has them. He eats whatever he wants out of the fridge. He even has his own room. With cable TV!" Although I was serious, she giggled at the high pitch of my voice on that last statement. "But the best he can give you is a cut screen and an open window? The best he can do is force himself to be a criminal? There are kids out there that have to do that to live. He's doing that for fun."

I stopped to let her say something. She still didn't have anything to say, so I continued to let my heart pour out its precious contents. "And you're right, only God can judge him. But I can judge that he has become a threat to our household. We got cops knocking on the door and calling all hours of the morning. Nobody should be calling us at two a.m. in regards to our sixteen year old. You look through his room and find Black & Milds tobacco and weed and notebooks full of gangster rap lyrics that he wrote. The same people we told him not to be like is the same people he is trying his hardest to be. When he brings death to our door, maybe then you will say 'no more'." I quickly opened the glove compartment and handed Mary a tissue. Her cry was more of a whisper.

"But this isn't my issue," I continued. "This isn't your issue. It's our issue. Andre is not the little boy I met seven, eight years ago. I don't know where that little boy is. But this person we are dealing with right now is going to make or break us. I pray every morning to God to let this boy make it. Let him stay out of the troubles and pitfalls we see on the news, on the streets and in our families. I pray that this doesn't end our marriage because you can't have it both ways. You can't have your son as a criminal and me as your husband. And if you choose me, he definitely can't have it both ways!"

Mary pulled up to the 23rd Precinct. I pondered about how I got to this place in my life. Why am I here? Why are we here?

After Mary checked him out and gathered his items, we all got into the car to head home. I was so mad at Andre. I didn't want to have to say anything to him, so I drove to preoccupy myself. But I couldn't just sit there and let the silence fill the car up and say nothing.

"So how is it that you got caught stealing from the same store they suspected you of stealing from less than two months ago? You do realize that you have to go back to court for a preliminary hearing on the same day you have to your adjudication hearing for the exact same store? Andre, this is senseless."

"It's not the same store..." Andre said blowing out air. His nonchalant words reeked of carelessness while his breathe held onto the remnants of stale Black & Milds and marijuana.

"What?" I was more disturbed by how he was talking to me instead of what he was saying.

Mary cleared her throat and spoke up for Andre. "He got caught in a stolen car with about four hundred dollars and an ounce of marijuana. His friends were robbing a liquor store. A different store. He was just driving the car." I was astonished. Her voice had a tinge of attitude in it like she was taunting me. Plus, she was correcting me in front of Andre. I hated that. It embarrassed me that I didn't know what I was talking about, but I was more embarrassed that I didn't know what I was talking about and my wife was using it against me in a taunting corrective tone.

When I held her hand on our wedding day, I promised to protect, love and respect her. Sitting in this car, I had to enlist the energy of those words to counteract the eidolon that inspired me to erupt. It was one thing for Andre to talk to me like he had no respect or regard for what I was saying, but when Mary corrected me in front of Andre, it made me cringe. It made realize that she had Andre's back unconditionally, and she only had mine when it didn't conflict with having Andre's back.

"Well, why are to doing this to us?" I still wanted answers. He didn't respond. Instead, he kept blowing his stinking breathe throughout the car and shifting in his seat.

"Andre, you better say something real quick." I was about to stop the car, but I really wanted to get back home and go back to sleep before work. Tuesdays were the busier days at the shop for some reason. The last thing I needed was to go into that hectic environment half-tired from this mess. He still didn't respond. Mary jumped in.

"Why are you not answering your father, Andre?"

"I don't have to answer Terrence. My father is Andre Maurice Johnson, Sr. Terrence Greene is just my step-dad because he's your husband...", Andre sighed. If he would have said that a couple a weeks ago, I would have been hurt. For some reason it didn't hurt at this point and time. I felt nothing. It didn't pinch, sting, or even stab any part of my heart or soul.

"Well, answer me," Mary quickly interjected noticing the meltdown in progress.

"What are you doing this for? This isn't how you were raised."

"Momma, I'm just a product of my environment. I gotta do what I gotta do, yadda mean? Me and my boys 'bout to flood the streets with our trap rap, you feel me? They say I'm like 2Pac when I'm in the studio. Verse after verse after verse. Yadda mean?"

I rolled my eyes and shook my head in disgust. I glanced over at Mary and wondered if she heard the same ignorance

I heard. When she didn't flinch at what he was saying, I went in on Andre.

"Oh? You're a product of a two-parent household? Where you still pee in the bed? At sixteen? O.K!" I couldn't resist throwing that in there. He hated that Mary kept me informed about this problem.

"Andre, please finish..." Mary said firmly while staring at me. That was the first time we made eye contact since the day before.

"Why do you do this to us?" I couldn't tell if she was asking me or Andre.

"Ma. I'm not doing anything to you. I do my dirt with my brothers. You don't have nothing to do with it." He was talking to the rear window of thc passenger side. About his brothers.

"So your mother had some kids I don't know about?" I laughed. "Better yet, Andre, if she doesn't have nothing to do with your dirt, then why is it that we're driving around at three in the morning to pick you up from your home away from home?"

As usual, Andre ignored me and spoke to his mother. "Ma. I'm just hustling to get some money to put my voice out in these streets. Tired of being broke. 2Pac didn't graduate from high school, and he madc it big with rap."

I didn't care that he wasn't addressing me, and I didn't care that he thought he knew everything there was to know about everything. "What!? What do you know about 2Pac? Did you know that he went to a high school for performing arts? Did you know that he liked acting and ballet? Better yet, you were about seven years old when 2Pac died because I married your mother the year after. So how do you know anything about 'Pac? Did you know he was homeless and sold drugs because he had to survive, not because he thought it was something cool to do with some fake gang? Did you know that besides the gangster lyrics that lead to his death, he was also a political activist? Did you know his mother was also a political activist that was a part of the Black Panthers. Do you know

who the Black Panthers are?"
"Cats in the zoo don't have nothing to do with the heat I'm bringing, yadda mean?" His laughter quickly turned serious. "But I wasn't talking to you... Terrence."
He said that right when we were pulling into our driveway. Perfect time to straighten him out. I jammed on the brakes, and we all jerked forward. I jumped out the car and jogged around to the back door on the passenger side. I snatched Andre by his collar and slung him into our front yard. As he got up and regained his composure I shouted, "That's the last time you disrespect me! Come here!," and I pointed right in front of me.
"What you gonna do, Terrence?" he shrieked. His voice always got high when he was mad. "Give me a whooping? I'll knock your old ass out. I've fought grown men before!"
"You haven't fought this one! Step on over here!" I was pounding my fist into my palm anticipating a bum rush.
His nervous laughter said it all. "Mama. Tell this man to back up. I wasn't even talking to Terrence in the first place. Secondly---"
"This is between you and him." Mary clipped Andre before he could include her into his conflict. "If you're going to talk to him like a man, then face him like a man. I'm tired of trying to keep this from happening. Y'all got to work this out..." She shook her head with a smirk and sauntered into the house. As soon as the door shut, I started stalking towards him.
"Old man, I don't want to hurt you." Andre blurted while backpedaling for the bushes. "I'm out."
I took two quick steps towards him ready to do damage. He hurried through the neighbor's yard and hopped the fence. After the neighbor's Rottweiler stopped barking, I fell against the car and threw my head in my hands. My tears were not for Andre, but for the fact I had serious intentions of injuring my teenager.
Even though we all had a hard night, I slowly rose just before the train slid through the sleepy woods. The train's horn slapped into my ears like the slam of a sledgehammer. I still got up to start my standard day at the shop. When I

looked in the mirror, it didn't look like my eyes were open. They were just two slits.

When Mary wasn't crying, she was praying. When she wasn't praying, she was crying. The gap between us grew by the day. She was sad for Andre, and I had no pity for him at all. She saw him as her baby that demons at had taken over. I saw him as a young punk chose to be a statistic no matter what. The house was filled with a deafening silence that I couldn't get rid of even with playing music or turning on the television.

The two of us weren't speaking, and that was a silence that my heart couldn't handle. We didn't talk. We didn't have sex. All we had between us was breakfast, and she only cooked those scrambled eggs. Eggs and hot sauce was my morning meal.

I found myself sitting in church one chilly, Sunday morning wondering how this chain of events would change for the better. Here I was, reluctantly going to church. I didn't like having to fake a smile. I didn't like feeling out of place with people who were fully invested in the church. They were not looking down on me, but I still felt like I belonged elsewhere.

When I first started going to church, it was because I could not have Mary otherwise. As the Sundays came and went, I started to soak in the teachings of the Pastor. I still didn't like all the sitting and standing you had to do. And I didn't like having to talk to my neighbor about whatever the preacher wanted us to say in unison. I just wanted to learn more about applying the teachings of the Bible to my life. The choir sang for what felt like hours. I always hated hearing a thousand people sing the same song. There was always bound to be one person who thought they were good enough to sing solo, so they sang a little differently than the rest of the group. That threw the song completely off. Plus, you have that one person who couldn't sing worth a lick.

As I chuckled at the overweight man who was obviously the wannabe solo singer, I noticed Mary started crying from the first words of "Glory Be to Jesus". Since it was their last selection, I paid more attention to it because I could sit down after they finished.

"Glory be to Jesus who in bitter pains, poured for me the life blood, from his sacred veins..."

I'd heard the song a couple times, but I never really listened to the words it. This time, I wanted to know what about this song could make my wife cry. Then it hit me.

"Abel's blood for vengeance pleaded through the skies, but the blood of Jesus for our pardon cries."

My whole life I wanted to see the people who hurt be hurt. My dad had beat me and my mom severely. I wanted to see him die with my own eyes. My cousin, Black, sold crack to his mother, my aunt. I wanted to kill him with my two own hands. Andre brought so much drama to our household that my wife was physically sick and, and I actually prayed that his kids did him dirtier than he'd done us. But Jesus stood before God to beg our Father to forgive us. I didn't know what was exactly right, but I knew I had to let go of my grudges.

"Oft as it is struck on our guilty hearts, Satan in confusion terror struck departs."

As the choir finished the song, I grabbed Mary's hand. She snatched it back to brace herself on the pew in front of her. Her sobs caused her to heave, and I almost cried with her. I rubbed her back knowing that it was not me. It was much bigger than me. I had to let go. I had to let go of the grudge I held against my father who died of a heroine overdose the day I graduated from high school. I had to let go of the grudge I held against Black who also attempted to rape me when I was nine. I had to let of my grudge against cops, especially the cop that pointed that gun at me when I was a little boy. I had to let go of my grudge against Andre who made the wrong choice and is sitting in prison facing adult charges for shooting a person during a carjacking gone bad. Grudges.

The pastor couldn't come out fast enough. I wasn't waiting to hear him preach, I had already received my message. Instead, I was inspired to write poetry. I was overwhelmed by the thought that my grudges held me back because I held on to my grudges. I wanted Andre to rot in jail because I felt he deserved it. After deciphering "Glory Be To Jesus", I realized that I had to keep an open line of communication. Jail or no jail, I had taken a vow and made a promise to love Andre as my son.

Everyone sat down after the choir finished that song. I ripped a few pages out of the notebook Mary used for notes and put my Bible on my lap to begin my journey. I didn't notice that everyone got up for the Pastor when he stepped into the sanctuary. I didn't care. I was already a sentence deep into what would become the letter to bridge the gap between Andre and I. The next two hours was spent writing and revising what I felt like was a masterpiece.

I let Mary read what I came up with as I drove us home. I knew she was curious but was too mad at me to ask to see it.

"This is nice." She smiled for the first time in weeks. "This is real good. I think Andre will like it. Especially coming from you."

"It hit me like when I used to write rhymes late at night," I said as I grinned at the fact that Mary was proud of what I'd done. I was grinning like a kids showing his mother good grades.

"I wish you would have paid attention in church. People think you are strange."

I wanted to say something rude, but that would have been me going back to my old ways too soon. "I am strange. We all are."

Instead of praising my report card, Mary hit me like a mother nagging about chores. "We go to church to get a message from the man of God. You didn't stand up when the pastor came in. You didn't listen to a word of his sermon. You could have written to Andre later."

"No, I had to get that out of me right then and there." I knew she wouldn't understand, but I couldn't be mad at her for that. "Not to start an argument or anything but---"

"You don't have to tell me that you hate going to church."

She was talking to me like I was on speaker phone again. I hated that.

"That's not it. I was going to say that we go to church to get a message from God. Many people put the preacher in front of God. The preacher preaches the Word. He is not the Word. God is. I sit in church sometimes and watch people look at Pastor Whitson like he's God. We stand up when he walks in. We sit when he says sit."

"That's called respect. It's like people speaking to you when they come to your house."

"That's the point I'm trying to make. The church is not his house. It's not the House of Whitson. It's the House of God. When the choir started singing Glory Be to Jesus, I didn't care to hear it. I saw you crying and wanted to feel what you felt."

I could see the light going on in her mind as she smiled sweetly. The same smile I'd seen at the altar that day came back. That smile was worth the trouble and drama.

"I pray everyday that you and Andre get it right." She put her hand in my lap. That's the first time she touched me in I don't know how long. It gave me a new strength.

"Hey, that's what this poem is. It's me reaching out to him in a way that he understands. This poem, to me, is the equalizer. We both love hip hop and rap for totally different reasons. 2Pac is the perfect example. I loved the lyricism. He loves the swagger. We both love the expression. If I would have sat there and listened to the Pastor, I would have lost the moment. Later would have been never."

"Let me keep it. I'll type it up and mail it off tomorrow."

She didn't take her hand out of my lap until we got home. Life wasn't perfectly smooth from that point on, but I had a new determination to give God and my family my best.

Poem to Andre

Nothing can budge us
from our grudges but us
Let God's love touch us

because God's love is tough
We are weak
speaking words we don't want to exist
Trusting in lust, too much to resist
Freedom isn't free, it's priceless
Worth more than gold and diamonds
to hang on your neck
This is about self-respect
Self-destruction and neglect
infects the intellect
Making rejects of your kids
and their kids not born yet
Keep your mind sober
Because intoxicated thoughts
brought on by cheap highs
will lead to your demise
Andre, one day the gun play stops
Leave crime alone
One day the gun may pop
Don't be deceived
You can be the receiver
of a bullet or a blessing
whether a sinner or believer

The Birthday Gift

Eddrick Dejuan

"You have reached Staci. Sorry I can't answer right now, please leave a message and I will call you back." Beep.

"Staci, this is the fifth time I've called you. I'm tired of talking to your voicemail. I'm hot, I'm tired and I want to speak to my wife and kids. Where are you? You're makin' me nervous. Amy's birthday is coming up and I want to talk with her. I'll be in Iraq for only two more weeks and then I'll be home…call me."

"Sergeant Brown…" a young, freckled-faced kid interrupted

"What Private Smith?!"

"What time are we going on the patrol?" Private Smith inquired nervously as he watched his superior angrily grip the phone in his hand.

Sergeant Brown tightened his jaw as he prepared to answer.

"I told you, we head out at 1900 hours!" he yelled.

"Yes Sir, sorry." The youngster said as he scooted away with his tail between his legs.

Sergeant Brown grabbed his rifle and began to clean it. He started to think.

Why hasn't this woman called me back? I've been over here thirteen months and she hasn't sent me anything;

no cards, no nothing. On top of that, I would do anything to hear my daughters' voices again.

Fed up and discouraged, Sergeant Brown decided to call his mother.

"Hello."

"Mama, how have you been?"

"Son, I'm so glad to hear your voice. How are you doing over there? Is everything okay and…" the older woman said as she caught her breath.

"Granny, granny, is that Daddy?" A little girl yelled excitedly in the background.

"Is that Amy?"

"Um…well, son…yeah it is."

"What is she doing over there? Did Staci drop the kids off with you?" He asked curiously.

"Yes, she dropped the girls off a week ago and said that she'd be back; I haven't heard from her since."

"Did you call the police? Maybe she got into an accident or something."

His mother sighed and then said, "I'm sure she'll return for the girlss we'll pick you up at the airport in two weeks right?" His mother said changing the subject.

"Why are you ignoring me? Mama, if something's happened to Staci, don't you think the cops should be the first to know? Call them report her missing or something." He said as a lump in his throat caught up with heavy-breathing. If it hadn't been for the fact that he was half-way 'round the world, he would have marched to every one of Staci's favorite hang-outs and demanded to know where the heck she was and why she would abandon her kids with his mother. But he knew better than telling his mother to do that. His head began to throb as he imagined what his daughters had to have been thinking throughout all of this.

"Sergeant Brown." Private Smith interrupted again, this time with his head bowed.

""'Wait a minute, Private, I'm on the phone with home."

"Well, here is your mail."

"Put it near my helmet."

"Yes Sir."

"You *know* something Mama," he said sensing his mother was withholding information.

"Well, I didn't want to have your mind heavy with things back home while you were over there fighting."

"Hmph, so Staci ain't missing?" He said as he smacked his teeth angrily.

"No, she left you Allen. She called after leaving the girls and told me she ain't coming back and to take care of myself."

The breath in Allen's body was slowly leaking out as his mouth dropped wide open. It wasn't like he and Staci had the perfect marriage, but he definitely didn't see this one coming. He felt his legs getting wobbly as he tried to figure out what he was going to do. Images of single father-hood danced in his head as he angrily slammed his fist into a nearby wall.

"Allen, don't you worry about us. We're going to be okay; you just get back here safely. Promise mama you'll do that."

Allen knew he should've been responding to his mother- simply out of respect- but he couldn't find the words to say. She was telling him to fight safely when his wife- the woman he had taken vows with- had given up on their fight to save their marriage; all without even telling him. Allen felt defeated.

Leaning his head against the wall, he lost his composure and began to cry.

"I'll call you back Mama." Allen said as his voice trimbled softly.

"Allen..."

"Mama, I promise you I'll make it back there. I'll call you back later."

He ended the call and took a knee.

"Why don't you sit this one out Sergeant Brown," Captain Longhorn said as he sympathetically eyed Allen in his vulnerable state. It didn't take a rocket scientist to tell-with his tear-stained face and trembling hands- that something had shaken Allen to his core.

Embarrassed by the thought of his commanding officer seeing him crying, Allen cleared his throat, stood up slowly and responded, "No Sir, I need to be out there with my men in the field."

"Are you sure? I only want you out there if you are in tip-top condition." The captain said as he slapped Allen on his back. "We've all got to be in this together."

Allen glanced up at the good ole' boy Captain Longhorn. He stood about 6'4', was naturally muscular and had salt and pepper colored hair that he kept neatly trimmed. Allen caught himself wondering what Captain Longhorn had to go home to. He envisioned it was a beautiful wife- who probably wrote him weekly and called daily- three well-behaved children and a house with a white picket fence. Allen caught his tears before they could surface as he thought about his new reality waiting back home for him. No longer was there a wife who had his back. All he had to look forward to was seeing his mother and daughters.

As if on cue, Allen snapped out of his daydream and shook himself free of all the thoughts of life back home. At that point, Allen had one mission: to have his guys' backs.

"I'm all right, I can still go out."

"Hoorah," The Captain yelled before leaving.

Allen picked up his helmet, sat back down, and decided to read the mail. Included in the mail was a letter from his wife, Staci. Butterflies bombarded his stomach, nerves were at an all time high. Allen ran his hands over Staci's familiar handwriting and stared at the white envelope, that looked like it had seen better days.

Reluctantly and anxiously, he opened the letter and read it.

"Allen- By the time you get this message, our daughters Amy and Sandra will be over your mother's house. I just can't do this Allen; raise these girls by myself, lonely nights, and having the water being shut off. I ain't never in my life had my water shut off, nor have I ever received an eviction notice. This marriage just isn't working

out for me. I mean everything was fine when you were here at home, your job at Dofttech was able to let me and the girls live comfortably, but now that's not the case. I told you to get out of the Army, but you wanted to stay in to get the retirement. Now look at you, over there fighting in the sand. You chose military retirement over me. You left me no choice. Sorry, but I have to go. I have needs that aren't being met by you. My cell number will be changed too, so don't bother calling."

After reading the last line, Allen crumbled up the letter, with little emotion crossing his face, and stared at nothing in particular. There was a deafning silence as he nervously tapped his foot on the linoleum tile. Where was the woman he'd married and who was this new-and-improved Staci?

As time passed and reached 1900 hours, Private Smith walked in and said "Sir its 1900 hours."

Allen slowly lifted his head up and said "Right, its 1900 hours, lets go."

He grabbed his rifle and headed out with his platoon for the nightly patrol of Iraq. The night was surprisingly quiet as if the enemy knew that life had brutally attacked the sergeant already. Walking down a quite street he turned to his left and saw two kids looking out of a window as they passed by. After a few moments the children's mother pulled them away from the window and closed the curtains.

A small smile went across his face as he thought, "At least I've still got my girls."

When Allen landed at Ft. Hood, TX, from Iraq, he was greeted by his mother and two daughters.
The sun felt brand new, as if he had been stuck in prison or a hospital and was just experiencing the beauty and relaxing feeling of sunshine and breeze. Allen threw his head back and inhaled the air deeply.

"Daddy, daddy!" Allen's oldest daughter, Sandra said as she skipped towards her father.

"Hey girls!" Allen grinned widely as he scooped up both his daughters and sprinkled kisses all over their beautiful faces.

"Are we going to pick up mommy?" Amy the youngest asked straightforwardly as they walked to the parking lot.

"Look what I made daddy!" Sandra interrupted as she pulled a piece of paper from behind her back.

He smiled at Amy and then looked at the drawing of him in a helicopter smiling picking up his two daughters and wife. "This is beautiful, baby girl."

The next day, He went to Dofttech to tell his boss he was back in town. He pulled out his security badge and quickly swiped it, as he had done hundreds of times before during his regular full-time position. The red light appeared. He tried the badge again and the persistent red light glared back at him. Confused, he walked around to the main entrance and spoke with his friend, Larry, the security guard.

"What's going on Larry, I think my badge needs to be looked at man; it's not working"

"What's up Allen, you back from the dessert?"

"Yeah for good this time."

"Let's see what's up with your badge." The guard says while taking the badge from him. Larry looked up Allen's information in the system. "It looks like they deactivated your account."

Allen's heart sank into the pit of his stomach. Something told him this wasn't good. "What do you mean it has been deactivated?"

"I don't know, man. All it says is that your account was deactivated three months ago."

"Can I use your phone?" Allen said feeling himself getting upset.

"Here you go."

"Hello." A man answered.

"John, this is Allen, my badge is not working."

"Welcome back from Iraq."

"Yeah, thanks, hey buzz me in."

"Allen, we sent you a letter about three months ago. We needed to fill that position quickly; I left you messages with your wife too."

"You're kidding me, right?" Allen replied, on the brink of losing it.

"I'll be sure to let you know if another position opens up."

"But I was in Iraq fighting for this country and now you say my job is gone!"

"Sorry, we were just short handed; Thank you for serving the country though. Hey I have to get back to work. Take care."

"Right." Allen said in disbelief as he slowly handed the phone back to Larry.

"Is everything OK?" Larry asked as he slid the phone back onto its charger.

"No, it's not." Allen replied as he put his head in his hands "I lost my job."

If there was ever irony in any situation, Allen thought as he peered around the building that had doubled as his employment home for years, this definitely took the cake. There he was, fighting for his life in Iraq when he should've been thinking about what life would be like after he returned home. First his wife, then his job.

"Here man, call my boss he may have something for you." Larry said as he scribbled something on a piece of paper and handed it over to a solemn Allen.

As Allen looked over the scrap piece of paper, he couldn't help but wonder why this was happening to him.

He walked into his mothers' house and heard her yell "Who is that?!"

"It's me, mama."

"Why are you back from work so early?"

"I lost my job."

"Have mercy Lord; please have mercy."

"I'll be okay mama."

"Well you can stay here until things gets better."

He sighed and went into his old room and closed the door. Allen knew that if he didn't have little people to take care of, he might have taken the news a little better. People lost their jobs everyday, he thought, but now that he had to provide for his daughters' he couldn't help but dwell on everything unfair about the situation.

He fidgeted with the number that Larry had given him and as he thought about his children, he dialed the number without hesitation.

"Hello."

"Hello, my name is Allen; Larry gave me your number and told me I should call you."

"Ok, yeah, he's a good guy. How can I help you?"

"He said that you may need some help."

"Right, it's a security guard job at the First Bank branch downtown, it's the night shift."

"How much does it pay?"

"I can pay you eleven dollars an hour right now and the hours are from 8:30 PM to 4:30AM."

"I'll take it!" At least I will be able to get my daughters ready for school, he thought to himself.

"Good, training starts this week; you will be meeting Damien."

Two days later a full moon was out and Allen showed up at his new job. As he stood outside of the bank, a big, burly black guy, with- what looked like- newly twisted dreads approached him and extended his hand.

"You must be Allen?"

"And you're Damien?."

"You got it! Well, here is your uniform, and flashlight. It's real simple; every hour you need to walk around the place and make sure everything is locked down. Any problems, call me on my radio. I'll be back."

"OK so when will training start?"

"You just had it man." Damien chuckled and then walked away.

Allen looked down at his new blue uniform not knowing if it was even the right size and then went to the locker room to change into it. He walked out and started his patrol of the building. As he paced throughout the building, following the poor training instructions, he began to get nervous. It wasn't a nervousness about someone hurting him on duty, or even being able to impress his new boss. Allen began to fear his new life. What if he couldn't provide for his two girls? What would he do to Staci if he saw her again for abandoning their kids? Everything was coming at him quicker than any dodged in Iraq.

As he ended his shift and headed back to his mothers' house, Allen gave himself a pep talk. He could do this, although he really didn't have a choice, and he would. The sun was still resting while the night sky ruled supreme. He got out of his car and walked inside a dark house. He showered and closed his eyes for a quick nap. A peace fell upon him and in, what seemed like, a few milliseconds, he was interrupted by the sound of the girls' blaring alarm clock.

He walked into their room and woke the girls up. "Its time to get up"

"Huh" Amy said as she yawned.

"It's time to get up and get ready for school, girls."

The girls wiped the sleep from their eyes and readied themselves for school. As they were about to leave, their grandmother yelled, "The girls didn't eat breakfast Allen."

"They'll get something at school; we gotta go."

His mother began preparing the food for herself anyway. He hurried his girls into the car and drove them to school.

"Here are a few dollars, buy something to eat." He said as he pecked the girls on their foreheads and scooted them out of the car towards school.

He drove back home and fell into a deep sleep. The kind of sleep that makes you feel like you lost years of your life in a comfortable bed.

Even though he felt as though he had been sleeping forever, Allen's short sleep was interrupted again by a loud thud.

"Mama!" He yelled and then ran to the source of the loud crash. His heart sank at the sight of his mother on the ground in the kitchen, face-down.

His hands shook in fear as he dialed 911.

At the hospital, the doctor approached Allen with an uneasy look on his face. Slowly, Allen lifted his head up and braced for the news.

He could take Staci leaving him and girls, he could take losing his job due to unfair circumstances and he could even take having to wear a too-small uniform in order to provide; but he could not take losing his mother. Not now; not like this.

"Well, your mother is in critical condition. She suffered a stroke. We will be monitoring her. Do you have any questions?" The doctor explained as his eyes scanned over a clipboard in his hands.

"Do you know what caused it?" Allen inquired

"More than likely it was high blood pressure; she just needs to watch the food that she eats."

"OK." Allen replied as he thought about everything that was happening.

Here we go again, he thought, if the girls would have sat down and ate the breakfast instead of mama then she would not be in here. Allen knew his reasoning was far from having any validity, but it was the only thing he could connect his heart and mind to.

Hours later, he looked at the time and noticed that it was almost time to pick up his daughters. He walked inside the hospital room where his mother lay and sat next to her. Tubes were coming from everywhere on her body and Allen stood silent, staring at her, before speaking.

"I can't lose you right now mama, I just can't, please do whatever it takes- whatever you can- to fight this and come back; I need you mama. I have to pick up the girls and I'll be back. I love you."

Later that night Allen spoke with Sandra.

"I need to go to work, Can I count on you to look after your sister?" It wasn't the best decision, but it was the only thing he could think of. He didn't have money for a babysitter yet and there was no one he could think of to call on to watch the girls. Sandra was getting older, he reasoned to ease his worries, and she should be okay watching Amy.

"Where's granny?" Sandra asked nervously

"She's in the hospital?"

"Why?"

"She had a stroke"

'What's a stroke, daddy?"

"A bad thing, look, go to bed." Allen yelled. He wasn't meaning to take his frustrations out on his girls, but everything was becoming a bit too much.

'Where's mama? Is she in the hospital too?"

"No, I need for y'all to go to sleep now!"

"It's 7 PM daddy, granny lets up stay up until 8" Sandra happily volunteered.

The youngest daughter Amy started to cry. "I want my mama."

"See what's wrong with your sister, Sandra I have to go to work."

"Don't leave daddy I'm scared." Amy cried.

Faced with a difficult situation he caved and called Staci's sister, Lisa. They hadn't ever been really close, but he trusted her with the kids and he knew she loved them.

"Hello."

"Hey Lisa."

"Allen! When did you get back from Iraq?" She asked.

"Four days ago. Where is your sister?'

"Umm, I haven't seen her in a while." Lisa stuttered.

"Don't play with me; where is she?"

"She's with Stan."

"That mutha-, so she's been cheating with the youth minister?!" He said sternly with anger being felt through the phone.

"It's sad aint it."

"Well, look, I have go to work and I need someone to watch the girls; my mama had a stroke."

"My God, is she alright?"

"She's in critical condition. They said she should pull through okay."

"And you are still going to work while she is in the hospital?"

"I have to feed my kids, Lisa. Life still goes on. Do you think you will you be able to watch the girls, please?"

"Alright, bring them over here." She agreed.

He gathered the girls belongings and dropped them over Lisa's house and made his way to work still shaken over the thought of Stan and his wife being together. Staci hadn't ever really paid attention to Stan, but he had definitely caught Stan looking at her one too many times in church. Stan had everything that Allen used to have- a good job, plenty of money in the bank, a nice home and his wife.

He looked at the clock and realized that at 9:20 PM, he was almost an hour late. He looked around for Damien to explain why he was late but he was nowhere to be found. He started his security checks and patrolled the halls. He walked toward a corner office with the lights still on and curiously stuck his head in to investigate. As he peered in, a woman looked up and their eyes met.

"Can I help you?" She asked.

'I'm doing security checks, is everything fine?"

"Yes sir…you must be new."

"Yes ma'am. How long will you be?"

"I'll be here for another hour; can you come back and walk me out?" She asked professionally.

"Yes ma'am."

He closed the door and continued to patrol the building. He peeked outside and finally discovered Damien sleeping in his truck. I should be doing the same thing, he thought to himself. The lack of sleep was definitely making Allen's life harder to maneuver through.

After the checks, he snuck inside a utility closet and sat on a bucket and began to cry. "What did I do to you God, huh? What could I have possibly done to you to deserve this?" He said quietly to God. The hour passed, he wiped his eyes and left the closet.

He walked back to the corner office and opened the door.

"You ready?" He asked the lady.

'It's been an hour already? … Well I need to go."

She gathered her belongings and locked her door behind her. She looked Allen in the eyes. "OK, I'm ready. Have you been crying?" She asked with caution.

'Huh?" He responded with a crack in his voice.

"It's OK to cry sometimes, it's natural."

"Hmph…what's your name" Allen said while laughing off the comment.

"I'm Vanessa. What did you do before working here?" She asked while looking at his name tag.

"I worked at Dofttech and I am in the Army reserves. I had to go to Iraq for 13 months, I came back and they filled my position with someone else, my wife left me and my mother just had a stroke today. I'm sorry, I'm saying way too much."

"It's OK, I'll pray for your mother; what's your name?"

"Allen, and thank you, I guess." Praying for me won't do a thing woman, he thought as he glanced at Vanessa's pretty face.

Vanessa wasn't overly pretty, but she had a subtle beauty that would make a person stare directly at her in order to take it all in. Her cocoa skin was smooth as any chocolate candy bar Allen had ever enjoyed. She had hair that hung to her chin and was neatly in order. Allen tried to distract himself from staring at Vanessa as he helped her put her things in the trunk of her car. The last thing I need, he thought, was another person to add to this messed up equation.

At the end of his shift he packed his belongings and headed to pick up his girls from Lisa's house.

"Any word on Staci?" He asked her.

"Yeah she called and spoke to the girls."

"Why didn't you call me so I could talk to her?"

"She didn't want to talk to you, Allen."

"Let's go girls" He said annoyed.

He dropped the girls off at school and went straight to the hospital. He entered his mothers' room and saw her pastor praying over her.

"How are you doing pastor?"

"I'm blessed."

"How did you know that my mom was in the hospital?"

"I'm on her emergency contact list and besides, she didn't call me for her daily prayer and I figured something was wrong. It's been a long time since I last saw you; you're in the service right?"

"I'm in the reserves right now. I just returned from Iraq."

"Welcome home brother."

"Why is this happening to me? Why is my mother lying on a hospital bed when she needs to be at home helping me with my daughters?"

"Sickness is as much a part of living as healthiness; we should just continue to pray that God renews her body and strength. Where is your wife?" The pastor said looking over Allen's shoulder.

"I thought God spoke to you man; didn't God tell you that she left me for another man- just so happen to be a so call man of God too? She left with the youth minister at my *now* old church. I guess that dude acted like a youth minister so he could get close to the church children and their mothers. After he gets comfortable with them what do you know, he's sleeping with them, married and all."

"It's unfortunate that this happened to you, Allen. But please don't mock me about my conversations with the Lord. Your mom and I wanted you to stay at my church; it may not have been as big as your now former church, but we are a family there"

"Whatever; come to think of it, why would God even consider talking to me? I asked him questions last night but he didn't answer. I didn't know that we served such a shy God."

"Some things happen in this life to test our faith. God wants to know just how deep our faith is. In the Bible God tested Job, God took his wealth, his family and his health, yet Job still trusted in God. This is your test my brother, let me help you ace it."

"Listen preacher man, I'm not nor do I want to be Job, I'm Allen. God got some nerve testing me when I did not ask to be tested. I need for the Lord to stop working on my nerves. Tell him that preacher man since you seem to know him and converse with him."

"I will pray for you brother."

"Yeah, yeah, you do that. I have to go home to take a nap so I can be rested to make eleven dollars an hour. Not everybody can ask for tithes and donations on Sunday morning."

As Allen walked out the door the pastor shook his head and prayed. "Please forgive Allen for he does not know what he is saying Lord. Please take the blinders off of his eyes and reveal to him that things will get better. Lord, renew his strength in you and strengthen Allen's faith. Whatever it is that you need him to learn, let him do so quickly. In Jesus name, Amen."

Later that night, Allen dropped his daughters off at his sister-in-laws house.

"Hey, umm, are you going to start paying me? I don't mean to be acting funny and all, but if your girls are going to be staying over here and eating my food, I need to be taken care of with some money. You know what I mean." She explained.

"Why don't you ask your sister?" Allen shot back.

"She said she ain't got no money."

"I ain't got no money either, why do you think she left me?"

"Just take care of me like I'm taking care of your girls."

"I have to go earn my pennies now." He said as he jumped in his car and left.

At work, Allen started his nightly security checks and noticed that Vanessa was working late again. He walked towards the door and peeked inside.

"Hey Hey"

"Hey Allen, how are you?"

"I'm making it." He replied.

"Listen, I was talking with my friend about you losing your job and he said that since you were called to duty and were deployed, your employer has to give you your job back."

"Really?" Allen said shocked at the information.

"That's right, I can have him send a letter requesting your job back and if that does not work you can sue."

"It sounds so easy! Just sue em'" Allen chuckled

"Yes, you attempted to go back to work right?"

"Yes."

"They knew you were in the reserves right?"

"Yes."

"Well, the next step is to pursue your legal rights."

"Why are you helping me?"

"You did what most brothers wouldn't do, you helped your country, so let me help you; besides, your cute" She handed the lawyers card to him.

He began to blush. "What time are you leaving tonight?"

"In about 20 minutes, you can come back and walk me out if that's okay with you. ."

"Sounds good to me."

Later that week Allen received a call from the attorney.

"Allen. I have good news for you."

"I like good news."

"Your former employer is willing to settle out of court if you would accept 2 years salary plus cash equivalent of benefits worth $100,000 plus pain and suffering so the total would be $300,000"

"That was quick, what made them bend?"

"I threatened to make them famous for refusing to give a veteran his job back; they did not want to lose their government contracts."

"I'll take it." He said enthusiastically.

He ended the call with the lawyer and eagerly called Vanessa

"Are you my guardian angel or something?"

She laughed off the comment, "How are you?"

"I'm great, man."

"Great, huh? Why is that?"

"Your lawyer friend reached a settlement with my old job."

"That's great, Allen! You deserve it!"

"Isn't life good?"

"All the time; I'll see you tonight at work."

"Of course."

He drove over to the hospital where the preacher was visiting again.

"Hey man!" he said enthusiastically.

"It appears as though you are in a good mood."

"Things are looking up; things are finally going my way."

"Praise the Lord."

"Yeah," Allen said nonchalantly.

"Is that you Allen?" Allen's mother said weakly as she lifted her head up to see her son smiling widely.

"Mama, you had me scared for a while." Allen said as he began stroking her soft grey hair.

"Nobody's going to see Jesus right now in this family." Allen's mother said sweetly.

The comment brought a smile to both Allen and the preachers' face. "I had a dream that you were cursing and fussing at the Lord, boy it was a nightmare."

"You need to rest mama; everything is going to be OK now."

"Let's step outside and talk Allen." The preacher said.

"Okay, cool."

"This is typical behavior God does not like, you were down in the dumps and you didn't want anything to do with God, now that things are a little better, you still stubbornly don't give God the credit, don't play with something as powerful as your soul, you need to acknowledge who is with you Allen."

"Yep, sure thing preacher man; for your information, I didn't even pray for things to get better. I- yes I said *I*- made these things happen, what do you have to say about that?"

"I prayed for you, on your behalf."

Allen remained silent for a while as the preacher deflated his confidence. He soon followed the preacher back inside the hospital room and said to his mother.

"I'll be back mama to bring the girls up here; you know its Amy's birthday this weekend."

"Alright, Allen. I'll be here." She said in a faint voice.

Allen got in his car and begun to think. I am really something, God spare my life and limbs in Iraq, he spared my mother, and he got me this settlement and who knows, he may be saving me from a bad marriage. I need to really get it together. As a man, it was hard for Allen to accept that he hadn't done anything to get him in his current state; but it took a man, Allen reasoned, to realize where your blessings really come from.

The sun was shining something crazy as Allen watched his daughters fight over a swing at the park. After everything he had been through, Allen couldn't believe it was already Amy's birthday and he was happily celebrating with the two most important people in his life. Gone were his fears, doubts and worries.

As he watched his girls play, he took a moment to call Lisa.

"Hey Allen, do you have to go to work tonight or something?" She asked.

"No; don't sound to enthusiastic to hear from me." He said sarcastically. "I'm calling to let you know that I got a big settlement coming and I will be taking care of you with a little cash for watching the girls."

"How much is the settlement?"

"Don't worry about it. Bye now."

He ended the call and yelled to Amy, "Come Here Amy and Sandra!"

The two girls ran to their dad who looked them in the eye.

"Amy happy birthday, I know that things may be a little confusing with your mother not being here; I want you girls to promise me that when you grow up that you will take responsibility for your actions and if you commit to something or someone, you stick with it, no matter what. Do you understand me?"

They both said, "Yes daddy."

"Even though this is Amy's birthday, I wanted to give you both a birthday present. I have recommitted my self to

God and vowed to be a better father. I have given God the credit for every opportunity and blessing that I have been given in this life and I will teach you two to do the same. I know this may not make sense right now, but it will later in your life. How does a trip to Disney World next month sound to you two?"

The girls squealed with excitement as they jumped all over their father and showered him with kisses and hugs.

Allen watched his two girls run off to play in the park when his cell phone rang.

"Hello"

"Hey Allen when did you get back in?" a familiar voice asked curiously

"Staci?"

"Yeah, it's me."

"Where the hell have you been? I've been home for months now and your girls have yet to see you."

"I just needed some space."

"Did Stan show you a good time in my absence?"

"Very funny Allen; where are my girls? I want to see them."

"You are a piece of work Staci, you had the audacity to just get up and leave your kids and husband just stranded and now you want to see them?"

Ignoring the accusations she said,

"Well, we are still legally married and I heard that you got some kind of settlement."

"I know where this is going; don't even try it Staci. There is no way you are taking half. You know we made a vow to be with each other for richer or poor, sickness and health. I upheld my end of the bargain and you bailed out. Anyone with a pair of eyes will see that you abandoned life when it got too hard, making your kids and your husband pay the price and only want money now that it's here. I just need for you to sign the divorce papers when you get them. I'll talk to you later, you take care of yourself." Allen said politely as he ended the call.

He wasn't bitter anymore at Staci for leaving him and girls, because, in all actuality, it might have been the best new start any of them could've wished for. He stared at all of the kids and parents out playing on the playground and wondered if he would ever find a woman to be a proper partner and parent to him and his daughters. If anything, they deserved that much. Taking out his phone, Allen sent Vanessa a text message asking her if she wanted to go to Disney World with him and the girls. When she replied, Allen glanced at the message and grinned.

"I'd be delighted to go." He read out loud.

Allen looked down at the phone and then back up at his daughters and sat there looking at them and thought, I may not be perfect, and I know this will take some time, but starting today, I will give full credit to God for every opportunity that I get in this lifetime and rely on him through thick and thin. And I vow that my soul will triumph over any obstacle thrown my way.

BOTTOMED OUT

Marc Lacy

"Buford! Man, we need to get a move on if we're gonna meet our quota for the day. Plus, I'm tryin' to bounce over to Southside Youth Center and watch my little nephew and 'nem compete for The Lafayette Pee Wee League Basketball Championship," said Hank.

"Okay boss, you know I'm gunning it as fast as I can. We'll get it done. Don't worry," mentioned Buford in his usual unexcited and solemn tone.

"Buford McDonald! Man if you weren't such a nice humble cat, and a great lead technician, your butt would have been sent packin' like a Mayflower moving truck...about a year ago! Alright. It looks like we'll make it after all...like we always do! You know I can count on your two gear having behind Buford," stated Hank as the rest of the assembly line crew laughed out aloud.

National Engines Incorporated was one of the more popular and thriving businesses in Lafayette, Indiana. Buford's seventeen years of experience was the most for the product line on which he worked (Cheetah Model eight cylinder/four hundred horsepower engines). Hank Boston, the shift leader, knew that Buford could not be replaced...even though management felt that he could do more, Buford still managed to satisfy them just enough to get the job done. But one thing about Buford, when it was time for him to *really* make a point...sometimes he would take it to the extreme. Everyone knew that in order for such activity to transpire, Buford would have to certainly be pushed to the limit.

The McDonald Family resided in a very modest two-bedroom ranch-style home in an old neighborhood called *Keel Estates* located just on the outskirts of the Southside of Lafayette. Buford and his wife Fancy have been married for approximately twenty years. Fancy was a clerk at a local Wal-Mart. They had a very strong marriage that really couldn't be earmarked by any blemishes other than the fact that Buford, Jr. or *JR* as everyone called him, was experiencing serious peer pressure as a ninth grader. The McDonalds made sure that JR stayed in church. It didn't matter whether it was regular service, Sunday school, or a special program--if JR was not in church, he'd have had to have the greatest excuse in the world because Sr. and mama didn't play that. But they did learn to live with the fact that regardless of what went on at Soldier's Faith Baptist Church, the kids were going to try to do what they wanted to do at home and everywhere else. The McDonalds understood that kids would be kids and that all phases of growing up had to be experienced; but JR had a small issue that had "big" potential.

"JR, I'm going to assume that you've got everything prepared for your game today and that you'll be ready to go once your father gets home."

"Ma, you act as if I'm senile or something. I got it under control. It's all good."

"I'm glad it's all good, skinny boy. But it'll be even better once you learn to pull those blasted saggin' pants up!"

"There you go. My saggin' pants don't make me a bad kid. Shoot, at Southside, all the hoopers, swaggas, and cats who like girls don't wear no snug pants. Now if I didn't like girls, my pants would be tighter than dad's wife beaters. I bet that you and dad wore things that your folks didn't approve of...or at least tried to."

"We probably did; but that was then, and this is now. Have some respect about yourself boy. Quit doin' what the rest of those Southside knuckleheads do. Your daddy hasn't said much; but I'm going to pray that you don't keep pushing the limit to set him off."

"Dad? He won't do anything. He knows that times have changed. I mean, just let me be a kid...please?"

Normally, Buford and Fancy would give passive reminders to warn JR that he would have to cease his pant sagging habit, or use his own money to purchase medium and small pants and shorts that better fit his parents' standards. But somehow over time, JR would slip back into his old habit.

One of the most heated rivalries each year was Southside Trojans versus Woodbridge Cavaliers. On this particular night, Woodbridge Memorial Gymnasium was packed to capacity, even during the freshmen game. The McDonalds smiled as they watched their son and his Trojan teammates bolt out of the locker room and perform sweat breaking warm-ups. There he was, JR McDonald, running through the lay up line like a deer. Going in for a shot, slapping the glass, and pulling his baggy shorts up as he landed.

"There goes my baby!" yelled Fancy as she proudly clapped.

"I don't know where that boy is getting his height from; but I'm glad he didn't take after his stocky dad," joked Buford aloud as he and Fancy shared a laugh.

Normally the McDonalds would be irked at the site of JR's shorts hanging off of his butt; but the excitement of the new season sort of diffused the effects of his slouchy tendency--that is--until the game started and it was time for him to sub in.

"McDonald! Go get Davis," ordered the coach.

"I'm comin' coach," replied JR while pulling off his warm up top.

Buford and Fancy both moved towards the edge of their seat with the highest level of anticipation. As JR came to the table to check in, he wiped his feet on the sticky board, chalked his hands up, and then pulled his shorts up--once again. When the ball made it into play, JR threw a pass that was picked-off by a Woodbridge player.

"Oh no, baby!" screamed Fancy.

As the opposing player dashed to the basket for an easy layup, JR trailed right behind him in an effort to foul or strip the ball. He took a swipe at the ball, missed, and ended up sliding face first on the slick floor. As the coach marveled at the good hustle, the entire gym erupted in laughter as the friction from JR's dive, not only pulled his shorts down; but his stripped boxers as well. When JR finally stopped sliding across the court on his stomach, he looked back. JR panned slowly to see everything. He looked up and saw that the player had actually made the layup. "Dang man!" iterated a disgusted JR. Then he glanced to the back left and right and saw people covering their mouths. Lastly, he peered straight back over his shoulder and noticed the source of everyone's laughter. JR McDonald was shooting a moon to the entire gymnasium.

Oh snap, I need to wakeup from this nightmare like yesterday! This can't be happenin', thought JR to himself.

With cheerleaders staring at JR feverishly, the referees blew their whistles as if to signify an injury time out. Immediately, without exposing himself too much, while still on the ground, JR slowly pulled his boxers up followed by his uniform shorts. As he felt an embarrassing tingle within his spine, JR got up, passed the ball inbounds to his teammate, and trotted down the court as if nothing happened. Meanwhile, Buford and Fancy took deep breaths, glanced at one another and continued watching the game.

"Make up for it right here son!" screamed Buford, Sr. sitting in anticipation.

"You're gonna make a great play right here JR! You can do it!" bellowed Fancy. During the next possession, the Southside point guard launched a three-pointer. The ball bounced off of the side of the rim and JR, with a running start, skied as his mouth was wide open and legs spread eagle, tipped the ball against the backboard and scored a basket. People cheered loudly; but followed it up with a laugh as JR landed, knees bent, beating his fist up against his chest--and shorts on his ankles as if he were squatting in the restroom stall. The referees blew the whistle, signaled for JR to come over to the sidelines to meet the coach.

The head ref made it plain and simple: "Coach, if your player does not have another pair of shorts that he can tie up, he simply cannot finish this game. Bottom line."

"Well they wanted the shorts big, so we ordered them big," the coach argued.

"That's not our problem. The rules of this venue along with what's captured in our officials' handbook clearly state, that a player's shorts cannot sag in a disrespectful fashion. The rules also stipulate that the shorts cannot be so loose that they cause the player to pull at them constantly. Coach, I'm afraid that your player must go to the dressing room and change in street clothes if he is going to remain in the gym."

"Okay. If those are the rules, they're the rules. McDonald, please head to the showers son."

"But coach, I was hustlin' and everything man."

"That's not the point son. We cannot participate if we're breaking the rules. Now please go."

"Aww man."

JR then trots to the dressing room as the entire crowd stood applauding. Buford and Fancy both had very disappointed expressions on their face. If that weren't enough, one parent stood up and screamed:

"Not only should he be ejected, put his parents should be escorted out of here as well! We're trying to encourage good hard clean competition here. This young man is running around like he's a thug or a gangster of some sort. It seems like his folks may have gang affiliations or something to the effect!"

Buford was clearly very upset as veins surfaced on his forehead like whales on water during mating season. All he did was push his glasses back, straighten up his ball cap and politely asked Fancy if she were ready to leave:

"Yes baby. I cannot take sitting here any longer. But let's wait 'til half-time so that it will not be so obvious."

"Alright dear."

Once the clock read zero at the conclusion of the second quarter, the McDonalds headed for the exit with JR in tow. Now, one could only imagine the exchange on the way home.

"Man, ya'll I wanted to stay for the rest of the game. Why did we have to leave?"

"JR, if the embarrassment did not send a signal to you, I don't know what will," a frustrated Fancy began. "Why do your shorts and pants have to be the loosest of anyone's in the building?"

"Ma, ya'll don't know anything about swag. This ain't the old days. Get with today. It's just a part of my style."

Buford remained deathly silent as he kept his eyes on the road while listening intensely.

"Boy, that swag of yours cost this family the worst embarrassment ever. As you were going to the locker room, other parents started hurling insults at your father and I as you did your cool boy jog to the locker room while pulling up those baggy shorts."

"Man, they don't know what time it is. This is what's in."

"Oh yeah? Since we're talking about time--it's time to take away your cell phone and that doggone Game Cube. That's what time it is."

"Ma, you trippin'."

"Oh, Junior I hadn't tripped yet. Just wait until I finish my spill here--then you can say I'm trippin'."

"What chu talkin' about?"

"Oh, you didn't know? Your Facebook and Myspace accounts will be canceled as soon as we get home. Oh--and if we decide to let you continue to play ball, you better hope that practice does not interfere with your part time job."

"Part time job?"

"Yes sir! How do you think your new clothes will be paid for?"

"What new clothes?"

"Some doggone pants that will fit your totem pole behind!" yelled Fancy as she turned around as if she wanted to swing her purse at JR while he ducked to the left.

"Your father and I work too hard for you to embarrass the family like that. Not to mention the fact that everyone from Southside High saw what happened tonight."

As they pulled up in the driveway, Buford thought to himself:

That boy has gone way over the edge. I don't want to say anything because my words may come off too harsh. I think his mother's words have caught his attention; but this time, I need to make sure that he has learned his lesson.

As time passed, Fancy and Buford never really addressed the issue with one another directly. However; over the years in their marriage, they learned to just feed off of one another and only give special attention to problems when it was absolutely necessary. At this juncture, it was implied that the verbal scolding coupled with restricting certain things in JR's activities was doing the trick. However, Buford thought long and hard about how the deal could be sealed. Although he never really expressed his feelings to Fancy, he had a plan brewing for about a week. Parent/Student day was vastly approaching at the academy. It was mandatory that the each parent sit in class with their child and introduce themselves to the teacher and the rest of the class as well as engage in group discussions.

The time was 7:30am on Parent/Student Day. JR dawned his usual jeans and polo shirt. Meanwhile, Buford had on a green blazer, white button down shirt, and some very big kaki pants, and Fancy wore a dress suit. As they were on the way to school, no one really said anything as the radio blared NPR News. Once they parked, the McDonalds made their way up the sidewalk and eventually under the ramp. All of JR's friends waved and spoke as he was a very popular student. All the while, Fancy maintained very politically correct smile on her face as she knew that mischief was behind the smiles on some of the kids. Buford was his normal cool self until they migrated halfway under the ramp. Suddenly without a hint of warning, Buford's kakis dropped to his ankles. He kept walking as a collective hysterical laugh rang out from the masses of onlookers. Even some parents received a giggle out of it. Buford continued walking as people laughed. All they saw was this family of three walking into the building--with a father in a green blazer, raggedy looking boxers, ashy legs, and kakis around his ankles. As people stared and laughed, the only adjustment Buford would make would be to push his glasses up. Once they entered the lobby, Fancy and JR finally noticed what the fuss was about and were extremely embarrassed.

"Dad. Yo man! What are you doin' dude?"

"Oh, my bad son. Let me pull my pants up. I didn't know they were that loose."

As all of the parents, faculty, and staff peered in a quite shock, the McDonalds made their way to JR's homeroom. As they walked down the hall, Fancy did not really know what to think.

If this is Buford's way of sending a signal to his son, I really don't agree with the timing. However, JR must be taught a lesson.

"Okay, here's my class. My desk of course is located there in the back," explained JR.

As the McDonalds got settled, JR's classmates and their families slowly trickled in. The McDonalds could feel all eyes on them as the student's snickers had gotten louder and louder as more of them filed into the room. JR could not really hide his embarrassment any longer as he rolled his eyes at his father and sighed. Meanwhile, Buford sat proudly and un-phased by anyone who may have been uncomfortable around him. Fancy, tried her best to tune out all externalities and focus on the goal of the special day.

Once the teacher called roll and had certain students provide opening remarks, she summoned parents up two by two. The reaction of the students for each presentation thus far was pretty nominal and respectful. But as soon as the teacher called the McDonalds to the front of the room, the laughter that resonated at that juncture was similar to that which one would see at football game with seventy-thousand plus fans about to do the tidal wave. All parents cut eyes at one another as each child laughed uncontrollably. The teacher attempted to calm them down; it was no use -- because Buford did not retrieve his fallen trousers until he made his way to the front of the room. After Fancy introduced herself and told a little bit about what she does, it was time for Buford to make his spill. As he stepped forward, the students began snickering once more before the sounds were doused by parents' "shushing" efforts.

"My name is Buford McDonald, Senior. I am JR's father and I got that swag!"

The students burst into another round of laughter. Once they calmed down, Buford attempted a "krump" dance move; which jarred his pants loose, and yes--once again they sat around his ankles. This time the room was filled with mass hysteria. Students were laughing so hard that they would have to gasp for air. Fancy could not watch and commenced to placing her face firmly within her hands as she stood flanking her husband. The teacher called school security and the portly little man politely escorted Buford out in the hall and asked him to leave the school property. Buford consented; but not before he requested to go back into the classroom and tell his son goodbye. As they agreed, with Fancy standing in the hallway ready to go, Buford calmly walks back in the classroom and just blurts out in front of everyone:

"Yo Junior! Me and your moms are about to bounce! Keep that swag goin' mane! We'll catch you at da crib! Oh, and stay up dude. Don't let life getcha down baby boy!"

Again the uproar of laughter sounded like a rocket leaving the launch pad. Every parent looked in total astonishment. But it wasn't over until Buford turn around, flashed the peace sign, gangsta walked out of the class, with his sagging pants still falling down.

As Fancy watched her unbroken husband literally make a total clown of himself, all she could do was shake her head. As the McDonalds made their way down the hall headed to the parking lot, Buford was greeted by two Lafayette Police Officers at the principal's office. They spoke to him briefly and cuffed him before they walked him outside. At first Fancy meditated quietly to herself, but then she really gasped for air when she noticed news cameras capturing the footage as Buford was being led to the police cruiser. As she walked outside, Fancy just about fainted as her husband's baggy kaki's slowly made their way, once again, down his legs. The cameras were aimed like sniper rifles as the officers had to help the cuffed Buford pull his trousers up and tighten the belt.

Fancy presented the bail money, retrieved her husband from lock-up, and quietly drove him home. Buford was straight faced and emotionless as they walked into the house. The time was about 5:30pm. JR was sitting on the couch with a pout so deep; one could have assumed that his feet were being dipped in acid. Once Fancy and Buford walked in, the news was just getting cranked. Of course among the local headlines, was the fact that a Southside High parent was arrested for not abiding by the school/city sagging pants ordinance? At that point, JR stood up and shouted:

"Man, thanks! Thank you! Thaaaaaaank you for embarrassing the hell out of me! Go ahead! Ground me! Scold me! Take away my video games! Kick me out of the house! You cannot do anything worse to me now than what you've already done!"

Junior's eye's watered as he breathed heavily. Fancy took off her coat and sat down at the dining room table just watching her son. Buford looked at JR, walked right passed him, and asked Fancy what was for dinner.

"I can't believe you man! How are you not going to acknowledge what you did! You are my father! What gives you the right to come in there, dress like a freakin' kid, and have me the laughing stock of the school?"

Buford calmly removed his blazer, headed into the kitchen and pulled his trousers up once again while looking in the pantry for some rice.

During dinner, Buford laughed while reading funny articles in the newspaper, Fancy remained calm with a concerned look on her face...while saying nothing. JR pouted, sulked, huffed and puffed while eating his red beans and rice.

Shoot...man! I should have run away from home after I threatened to do it two years ago. Here I am at a prestigious school, and my friends will take me for a joke from here on out. This clown is acting like a little kid...my father. I couldn't imagine ever doing something like that to my children. What gives him the right? This is crazy. I can't wait 'til I graduate. I ain't ever coming back to this camp.

Later that night as JR lay in his bed, peering at the ceiling with a blank look on his face; there was a faint knock at the door.

"Come in."

"JR, I just wanted to tell you that your father is going to be doing some serious housework during the next two weeks or so."

"And?"

"And, I'd like for you to at least lend a hand on nights when you don't have a lot of homework."

"May I ask why he's trying to get all of this housework done suddenly? Is it the guilt from embarrassing me?"

"Don't know. It might be," replied Fancy facetiously. "I do know that your father has been suspended with pay from his job."

"Dang, who did he go off on at the job?"

"It had nothing to do with what took place at work. Besides you know your father really doesn't get down like that."

"Oh yeah, for what then?"

"He got suspended because of the embarrassment he caused his company. You know--with the sagging pants deal."

"What? I can't believe that. Even though it was stupid on his part, how are they going to suspend him for wearing sagging pants offsite?"

"The same way your school just informed us of how you've been suspended for three days from the classroom and indefinitely from the basketball court. I'll let you guess why."

As Fancy exited the room, JR sat up with his mouth open, and an extremely stunned look upon his face.

After two weeks, Buford was back at work in full capacity as JR once again matriculated the halls of Southside High. The two of them never really talked about the incident, nor was sagging pants ever an issue in the McDonald household again.

I Used to Love H. E. R.

Jarold Imes

2Pac wakes Calvin up from his nightmare as he sees death around the corner. The phone has been vibrating all through the night and his wife hasn't heard a peep. He looks at her nude body and thinks about his five in the morning woody that is demanding some attention. He is about to wake her up with an early morning rump but that phone just keeps on vibrating and getting on his everlasting nerve. Calvin sits up and looks at the text message:

I'm sorry about the problems I caused between you and your man... but at least he knows now that your heart belongs to me and with me is where you need to be...

- Bilal

"Uggh," Calvin growls as he throws the phone against the wall and watches it crack and fall to the carpeted floor. He is beginning to regret getting in bed with his cheating Spanish Kimora Simmons knock off laying next to him. Calvin had been trying to forgive Maria for cheating on him but every time he did, all he could picture is the night that he caught his wife and a deacon from another church rolling around in bed... his bed; the very bed in which they conceived their second child and shared many a moment as husband and wife.

Lately, those moments had become less and less as they struggled to get over the death of their son. He had been the second child they had lost as their first son died as a result of sudden infant death syndrome. Calvin and Maria longed to raise beautiful sons and daughters, but their failure to deal with their children's deaths were part of the problem they were having now. Problems that were keeping the black and Mexican couple from achieving true happiness. Having a child had meant the world to them and they'd gone through any length to get one. Maria had been through a lot to give them a family; two infant deaths and two miscarriages but they kept trying.

Calvin often wonders if this is the reason that Maria was cheating on him… so that she can have a baby by someone else, but he shakes the thought aside.

"What's wrong baby?" Maria wakes up and starts massaging Calvin's pound cake colored member.

"I want to talk about ol' boy."

Maria quickly turns over and huffs, "I'm not going through this again. I said I was sorry."

"Why does he keep calling?" Calvin gritted through his teeth and then looked at the clock. "It is 3:45 in the morning, can't he respect me enough to call when he thinks I'm at work at least?" Calvin turns over and feels the breeze on his nude body as Maria snatches more of the sheet to cover herself with. "I should have messed him up when I had the chance."

Maria looked at him disturbed. All her husband seemed to care about was the fact that he caught her cheating. At times she wished that she had just run off with Bilal, an action that would have given the members of both her church and his can end their speculation about their relationship. Calvin turned around, met with the grit on her face and turned back on his side of the bed. And just like that, he was seething mad as he watched his wife disrobe and step into the shower in the bathroom. If only he had the heart to leave her; maybe he could have a shot at being happy with someone else. He noticed that she no longer took pride in being able to go downstairs and fix his breakfast, and he contemplated whether getting a divorce would be the way she was going to get a break fast. Calvin decided that instead of arguing with his wife about the issue again, he would do best just to go to work early. Going to work kept him out of trouble and more money in his pocket and sometimes, that was the best decision.

Maria made sure her husband was long gone from the house good before she placed her call.

"This is Bilal speaking," the adulterer picks up the phone on the first ring.

"Good morning, I was wondering if you could come by and see me," Maria purred into the phone seductively.

"You know I can't do that, I got some business to handle."

Back in the day before she married Calvin, Bilal and Maria had both lived in Denver, where they had hung together pretty tight. At her suggestion, he accepted a job at Bank of America and a chance to go to divinity school at Duke. She wanted to make sure she kept tabs on her "investment."

"You mean you can't meet me somewhere and just hang out. Get a drink or something?"

"No, we can't, Maria," Bilal sounded agitated. "I like you as a person, but I respect the fact that you are married, so we can't do that no more. Besides, I just came out of church, so I don't need to be thinking about that no way."

"Okay deacon," Maria tried to be coy on the phone, "I just wanted to give you a late Christmas present."

"You got me some money," Bilal was laughing at his own joke. He knew the mere mention of cash would upset her. Maria knew he was pulling her string so she tried not to sound upset.

"I got lotta money, do you have lotta man?"

"See," Bilal was mad cause now she was pulling on one of his sensitive spots. "I know mine work, can't say the same for your husband." Maria conceded defeat on her man's ability to stay up as long as she wanted him to. She often complained about their lack of lovemaking, their lack of time spent lovemaking, their lack of unity and togetherness. "When are you and Calvin coming to church with me?"

"As soon as I can keep him from kicking your butt... you know you can't take him?"

"Why don't you come?"

"I want to really bad, but you just won't cooperate," she tried to sound seductive like Marilyn Monroe.

"To church girl, I'm not talking about that." Too bad it didn't work. "Even if he don't want to come, you owe it to your self and to the Lord to come to His house."

"Boy please, you know you want me to hear you sing."

"I've given you plenty of private concerts already."

Maria was frustrated, sexually, "You know what I mean... well, why don't you sing me a Christmas carol?"

"Chestnuts roasting, on an open fire..." Bilal began to belt.

"Oh Bilal, why don't you just come over here for a few minutes. That's all I need is a few minutes."

"He's got lots of toys and goodies on his sleight," Bilal continues to sing and laugh. "Naw, but for real. Surprise your husband. Do something exciting. It might be the last time you get to spend with him alone."

She knew he was telling the truth. Earlier this year, Calvin and Maria had talked about leaving for a getaway and spending Christmas and New Years in the Bahamas or Bermuda. They hadn't had a trip to themselves since their honeymoon three years ago.

"Aight, I'll get something together for him. I'm upset that I can't spend some time with you though," she sighed with a pout.

"Maria, you know the rules," Bilal reminded her, "When you married Calvin, you became taboo. Even if you were to divorce him, you and I could never be the same cause you married him in the first place."

Maria exhaled, "Okay, I call you later on."

"Bye Maria."

Maria hung up the phone. She still couldn't figure out where or how she was going to get her sexual fix, but she knew that she needed going to get it soon.

Chapter Two

While D'Angelo was letting the woman of his dreams know that she was his "Lady," Calvin was contemplating how he was going to tell the woman sitting next to him the same thing. He and his wife had been having difficulties in their marriage off and on for the past two years and were just two steps away from a divorce. Calvin tried to reach out for her hand and was promptly dismissed. They stared at each other knowing the love that used to exist between them was starting to dwindle away. Calvin exhaled and reached for the radio and turned on the CD player. Toni Braxton started singing about how her man was "Trippin'" and Calvin was hoping that Maria got the message.

"How are we going to make this marriage work if you won't communicate with me?"

Maria started mumbling and complaining about her man in Spanish in an attempt to get a negative rise out of him. She looked into Calvin's murderous eyes and she couldn't believe that she married or had kids with the murderer.

Calvin shook his head and began to inhale the lavender scent from the air freshener that dangled from the rearview mirror as he continued the drive to their counselor's office. Calvin initiated the marital counseling when he discovered that his wife had cheated on him with a another man. When he walked in on their tryst, he had become heated—so heated that he had a flashback to the time in which he killed a man. He was twelve and was living with in Colorado at the time. Calvin and his friends were being terrorized by a group of Crips . One of the terriorzers, Garfield, had killed his older sister, Carla, because she was dating a member of the Bloods gang. For months Garfield and his friends had sought revenge on the sixth graders at Calvin's school. In the escalation of tension, Calvin stole a gun from one of the Bloods in the middle of the affray and challenged Garfield to a duel. Being fast with the fingers, Calvin shot off two bullets, killing Garfield before the boy could think to pull the trigger. Calvin had escaped prison because of the selflessness of his older brother, Carlton. Carlton had taken the gun from Calvin after Garfield had dropped to the ground and shot at the dead body; to later claim responsibility for the murder. Calvin had sworn that he'd never kill another person again, but seeing another man on top of his woman that night, enjoying what should have been his and only his, almost caused him to renege on that promise. The only thing that kept him sane was the thought of his brother getting out of jail soon. He would prove Carlton's prison sentence vain, by murdering again. Nothing would keep him from seeing his brother outside of prison walls, so he had kept his cool and let the adulterous deacon live.

Maria weighed her options and decided that it was best for her to get out of her marriage now. She hadn't loved Calvin for some time and she knew that she would not be happy if she continued to live with him. She wanted a divorce and she was willing to do it at any cost.

She also didn't want to risk Calvin getting angry enough to kill Bilal, so she decided that she would surprise him. She had a nice lasagna meal for Calvin complete with turkey salad and red wine. She made arrangements with a drug dealer friend of hers to get one of the popular "date rate" drugs, and she meticulously followed the written instructions that was provided as she blended it in to his drink.

Upon Calvin's arriving home, she made sure she was spontaneous and gave him something he could feel while Aretha was singing one of her most famous tunes in the background. When they were done with their grownup games, she decided it was best if she listened to Beyonce, Kelly, and Michelle's advice and catered to her man by feeding him on the couch as she sat in his lap. She continued her role as the innocent housewife as she waited for the drug to take affect. Once Calvin was out cold, she called Bilal.

"It's done."

"Really? You told him you want a divorce?" Bilal got excited. "You told him you wanted to be with me.?"

"He got the message. Can you pick me up as soon as possible?"

"I'll be there in ten minutes." Bilal replied and hung up the phone.

Maria went to the desk and she quickly composed her Dear John Letter informing Calvin of the reasons why she wanted a divorce. Then she rushed upstairs and threw all the clothes that she thought would fit in a bag and she grabbed her credit cards and some cash. She also made a mental note to search for pawn shop so she could cash in on her engagement ring and her wedding band. As soon as the doorbell rang, Maria opened the door and Bilal immediately made himself useful by helping Maria carry Calvin and put him in bed. Maria place her letter on the pillow feeling a slight tinge of guilt as she thought about the fact that Calvin's brother was getting out of jail in seven days. She was walking out on him on only days before their planned trip to pick Carlton up and bring him to Winston-Salem. Calvin was especially excited because Carlton expressed interest in joining the Street Disciples Ministry and passing out copies of "The Upper Room" to sinners and saints on Dr. Martin Luther King Boulevard. Maria loved watching the men dressed in street clothes as they talked about the Lord. She was particularly fond of Donte Eugene Sparks, who in his past life lived his life as an adult video star. She thought of the five ten sexy young thang and all of the videos she wished she had made with him before he retired.

"We need to go." Bilal was firm in his command as he gently grabbed her hand and led her out of the room she shared with her husband. When she looked at Bilal and thought of the money and the great sex she had with him, she felt confident that her decision to leave him was the right one.

Chapter Three

Calvin woke up mad as hell and Madea was right, he was not over it yet because he still wanted to kick Bilal's butt. Last night, he had cried himself to sleep. His wife was putting a hurting on him that he was in no way prepared to deal with. In fact, he could not remember any other time in his life where he had ever hurt as bad. When a man loves someone the way that he loved his wife, he's willing to do anything it takes to keep her, not matter what it may cost him in the end. At first he thought money was the reason Marcia cheated, so he considered applying for a part time job at a grocery store just so he could have enough money to pay *their* bills; as well as a little extra for Maria to play with.

He ignored his ringing doorbell—something he become accustomed to doing since Maria left.. Calvin desperately tried to avoid his mother or anyone else who had something negative to say about his situation. He preferred to sit around the house and listen to Mary J. Blige, she seemed to be the only one who could identify with his problems—problems that. he knew eventually he would need to deal with his problems. After twenty four hours of Mary and her life, Calvin got up and looked through his CD rack and finally decided to put in Toni Braxton's latest CD. She got it right on the first track when she reminded him that he gots to breathe and move on with his life. The doorbell rang again and he could hear a set of keys jiggling and trying to fit into the door knob. He knew he couldn't ignore it and hoped that maybe Maria had come to her senses and realized that their marriage wasn't over, and that they could save it. The minute he thought about the fact that he was naked, his stick got a little stiff and he realized that she could see him through the window. At first he thought he should get some pants on, but then he decided that maybe some spontaneous loving was exactly what their marriage needed. Maybe the answer to their marital problems lied between his legs.

"I've been trying to get at you for a few days?" Martin walked in and gave him a hug. To say that Calvin was disappointed to see his best friend was an understatement given his present condition. After all these years, he couldn't believe that his boy looked so much of Tyrese, especially now in his muscle shirts that allowed the world to see his "Ain't No Punk Christian" tattoo on his right bicep.

"Let me get decent," Calvin said in defeat. He had almost forgotten that he had given Martin a set of keys to assure his mother and father that he would be safe in Winston-Salem. It has been almost four years since they graduated from college and he had never asked his best friend to return the key back to him.

"What's Good?" Toni Braxton sang through the stereo. Martin shook his head as he picked up a current issue of *Black Enterprise* from the coffee table. Martin was a little ticked that Calvin had been rude and not invited him in or at least warned him that he was baby boy fresh.

"Have you packed to go to the airport tomorrow?" Martin asked when Calvin returned to the living room. Calvin looked at him, shook his head to indicate that he hadn't and took a seat on the couch. "So I take it you aren't trying to go to the ball your frat is having with the AKA's tonight either?"

Calvin had been so depressed in his funk that he forgot about the Diamonds & Pearls Ball which his alumni chapter and the local AKA chapter used to raise money for academic scholarships they give to students attending their alma mater, Winston-Salem State University. Calvin got to thinking about how long it's been since he been to a fraternity function.

"I'm surprised you're not dressed in your black and gold," Calvin replied. "I haven't been thinking right since Maria left, man."

"Look man, you can deal with Maria and the divorce later," Martin back tracked when he thought how cold his words were. "You can't let a woman who doesn't appreciate you bring you down. I mean, I haven't been through a divorce but you can't let the divorce consume your life." He noticed the foul odor coming from his friend. Martin was not used to seeing his friend down in the dumps like this.

"Let's get you ready to go," Martin encouraged him. "You go take a shower while I find you something to wear."

"But what about my hair? I need a shape up." Calvin came to the reality of how unkempt his appearance was.

"Calvin, when have you *ever* walked out of this house looking a mess?" A reminiscent smile spread across Martin's face. "I remember when you were Mr. Ram, you had a new hairstyle every three or four days it seemed like and you always had something fly to wear."

It was true. Calvin remembered those days fondly. Even though he was a newlywed and getting ready for the birth of his son, he still felt the need to keep sexy coming back. Calvin walked up the stairs to the bedroom, stepped into the bathroom and turned on the water. Calvin looked at himself in the mirror… he looked and felt a mess. He could hear Toni singing about how he was so stupid and he had to agree with her.

Calvin reached for the Nubian Heritage Indian Hemp & Haitian Vetiver soap and inhaled the smell as a means to calm his body. He allowed the light bristles to attempt to scrub away the pain of his divorce. The fragrance smelled so good and he felt like falling a sleep right there but he couldn't. He breathed and exhaled and felt the weight of all his drama and stress roll off his back and fall in the tub. If only he could see it going down the drain. He scrubbed away washing off Maria and Bilal and every mean and evil thing that has happened in the past two years.

Calvin grabbed his robe and put it on over his undergarments, then he brushed his teeth and rinsed, humming along with the songs as the CD played. He walked to the room and sat on the bed and put on the same scented lotion as the soap that he had scrubbed with in the shower. His allergies to regular perfumes and fragrances were so severe that over the years he had probably become the most faithful consumer of Nubian Heritage Indian Hemp & Haitian products.. He looked over to the left and noticed that Martin found the white and crème Armani suit that he thought he got rid of after he and Maria got married. Calvin really didn't want to wear it at first but once he put the suit on, he was surprised that he still looked good in it after putting on a few extra pounds.

"Yo!" Calvin was excited. "I still got it."

Martin had the look of the proud father when he saw Calvin admiring himself in the mirror. Now he remembered why Maria bought the suit. He smiled and started dancing to the music.

"This is what I needed." Calvin admitted.

"And we are going to make sure you stay *needed.* You look really good."

"Thank you."

"Pull out those diamond cufflinks and my crushed red diamond tie, they go good with this suit."

Martin did as he was told. He also came back with some hair clippers. Calvin took the suit jacket off and Martin got to work giving Calvin a much needed shape up. He wished he had thought to do that before Calvin got in the shower but it would be alright. Martin was just happy to see his friend smiling again. Calvin changed undershirts and went to the bathroom to dampen a towel so he could go over his hairline. Once he completed that task and put his shirts back on, Calvin was ready to go. When Martin came back into the room, he wore a dark crème suit with matching shoes with a black shirt and gold tie.

"If I didn't know any better, I'd think you were trying to outshine me."

"I got to do my best," Martin remarked. "I am single and I need to find a nice Christian girl I can bring home to mama."

"And you think you are going to meet her at the ball?"

Martin looked him over, "With the way you are dressed, I should be asking you the same thing."

Calvin punched Martin in the arm and they went about play sparring, as if they were kids again. When Martin landed a blow to the chest, they both knew it was time to stop.

"For real, I'm not looking for another woman, but if I do find one, it'll make it easier to forget my whole situation."

Martin nodded his head and the gentlemen left the house. Calvin deeply inhaled the air and when he exhaled, the thoughts of his pending sin in granting Maria's request for a divorce slipped his mind.

Chapter Four

Calvin and Martin walked in to the ballroom and were greeted by a fabulous and thick sista interpreting "And I Am

Telling You I'm Not Going." Calvin began to miss Maria and the way she used to sing to him when they first got married. That was his favorite song to hear her sing because of the way her the way her beautiful voice carried the song. When she sang that song—when she sang *any* song, Calvin felt like he was the only man in the world.

When she was done, the mood changed as Usher's voice began to pump from the speakers massive speakers that lined the edge of the stage. He was telling the ladies that they didn't have to call, and the upbeat tempo made Calvin want to cut a rug. The new initiates of Calvin's fraternity were rocking suits with vests or nice button ups and slacks in their fraternity's colors and began doing a stroll on the dance floor. Calvin joined in with some of the alumni members who knew the stroll. He felt good being amongst his brothers and began to remember his days as an active member of the collegiate chapter. When they were finished and the DJ switched the song to another selection, Calvin spotted Martin sitting at the table talking to two women of another sorority.

"Calvin, this is Kima and Keisha." Calvin shook their hands sat in the empty seat next to Kima. "Vincent went to go bring back some drinks for the ladies while his lady, Pam, went to go freshen up," Martin announced to Calvin.

"Vincent… as in Minister Farrakhan Vincent?"

Keisha and Kim chuckled at the disappointed look that Martin gave Calvin..

"That is foul and un-Christ like Calvin. We're supposed to treat others as we'd want to be treated."

"That's right, it is un-Christ like," Kima tried to agree but couldn't stop the chuckling.

"All Muslims are not Minister Farrakhan Calvin," Keisha appeared to be genuinely offended by the comment. Calvin was confused because a few seconds ago, she was laughing with her girl.

"Please be nice to Vincent," Martin was serious and began nursing the glass of water he was cradling, "I can't have my best friend and my line brother fighting at this function. My sorors will never let me hear the end of it."

"Um-um… naw, we not trying to have that." Kima seconded as she began to take an interest in Calvin. She was trying to figure out the fragrance he was wearing but she couldn't place her name on it. She knew it wasn't cologne but whatever it was, it smelled good on him. She was sizing him up and he passed the inspection until she noticed the wedding band on his left finger. "How long have you been married?"

Calvin looked at her dumbfounded. He hadn't told her that he was married but took the hint when she gave a subtle reference to his hand. He looked down on his reminder of his vows and his promise before the Lord to honor and to love his wife until death did him part. He was sad because one thing Calvin tried to do was avoid lying to God. He know that God could see everything and hear everything, even the whispers of his heart but he felt that he was letting God down by allowing Maria to leave him and finally excepting that she was gone. It still wasn't easy. It hadn't been that long since she left, but he knew that he had to let go.

"I'm in the process of getting a divorce," Calvin finally verbally acknowledged the transition of his life. He took the ring off and put it in his pocket. "I've been so used to wearing this thing every day because it meant so much to me, but I'm finding that the ring doesn't mean the same thing to everyone. My wife left me a few days ago."

"I'm sorry, I didn't know." Kima apologized but the damage had been done.

"No, I need to accept that this is where I am at with my life and move on and maybe meet the woman God intends for me to spend the rest of my life with."

Calvin stared at the imprint of his wedding ring and realized it was the first time he had taken it off in a few days. He often left it on when he showered so moments were few and far between when the ring was parted from him. He was beginning to regret being so adamant against getting a prenuptial agreement as he thought about not only of his wife cheating on him with another man, but them enjoying half of everything, even if it wasn't much, that he had spent his entire life since graduation to build. Marriage, like an initiation in a membership of a black Greek letter fraternity, was supposed to be a life time commitment; a prenuptial should not have been necessary.

"Well if you need space, I can give you that."

An uneasy discomfort came over Calvin's eyes as Vincent's arrived to help Pam sit in her seat across from him. Vincent equally displeased to see Calvin as well.

"Nice to meet you Pam," Calvin extended his hand to greet hers and she smiled. He tried to remember where knew three other women named Keisha, Kima and Pam but couldn't see it. No one else came to mind so he decided to enjoy their company. "I don't need anymore space," he replied to Kima's offer. "I'm gonna be fine."

"Well that's good."

"Now that we got that out the way," Martin popped open a bottle of sparkling grape juice that had been on ice in the middle of the table. "I say you get to know her," Martin pointed at Calvin and Kima. "I'll get to know her," he referred to Keisha as he poured some of the juice in their glasses and acknowledged Vincent and Pam. "And ya'll do what ya'll do."

Chapter Five

Martin probably should have been more specific when he said "get to know her." Martin and Keisha made plans to leave the party and to go sight-seeing; just the two of them. Vincent and Calvin were never going to be much for a conversation, so he and Pam dipped on them shortly after Martin and Keisha left. As for Calvin and Kima, the drinks led them to the dance floor , along with some of the other people who came to the Diamonds and Pearls Ball. After they danced they went to T. G. I. Fridays where they had a nice meal and mingled with some of the other people from the ball who ended up there afterwards as well.

When dinner ended Calvin and Kima were both a little tipsy, yet Calvin took the risk and drove Kima back to his place. It was after one o'clock in the morning and yet he felt guilty because he almost expected his wife to be home.

When he didn't see her car, Calvin felt safe and he Kima inside.

Only a few minutes earlier, he had been struggling to write a message for the next youth meeting—a message that it didn't look like he was going to be able to write—or even be able to attend the next youth meeting. He could feel the breeze on his legs letting him know that he had left the window open. He looked over to the see that the maroon curtains were closed but flew into the room just a little bit. He started to reach out to close the window when he was brought back to the reason why he couldn't concentrate on the paper he was supposed to be working on. He was trapped in his seat by a pair of arms that had reached out to grab his chair. His legs were shaking and his eyes were rolled back as he looked down at the bald, caramel head that was bouncing up and down on his midsection. He was scared that it might have been a man that he was with until he smelled the familiar scent of a woman and he relaxed knowing that he was cool. As he grabbed her head with his left hand, he looked to his right to see his pants were laying across the floor and his dress shirt hanging on the stair railing. The woman with the caramel head was not supposed to be pleasing him like this… especially since he'd just come to grips with the idea of getting a divorce, He was, after-all, the one teaching teens how to abstain from sex in the church. She had his lips on Calvin's precious jewels with his legs over her shoulders, rendering him helpless.

It dawned on Calvin that he and Maria had not sex in almost three months. It was not celibacy by choice, either Calvin was too tired or Maria came home too late to give him any, but today he had given in to that temptation in lustful sin. Now not only was he getting a divorce, he was committing adultery. Trust, it wasn't planned. He hadn't even been thinking about sex. Calvin was the kind of guy that avoided all of the bars and clubs he used to hang out at when he was single. He had avoided some of the ex-girlfriends that he used to give a little piece of himself to. When Calvin got saved and agreed to help with the youth ministry, he wanted to be a role model, an inspiration, and a goal for what a man had to look forward to when they saved themselves for marriage, but he could relate to those who found it hard not to give into temptation.

As he threw Kima on the couch and got on top of her naked body, he reached behind the cushions for his stash of massage oils. Like R. Kelly, he was feeling on her booty while trying to feel around for the oil and some rubbers that he now realized that he had thrown away. With this realization, he stopped—he stopped touching her completely, and he moved her legs so he could sit on the couch. Calvin looked at the hair on his chest and the happy trail that pointed at his sword in the sky that was anchored by a nice set of boulders. He looked at the little fuzz that he let grow back… and remembered that back in the day, the rule was that he had to be bald everywhere. Then he looked ahead and saw the picture of Jesus hanging on the wall. He saw his colored body hanging on the cross for his sins and Kima's. As the she put her lips at the tip of his sword, Calvin brought her head up and shook his head. He looked at her body and had admit, she had nice shape and probably went to the gym more than he did. Calvin had always a nice body frame … not necessarily muscular but sort of how Gary Dourdan looked in *Trois*.

"Yo, what's up, I thought we were going to get down?" Kima asked and Calvin could see the disappointment on her face.

"Nah, I can't do it," Calvin was happy that his penis finally decided to agree with his thinking brain and go limp. "Just because my wife cheated on me in our bed doesn't make it right for me to do the same to her." Calvin turned to face Kima and lifted her chin up. He could see tears beginning to form in her eyes.

"I'm sorry but I can't have sex with you now. I want to and you are a pretty lady but right now, I'd only let God down and hurt you in the process."

Calvin sounded nice trying to let Kima go gently, but on the inside, he wanted to slap his own face because he was getting ready to let a nice looking woman go. Calvin really wanted to take Kima and let out the frustration of not being able to know his wife's body for three months. He wanted to use Kima to feel the void; get to know her very well, but he that is would have been wrong. Calvin expected her to jump up and go crazy on him because he got a little sexual healing and didn't give her any, but she surprised him..

"We cool," Kima said while touching his chest. Calvin was trying to remember how they had gotten to his house to begin with. It certainly wasn't to have sex, it was for something else… then Calvin remembered that they both were a few glasses short of too much wine and it didn't help that she and Calvin had taken shots of liquor while attempting to discuss their problems. While Calvin was going through a divorce, Kima was battling with an abusive ex-fiancé that could not deal with the fact that she looked like a beautiful, light skinned version of India.Aire. She too was now looking at the wall and facing the same picture of Jesus that Calvin was facing. "Sometimes, when I know I'm going to give in, I take the pictures down."

"But don't you feel guilty afterwards though? I mean, He sees and knows everything. Do you repent?"

"It's a part of who I am. My desire for sex does not change how I feel about God," Kima got up and Calvin watched her walk away to the bathroom. Calvin was getting stiff again and the old him would have gotten up and pounced on that one time. His sword had returned and he sure enough wanted to attack the enemy… stab it a few times until he felt satisfied that he had put it to rest, but he couldn't get the words out of his mouth. Kima turned around and saw him looking at her. Calvin was fixated on the nice plump triangle that was at her midsection. His mouth salivated at that thought of returning the favor of the feeling he had been giving him, but Calvin knew he didn't want to go back, for he might not just stop at putting his mouth there. Calvin felt bad that he didn't satisfy her like she had done him, but what was he supposed to do? He touched his sword and voluntarily swung it from side to side. He remembered that he hid a large size condom in one of the cushions.

Calvin wasn't that big but he saw nothing wrong with pretending like he was. Calvin knew he could put the condom on, handle his business and make sure she was satisfied in the process and let her go but he also knew he couldn't handle that if the roles were reversed. Calvin's sword said if he was going to do this thing, stay on top so he could quit if he wasn't feeling it. But his mind, the one in his head… that still grappled with the idea of actually going through would could be a very nasty divorce… the one that thought about Bilal entering Maria at this very moment and having his way with her… the one that knew that he would be stuck with paying all of their marital bills regardless of what happened, said no. "Are you changing your mind?"

Calvin got up and she met him halfway and they kissed. She was a great kisser--one of the best Calvin had ever kissed. They took turns jockeying for the dominant space on the wall and like warriors they took their battle to the floor. Calvin grabbed the condom from Kima who picked it up from the floor during their wrestling match, tore the package open as she got on her knees. She backed her mound onto him and rubbing it up and down his shaft. Calvin tapped it twice and then told her to get on her back. He had to admit, it had been a while since he covered his member but like they used to say, it was just like riding a bike. Calvin put her legs up over his shoulders because he always liked looking at Maria when he went inside of her. Just to see the look of surprise and fear in her eyes was enough to turn him on. And just when he was getting the head in good, he looked in her face and all he could see was Maria and he backed away into the wall like he had seen a ghost. Calvin bumped his head against the wall and his heart was racing. Calvin tried rubbing the spot that made contact with the wall to make it feel better but instead, he made it worse.

"It's alright Calvin, we don't have to rush this," Kima said as she got up and walked to the bathroom. As he could hear the shower running, Calvin took the condom off, and at that moment, he thanked God that he wasn't Catholic cause he had no idea how many Hail Mary's he was supposed to say for this. When Kima turned the water off, Calvin quickly asked for forgiveness from God and got up off the floor. Calvin faced her eye to eye as she walked out of the bathroom.

"You alright?"

"Yeah, I am."

"I don't want you to hate me or feel bad about yourself. Everyone gives into a temptation at one point or another... this just happens to be the one we share."

"Yeah," Calvin responded. In the back of his mind, he was criticizing himself for breaking his marital vow. Calvin knew he needed to save himself again for the moment when he could get married to the right woman and eventually make him some babies.

Kima gave him a hug and grabbed her clothes and starting putting them on. Calvin did the same as he realized he did not have a lot of time to meet Martin and their friends, Franklin and Mike, at the airport for their flight to Denver to get his brother. After making sure that Kima was ready to go, he grabbed the bag he packed earlier as well as an outfit he could change into at the gym, where he decided he would take a shower after he dropped her off. Once they both were ready to go, they walked out the door and into Calvin's car.

Chapter Six

Martin was smiling when he seen Calvin adjusting his shirt when he stepped out of the car.

"Man, I didn't think you was gonna make it," Martin gave his best friend a pound. Calvin also gave a friendly grip to Franklin and Mike. Franklin had grown up with Calvin and Martin in Denver and was the first to move to Winston-Salem. It was here where he met Mike, a straight acting homosexual who had no problems letting him or anyone else know that he was more man than any Olympian or muscle bound dude could have ever hoped to be. At first, Calvin wasn't feeling the idea of Franklin being cool with Mike like that but once he saw that Mike wasn't going to "make Franklin gay," or turn him out as they say now, Calvin stopped tripping. Of course, the fact that Mike stood up to him during his freshman year at college for accusing him of being "soft" followed by a very stern and disciplining letter from Carlton helped out too.

"I've been waiting over thirteen years for my brother to get out of that joint." Calvin said as he pressed the lock button on his keypad and walked with his friends to Martin's black 2007 Nissan Altima. It was hard to believe that Martin had had the cover for over a year and it still had that fresh new care smell. "I can't wait to bring him home.

The young men started their journey by traveling twenty five miles east on I-40. They listened to Michael Baisden try to talk some sense into some caller who felt that black people were not intelligent enough to be entrepreneurs. That conversation hit a cord with both Martin and Mike as they both were successful business owners in their own right. Martin was a writer who owned his own publishing house that specialized in publishing Christian Fiction for both adults and teens. He was also a partner in a small barbershop. Mike owned and operated a group home for troubled gay teens and a small club and entertainment center that hosted gospel concerts and talent shows which; he allowed high school and college students to intern so they could get a taste of the entertainment industry.

"How she gonna say black people can't run a business," Mike complained. "Yeah, we're not all drug dealers with our pants off our behinds wearing Timbs and jewelry off our necks."

"Yeah, a lot of times folks assume that if we're black business people that we're either selling drugs or bootlegging videos," Martin added.

"Or that we're dishonest businessmen trying to rip folks off."

"You know what the problem is though?" Martin proposed, "When there is a shady brother or sister out there not honoring their contracts or playing games with peoples' money because they got emotional issues, they make it bad on all of us."

"We need to start holding our brothers and sisters who do bad business accountable instead of blowing off all the other brothers and sisters in the business and not giving them a chance to do the right thing." Mike added.

The men continued to listen as Michael Baisden and his guest educated others about the importance of reinvesting and supporting African American owned businesses. Once they arrived at the airport, they checked in, relaxed a little and boarded their plane.

"So what happened with you and Kima?" Calvin knew it would be a matter of time before Martin tried to get the 411.

"I was a respectable Christian man," Calvin responded sharply while glancing at Martin out of the side of his eye. "How were you and Keisha?"

"Keisha might be the one... I'm gonna try her out for a few more months and see where it goes. I already introduced her to mom and pops and plus she knows a little something about hair herself even though she's going to be a make up artist."

"Oh word."

"Yeah, she sells beauty products for M. Walker like my dad and she works with some local news anchors making sure they look right before they step into the limelight."

Calvin cut right to the chase, "You feeding me some bull man."

"Why you say that?"

"You not sleeping with her?"

Martin got dead silent because he knew the answer to that question was that they have had intercourse a time or two but they also agreed to remain celibate until they walked down that aisle, and made a promise to God to honor each other as man and wife. Martin also knew it was his fault for the line of questioning. So he answered the question the best way he knew how without bringing dishonor to Keisha, "we decided to wait until Holy Spirit brings us into that unity with Jesus."

"I'm not gonna front, Kima and I almost did it." Calvin made sure that Martin was looking him in the eye. "We really took it there, butt naked and everything and just when

I was about to put it in, all I could see was my wife and how wrong *I* would be if *I* did that to *her.*"

"Don't beat yourself up over it man," Martin could tell it was eating at Calvin that he almost gave into his flesh and fed it what it desired. "Rev. McClurkin was right, we fall down but we get back up again."

"I mean, I was *this* close to physically committing adultery," Calvin emphasized by bringing his index finger and his thumb about face and making sure there was very little space in between.

"I'm not one to talk about committing adultery… you done already seen me do that." Calvin briefly flashed back to a time where Martin was dared to have sex with an ex-girlfriend of his, and also remembered the scolding that Martin had received from his father because he hadn't abstained from sex. "Sometimes, I find that as Christians, we're not able to move forward because we keep reminding God about what we did. God will forgives us for it and then when we bring it right back to him he's like 'huh.'"

"You right." Calvin and Martin stopped talking long enough to take the drink and the peanuts from the stewardess. "You think God's gonna forget that Maria and I got a divorce."

"I can't answer that one." Martin took a sip and then continued, "but I feel that if you know that you made the best effort to save your marriage, you will be okay. I mean, you stayed with her after you discovered that she was messing around on you with another man, you tried to spend time with her, you tried to go to counseling with her. She left you in the middle of the night and Lord knows what she could have drugged you with."

"You think I was drugged?"

"You said yourself that you've never been a heavy sleeper ever since Garfield…" Martin stopped because he knew that he reminded Calvin of the afternoon when he took that young man's life. True, Garfield, being the leader of the Crips at his middle school was a true terror, but still, his life was gone and he did not have the opportunity to turn his life around or to get help. After a few years and with some counseling, Calvin learned to forgive himself for that and for the fact that he was responsible for putting his brother in jail. "You never sleep light. You used to wake me up paranoid when we stayed in the dorm."

"But I'm getting better with that though."

"Yeah?"

"Yeah."

Martin and Calvin continued to talk until their plane landed at Denver International Airport. The airport looked like it fit in with the Rocky Mountain backdrop. They later rejoined Franklin and Mike as they got their stuff and their rental car and left the airport.

Chapter Seven

The four young men enjoyed their stay at a nice five bedroom house in the Hidden Valley area that was owned by the award winning actor Darren Colbert. Darren was a tall, six foot nine dark chocolate A-list actor who had also sold candy with the boys when they were kids. He had already sent Martin the keys to his house and would be flying in this morning before they were to leave to pick up Carlton from jail. Darren had just finished shooting a scene for an upcoming movie based off one of a novels Martin had written when he was in college.

This morning, they were greeted by their mixed race, black and Mexican friend Juan Morales. Back in the day, he was the shortest one in the crew and was picked on for speaking both Spanish and English to his friends. Now, he is the second tallest at six foot five. After spending a stint in a homeless shelter, he focused on redeveloping his basketball skills, eventually being able to play college and professional basketball overseas. His three children who were all elementary school age were well mannered and his wife was working in the kitchen, making sure, "her men" as she liked to refer to them were well fed.

The only ones in the middle school crew that were missing were the twins Ray & Trey. No one really knew what had happened to them. Word on the street was that they were caught up in the gang violence and possibly ended up behind bars, but no one had been successful at locating them and finding out where they really were. Last year, Martin, Calvin, Franklin, Mike and his partner, Eric, had went to Colorado to bury their other friend Lester next to his little brother Sammie. They had made an attempt to get special permission for Carlton to be released temporary since Lester and Calvin's families were close, but the State of Colorado wasn't budging. That was a rough time for all of them because they knew that Lester's desire to defend our country from terrorism grew more so out of his perceived lack of ability to protect Sammie from getting killed by Garfield on an elementary school playground. That event was the catalyst for the war they waged against the gang when they were sixth graders and what eventually led to Calvin and Garfield having their shootout. Carlton had requested that they visit Lester and Sammie's gravesite before going to meet with family and friends so that he could pay them their respects.

Their other friends that they were able to keep up with in Winston-Salem, Second and Brenda, were enjoying married life with their children and had agreed to stay back to help prepare the home that Carlton would be moving into.

As they finished eating and reminiscing on their youth in Colorado, they made the two hour trip to the correctional facility that Carlton was being released from. Everyone was giddy with joy until they arrived at the big gray building that was protected by barbed wire and steel. Calvin thought about Abednego and his ministry working with young men in prison and remembered the parable that the good seeds were to grow with the bad and they should be separated at the Harvest. Calvin had often wondered how many lives were not given a chance to be cultivated behind bars because the rehabilitation that was supposed to take place wasn't to be. He thought about how common it was to see these young men on the corner, being misunderstood people who ministers, political leaders and others who claimed to profess Christianity or some "other faith" refused to give them the light. Only if Kanye could have given them the feeling…

The men were getting out of a white 2007 Yukon and they watched the peanut butter and caramel colored man leave the correctional facility for good. The folded brown bag held all of his worldly processions and in his right hand, the Word of God gave him the encouragement to put a little extra pep in his step. The taste of freedom that he hadn't had since he was a youth began to remind him of all the foods he wanted to partake in once he got home. Juan's wife had agreed to cook a down home southern meal and had enlisted the help of her sisters to make sure that they had a feast fit for a king.

Calvin met up with his parents at the gate and gave them a hug. They were enjoying their lives in Phoenix, Arizona and had tried to convenience Carlton to go back with them, but Carlton had a goal of pursuing divinity school at Shaw University, but he wanted to attend Winston-Salem State University as his brother and Martin had.

One of the pictures that Rahiem had sent him fell out of the Bible and Carlton kneeled down cautiously to pick it up. It would be a while before the custom and culture of prison life would wear off of him and he had given Calvin and everyone else a first taste of what they would be dealing with upon their return to Winston-Salem. And that was another joy Carlton had about getting out of jail, joining Rahiem's Street Disciples Ministry and spreading the Word and the good news of Christ in the streets as he did in the prison once he got saved three years ago. Once he had gotten saved, he had worked on both Calvin and their little brother, Casey's salvation. Casey was the easier case because he was pursing a professional bowling career, which had very little African Americans involvement and had very little support on a national level when compared to sports like tennis, golf and lacrosse. Casey himself didn't look bad bearing an ironic and striking resemblance to Tiger Woods, making his goal to be the Tiger Woods of bowling that much easier. Carlton became living proof that God, when given the opportunity to try him, can change any situation you *think* you are in and make it out for your good. True, he spent over thirteen years in jail for a crime he didn't commit, but when he thought about the children he hadn't fathered when he was getting with any woman who would give it up and baby mama drama that normally comes along with such responsibilities, or the STD's he didn't catch from having numerous unprotected sex encounters at a young age, prison wasn't such a bad thing.

Carlton gave his mother a long hug once he finally reached her and their father, Calvin and Casey joined in. Calvin shed tears of joy because his brother was finally free.

Chapter Eight

Everyone was getting into their cars after paying respects to Lester and Sammie. Just as suspected, Sammie's murder brought back fresh memories of that eventful day, but they rejoiced and healed knowing that both Sammie and Lester were with Jesus.

"I can't wait to taste some good food." Carlton said in a rich, high voice reminiscent of the comedian Katt Williams.

"My wife got it for you." Juan bragged. "You know her and her sisters can throw down in the kitchen."

"I believe it because her mother could cook."

"Yeah, she'd try to get you fattened up too so you could stop being a Casanova."

"Oh that's what that was."

Everyone enjoyed a laugh in the Yukon. The men continued to go down memory lane and talk about their days of selling candy. The teased each other about the girls they liked and the women they were dating now. Once they got to Darren's house, Calvin pulled Carlton to the side so he could have a short one on one with his big brother.

"You know why Maria is not here?" Calvin was hoping that he would not have to have this discussion with Carlton upon his release, but he thought it better now to get it out of the way.

"I know," Carlton confirmed, pulling out a letter that Maria had handwritten and handed it to Calvin. "She told me about Bilal and her reasons for wanting a divorce from you."

"I can't believe that…"

"It's no reason to get mad Calvin. I look at it like this. I know you are worried about whether or not what you are doing is the Christian thing to do. I say, let go and let God."

"I try but…"

"I thought you learned that poem about excuses."

"I did."

"Look at it this way… she's using Bilal as an excuse to do whatever it is she is setting out to do with her life at this time. She may come to realize that she made a mistake. You on the other hand, have to wake up every day with the desire to be a better man for the Lord than you were yesterday. Being a Christian means that you are free from being a slave to sin… it does not mean that you won't go through trials and tribulations or that you are immune to them. You remember that song at the end of *Diary of a Mad Black Woman* that Pattie LaBelle sings about being free?"

"What you know about *Diary of a Mad Black Woman?*"

"Boy you silly," Carlton grabbed Calvin and put him in a headlock, "I also know that if I was a woman, Mo'Nique could've been my cellmate too. Anyway, I love Tyler Perry and what that man is about and I can't wait to buy the DVDs and go the movies and support the plays."

"You must have been in the car with us before we got on the plane to get here."

"Who do you think has been schooling Martin and Mike about business?"

Calvin looked at Carlton and shook his head. He glanced at his hand and realized it had been bare for a week now. It was the longest that he's ever gone without wearing his wedding ring ever since the pastor declared him and Maria husband and wife and he kissed his bride. Calvin began to realize what his brother was trying to do other than get inside the house so he could get him some southern food to eat. On one hand, without the ring, Calvin was free to pursue a stronger relationship with God and to grow more within himself in Christ. On the other hand, Calvin was free to love Maria in a new way… to love her as his sister in Christ and as the woman she was destined to be.

REACHING FORWARD

Thomas Ashburn, Jr.

"Brethren, I do not count myself to have apprehended; but this one thing, I do, forgetting those things which are behind and reaching forward to those things which are ahead.
(Philippians 3:13 NKJV)

It was Saturday, 9:30 a.m. Shawn Michael Williams stared at himself in his bathroom mirror trying to wrap his mind around where he was about to go and what he was about to do. *I can't believe I'm doing this. Maybe I shouldn't go,* he thought.

His appointment was 10 a.m. He knew it would be rude to cancel now. He walked back and forth and all around his small one bedroom apartment. He glanced at the dirty dishes in the sink and lint on the floor. Then a light bulb came on in Shawn's head.

I know. I can call the office and say I have some important housework to do and can't make it. No, that's a poor excuse. I need to do this.

Shawn walked back to the mirror to give himself a pep talk.

"Come on dog, you can do this, it's no big deal," he said aloud. "A lot of people do this type of thing."

He still wasn't convinced. Now it was 9:40 a.m. Shawn had to make a decision. Call the office now and cancel or man up and leave right away.

I have to at least give this a try, Shawn pondered. He brushed his low cut hair, tucked his short sleeve polo shirt into his khaki slacks, and jetted out of the door. He jumped into his blue 1998 Honda Accord and he was off. Shawn was glad he was only ten miles away from his destination.

Shawn pulled into the church parking lot, took one last deep breath and got out of his car. He felt weird being there on a Saturday. He walked through the double doors, through the foyer, and started walking down a long hallway. He finally saw a young woman sitting behind a desk.

"Good morning," she said in a soft voice. "You must be Shawn."

"Yeah, I'm Shawn, what's your name?"

Shawn slowly grinned as he tried to make direct eye contact with the young lady.

"My name is Anita," she said.

She handed him a clipboard with a questionnaire and a pen attached.

"I need you to fill this out and give it back to me when you're done," Anita said.

"No problem," Shawn said. "You have beautiful eyes. A man could get lost in them."

"Thank you," she said with a shy smile.

"Are you busy later," Shawn asked. "Maybe we could go to dinner."

"I'm sorry, I have a boyfriend," Anita answered.

"He is one lucky man—I mean one blessed," Shawn said. "I meant to say one blessed man."

"You can have a seat if you like?" Anita said. "I'll let Brother Jones know you are here."

She got up and squeezed her petite frame through the small area between the desk and the wall and walked into the office across the hall.

I must be crazy, Shawn thought as he sat down. *Who in their right mind would want to date a guy who is getting counseling? He obviously has issues.*

Shawn tried to forget about the embarrassing moment he just had. He looked over the brief questionnaire. It was mostly basic things like, name, address, occupation, age, reason for visiting the church counselor etc. Shawn had to really think about why he was there.

That's a good question, Shawn thought. *Why am I here? I have a million reasons but I guess the number one reason is my problem with women.*

Anita came back to her desk and started typing on the computer.

Shawn filled out the last portion of the questionnaire. Then reality set in. He was about to talk to a counselor about his problems. He was always the type to keep things bottled up in side. He hoped this would go well and that all of his apprehension had been a waste of time.

Shawn got up from the small folding chair and handed Anita the clipboard.

"Thanks Shawn," she said. "Follow me".

Shawn followed Anita into Brother Andy Jones' office. Shawn had seen Brother Jones many times at church but never really had a conversation with him.

"How are you doing Brother Williams," Brother Jones said in a loud happy voice. "God bless you brother it's good to see you."

When Brother Jones stood, he was so tall it looked as though his head would touch the ceiling. He extended his hand across the cherry wood desk. Shawn gave him a firm handshake.

"I'm doing alright Brother Jones," Shawn said.

Anita handed Brother Jones the clipboard.

"It was nice meeting you Shawn," Anita said.

"The pleasure was all mine," Shawn replied.

Anita walked out of the room and closed the door tightly behind her.

"Have a seat," Brother Jones said.

Shawn sat down on the dark green love seat. There were two other single chairs in the room but he thought the love seat would be more comfortable. He took a quick look around the room at all the degrees on the wall.

"Let me tell you a little about myself," Brother Jones said leaning back in his large leather chair. "I got my bachelor's degree in sociology from Old Dominion University. I got my master's degree in psychology and counseling from Regent University. I've been a family counselor for the city of Virginia Beach for 20 years. Many of the church members would ask me for advice from time to time and about five years ago the pastor asked me to be the church counselor.

Brother Jones took a deep breath and continued.

"I have counseled married couples, single men, and single women from teenagers to adults. I have heard some stories that you wouldn't believe. I am saying this because I don't want you to hold back."

Shawn nodded to let Brother Jones know he felt comfortable.

"Don't be afraid to tell me anything and I promise our conversation will not leave this room," Brother Jones said. "Any notes I take will be locked in a file cabinet that only I have the key to. I believe that whatever issues you have God can work out."

Brother Jones glanced at the questionnaire. "It says here that you are 26 years old," Brother Jones said as he read aloud. "Single, no kids, no siblings, you are a customer service representative at USA Telecom, and you live here in Virginia Beach. Tell me some things about you that aren't on this questionnaire."

Shawn slumped down in his chair, looked up at the ceiling and tried to think of where he should begin.

"I was born in Norfolk," Shawn said. "Most of my family is from Savannah, Ga. It was always just my Mom and I. My Aunt Sarah lived with us for a little while but she went back to Savannah."

"What about your father," Brother Jones inquired.

Shawn sighed.

"I never knew him," Shawn said in a regretful voice. "I asked my Mom about him many times when I was younger but she would get upset, yell at me, or just change the subject."

Shawn's cell phone vibrated on his hip. He glanced at the caller id, it said Shaniqua. He hit the ignore button and continued talking.

"The neighborhood I grew up in was not the best," Shawn said. "There was a lot of drug dealing going on and a lot of violence. I mostly went to school and came home. I didn't hang out in the neighborhood too much. I also had a job at the grocery store down the street from our house."

"What about your education," Brother Jones asked. "Did you ever go to college?"

"I barely finished High School," Shawn said, trying not to laugh. "After I finished high school a lot of brothers I knew were going to jail, the military, or college. I couldn't see myself going to any of those places so I started working full time. I worked everywhere from department stores, to warehouses, and I did some telemarketing. I saved the majority of my money until I had enough to buy a used car and to get my own place. I would also help my mom out with bills or whatever she needed."

"That's good that you helped out your mom," Brother Jones said. "What is your relationship like with her today?"

"We talk maybe once or twice a month," Shawn said. "As I got older we drifted apart. She works a lot of hours as a nurse at Norfolk General Hospital. When she was off of work she was always out on a date with some man. That's why I worked and went to school and mostly took care of myself as a teen."

"It seems you learned about responsibility at an early age," Brother Jones said. "Do you feel like your Mom wasn't there when you needed her?"

"Definitely," Shawn said quickly.

Brother Jones read more of the questionnaire.

"It says here that you have problems with women," Brother Jones said. "Do you think that your relationship with your mother is the root of these issues?"

"Maybe," Shawn said with a puzzled look on his face. "I don't know. It's like I love women and hate them at the same time. Before I gave my life to Christ I was what they call a 'player'. I would meet women, sort of like them at first, use them for what I wanted, and then disappear. I wouldn't answer my phone, wouldn't respond to emails or text messages. I would just shut them out. Then after a month or two would pass, I would feel guilty about the situation."

"Wow," Brother Jones said. "It's hard to believe that you were that type of brother. I remember the first time I saw you at church a few months ago when the pastor did the alter call. You were so sincere when he asked did you want to give your life to Christ. We men at the church get excited when we see a man your age give his life to the Lord. Tell me how you got to that point where you wanted to be a Christian."

Shawn smiled as he thought back to when he gave his life to the Lord.

"I always play basketball at the community center not far from where I live," Shawn explained. "That's where I met Deacon Antonio Gray. We would play basketball for hours."

"Oh yeah," Brother Jones said. "Tony has been a member of the church for some time now. He loves to play basketball."

He was always asking me to consider giving my life to Christ and always inviting me to church, Shawn said. "I knew that I wasn't happy so one day I took him up on that invite."

Shawn reminisced about how he felt that day he gave his life to Christ just six months ago. It was a chilly day in February. The pastor preached *Let go and let God.*

"I felt like Pastor Johnson was talking directly to me out of the 300 plus people that were there," Shawn said excitedly. "When I gave my life to Christ it was like a load had been lifted off of my shoulders. I believe my life is moving in the right direction."

Brother Jones sat up straight in his chair, slightly loosened his tie and thought about his next question.

"You made a great decision," Brother Jones said. "When did you discover you had a problem with women?"

"After I gave my life to Christ I felt even worse about the way I treated women," Shawn said. "I called a lot of them and told them about my new life. Most of them laughed at me, but some of them said that it was good and they felt they needed to do the same thing. I apologized to them but I still didn't feel right. Now when I meet women I'm still tempted to do the same thing but I know God would not be pleased."

Shawn looked down at his cell phone. He couldn't believe it was 11:15 a.m.

"I think this is a good stopping point for us," Brother Jones said. "I have learned a little about your past, your present, and your problem. I want you to be encouraged. Keep coming to every Bible study and every service like you have been doing. If you have not already I would advise you to develop a daily prayer life and read your Bible at home often. You are on the right track, just don't stop."

Brother Jones always ended every counseling session with a prayer. He stood up and reached both of his hands across his desk. Shawn stood up, joined hands with him, and bowed his head. Brother Jones said a brief prayer and then sat back at his desk.

"I'll see you at church tomorrow," Brother Jones said with a smile. "I'll tell Anita to make an appointment for next Saturday at the same time if that works for you?"

"Yes, that's sounds great," Shawn replied. "See you tomorrow."

Shawn said good-bye to Anita, walked out the door, and headed for his car. He felt relieved having shared his problems with somebody he could trust.

God is good, he thought. *I can't wait to go to church tomorrow.*

Shawn's cell phone vibrated on his hip. The caller id said Shaniqua again. She was one of those old friends who laughed at his new life. She knew him all to well. He wouldn't dare answer it. Shawn hit the ignore button quick. He knew that if he answered that phone that she would persuade him to go out for drinks or to come to her apartment, but either way it would turn out bad. He was not going to let anything or anybody mess up his relationship with God. Shawn got into his car and headed home.

Shawn was one of the first people at Virginia Beach Christian Center Sunday morning. Church usually started around 11 a.m. He was there at 10:30 a.m. Church had become his favorite place over the past few months. Pastor Johnson always seems to speak about whatever problem Shawn had been going through the previous week. He always left church feeling inspired and motivated. Shawn rolled all his windows down hoping to catch a summer breeze.

Then a black SUV pulled up in the parking space beside him. It was Tony. Shawn grabbed his Bible and got out of his car. Tony got out of his truck. The sun was shining on his freshly shaved head.

"There's my main man," Tony said as soon as he got out of his SUV. "What's going on?"

"Nothing much," Shawn said as they shook hands.

"You ready to have a good time," Tony said with a smile. "You know how we do at V.B.C.C."

"No doubt Deacon," Shawn said while nodding his head.

Shawn went in and found his favorite seat, third row on the right. He flipped through his Bible and read a couple of scriptures and before he knew it, the 300 plus crowd had piled in and church had begun.

After the scripture and prayer, the praise and worship team starting singing led by Lakesha Parker. The team was singing *Because of Who You Are,* by Martha Munizzi. Shawn loved to hear Lakesha sing. Her voice was amazing.

All around the church people began to stand and praise God. Then right on cue Gabrielle Harris starting shouting and dancing all over the church.

"Hallelujah," Gabrielle shouted repeatedly.

Shawn thought Gabrielle was the most beautiful woman at church but he was always afraid to approach her. Shawn thought she looked a lot like actress Lisa Raye. He also felt that she was a little too spiritually mature for him. He knew he had just given his life to Christ and he had a long way to go before he would be on her level. But he still believed that if he were given the opportunity he would at least introduce himself.

After church was over Shawn was headed straight for the door. His stomach was growling like crazy and all he could think about was the left over spaghetti at home in his refrigerator. Just as he was about to go out of the door, Tony stopped him.

"Hold up a second Brother Williams, don't leave yet." Tony yelled from the front of the church. "I'll be right there I have to talk to the pastor first."

Tony was talking to a sweaty and obviously fatigued Pastor Johnson. The pastor had just preached for at least an hour. Shawn went out in to the foyer to wait for Tony. He realized he needed to use the restroom and made a quick right turn and bumped right in to Gabrielle.

"Excuse me, I'm so sorry," Shawn said quickly.

"I'm okay," Gabrielle said.

"Hi, my name is—"

"Shawn," Gabrielle interrupted before Shawn could say.

"How did you know my name," Shawn asked inquisitively?

Gabrielle looked Shawn directly in the eyes.

"I've been seeing you around for the past few months," she said. "I have my ways."

"Service was off the hook as usual, "Shawn said. " Pastor really preached. I saw you getting your praise on."

"Yeah, God has done so much for me I have to praise Him every chance I get," Gabrielle said with a smile.

"We should talk more," Shawn said.

Gabrielle pulled a pen and a small piece of paper out of her Coach bag and jotted her cell phone number down.

"Give me a call later on tonight," Gabrielle said.

"I'll do that," Shawn said.

Gabrielle walked away and Shawn just stood there stunned. *Did the most attractive woman in church just give me her phone number Shawn asked himself?*

He almost forgot he had to use the restroom. He went in, used the bathroom, washed his hands, and came back out to wait for Tony.

"There you are Shawn," Tony said as he was walking up. "I'm going to be starting a Men's ministry soon and I want you to be a part of it. We are going to meet once a week to study the Word, pray and discuss issues that men deal with. We're going to talk about issues like being single and saved, being a good husband, managing your finances wisely, and maintaining good health."

"Sounds great," Shawn said enthusiastically. "Just let me know when it starts."

"I'll let you know later this week," Tony said. "I have to go over the details with the pastor. He likes the idea he just wants to know a little more.

"That's cool," Shawn said. "I'll talk to you later."

"Catch you later Brother William," Tony said as the two slapped hands.

Shawn jumped in his car and headed home excited about the new men's ministry and getting Gabrielle's phone number. It had been a great Sunday.

When Shawn got home he tore in to the leftover spaghetti. He finished the last little bit of it on his plate, slumped down on his couch, and started flipping channels aimlessly.

Shawn pulled Gabrielle's phone number out of his pocket and stared at it. He glanced at the clock on the wall. It was 8:30.

I'd better call before it gets too late, Shawn thought.

He dialed the number and waited. Her ring back tone was playing some praise and worship music that he never heard before.

"Hello," Gabrielle answered. "Hello."

Shawn had gotten so in to the music he almost forgot he was waiting for her to pick up.

"Oh, Hi," Shawn said. "Sorry about that. I was feeling the music. What are you up to?"

"Nothing much," Gabrielle said. "Just curled up on the couch in my pajamas watching the women's channel."

"My mom watches that all day," Shawn said.

"Tell me about your mom," Gabrielle said. "I've never seen her at church before."

"We're cool, "Shawn said. "As far as church, she doesn't really go. "She works a lot of hours as a nurse at the hospital and when she gets a day off, she usually sleeps all day. Don't even ask me about my father, I never met the guy."

"I can sort of relate," Gabrielle said. "My mom and dad got a divorce when I was about five. My dad never sees me or calls. I was surprised to see him at my high school graduation. He sends me money ever month but that's it."

"At least you know who he is," Shawn said.

"You're right, I guess I shouldn't complain," Gabrielle said. "Where do you work?"

"I'm a customer service representative at USA Telecom," Shawn said. "I handle inbound calls for people who are having problems with their phone service."

"Wow," Gabrielle said. "What is that like?"

"Crazy," Shawn said. "You wouldn't believe how rude some people can be. They act as if I personally came to their house and messed up their phone service."

Gabrielle laughed.

"You're funny," she said." I work part-time at Hot Fashions in the mall and I go to Norfolk State University full-time. I'm a junior majoring in computer science. I'm kind of mad at myself because I should be working in my field right now. I took a couple of years off because I wasn't focused when I first started college."

"What made you lose your focus," Shawn asked?

"Too much partying and not enough studying," Gabrielle replied. "I learned my lesson and now I have a 3.0 grade point average. I can't wait to graduate and start making the big bucks."

"I hope you have all the success in the world," Shawn said. "I've really enjoyed talking to you. "What are you doing Friday night?"

"I don't know," Gabrielle replied. "Are you asking me out?"

"Yes I am," Shawn said. "I was thinking about taking you to Joe's Crab Shack. Do you like seafood?"

"I love it," Gabrielle said.

"I know this is our first date so we can meet at the restaurant instead of me picking you up?" Shawn asked in a confident voice.

"You can pick me up from my house," Gabrielle said. "I trust you. Is 7:30 good for you?"

"Perfect," Shawn said.

"Call me later this week and I'll give you directions to my house," Gabrielle said.

"Sure," Shawn said. "Goodnight."

"Goodbye," Gabrielle said. "Have sweet dreams about me."

"I hope so," Shawn said.

Shawn hung up the phone and a big smile came across his face. He was so excited about going out with Gabrielle that he wasn't even dreading going to work tomorrow. In his heart he thought this might be the beginning of something great.

The week seemed to fly by. It was 5:30 p.m. Friday and Shawn was almost home. He turned the radio up as loud as he could. He rolled all of the windows down and put the sunroof back. He was feeling good.

He got home, took a shower, sprayed on some cologne, and put on his favorite button up shirt and jeans. Shawn drove down Lynnhaven Parkway until he saw the sign for the apartment complex where Gabrielle lived. He pulled into a visitor's space and sat there for about five minutes. He finally walked up and knocked on the door.

Gabrielle opened the door with a big smile.

"Hi Shawn, come on in," She said. "Have a seat. I'll be ready in about five minutes."

Shawn looked around the apartment. It was much more spacious than his and the furniture was a lot nicer. Most of his furniture came from the flea market. He also saw some pictures of a girl who wasn't Gabrielle.

"I'm ready," Gabrielle said grabbing her purse.

"You have a nice place," Shawn said. "Who is this woman in some of these pictures?"

"That's my roommate Shauna," Gabrielle said. "She works two jobs. She's never home."

"In today's economy working two jobs isn't such a bad idea," Shawn said. "Wow! You look great."

Gabrielle was wearing a pink halter-top, tight designer jeans, and heels.

They went out of the door and Shawn quickly went around to open the car door for her. They got to the restaurant and had a delicious dinner and some great conversation. Shawn ordered shrimp and Gabrielle ordered crab cakes. It was 9 p.m.

"The night is young," Shawn said. "How about we go to the beach and walk on the boardwalk for a little while."

"Sure," Gabrielle said.

They got back into the car and they were off. They arrived at the beach, parked the car, and started walking on the boardwalk. It was a warm June night but a little breeze was blowing making the night comfortable. They walked and talked about everything from, church, to politics, to relationships, and Christianity.

"Do you see yourself married one day in the near future," Shawn asked?

"I don't know," Gabrielle responded. "I am 25. I guess I should be thinking about it. I'll have my degree next year in May. I'm thinking more about my career and just having a good time right now."

"I can understand that," Shawn said. "I'm excited about getting married and having kids someday. I want to be a good father and do all the things that my father didn't do for me."

"That's sweet Shawn," Gabrielle said. "You're going to make somebody a great husband someday."

"Thank you," Shawn said.

"I am really enjoying myself," Gabrielle said. "Do you want to go back to my place and watch a movie or something?"

"Sure," Shawn said. "Let go."

Gabrielle reached out and grabbed Shawn's hand. They walked hand in hand back to Shawn's car.

They arrived at the house and went inside. Gabrielle turned the lights on.

"You can have a seat, I'll be right back," Gabrielle said.

Shawn sat down on the couch and patiently waited for her to return. She came back in sweat pants and a t-shirt.

"What do you want to watch, action, horror, romance, or comedy," Gabrielle asked? "I have it all."

"I've always been sort of a man of action so I guess you can put one of those in," Shawn said.

Gabrielle put the DVD in the DVD player, turned off the lights and sat really close to Shawn on the couch.

"I had a really good time tonight," Gabrielle said. "Thank you for dinner and everything."

"You're more than welcome," Shawn said. "I hope we can do this again."

"I hope so," Gabrielle said. "The night isn't over just yet."

She leaned in and gave Shawn a kiss on the cheek. Then she kissed him on the neck. Then she grabbed his face, turned it toward her, and kissed him aggressively on the lips. Shawn pulled his face back.

"Whooooooa," Shawn said. "What are you doing?"

"I thought you were feeling me," Gabrielle said.

"I'm trying to have a good time but not that good of a time," Shawn said.

"Don't trip Shawn". "We are both adults here."

"I thought you were a woman of God," Shawn said with a confused look on his face.

"I am," Gabrielle said. "God understands that we have needs. He gave us these desires."

"I know that, but not like this," Shawn said. "I mean… I ...we can't just. I don't know what's going on right now. Thank you for a good evening but I have to go."

Shawn headed for the door as fast a possible. He went out of the door and closed it behind him. He got into his car and went home. It was almost midnight but he needed to talk to somebody. He pulled out his cell phone and called Tony. Shawn was waiting for Tony to pick up the phone. His mind kept replaying the night's events in disbelief.

Tony answered.

"What's up Brother Williams," Tony said.

"Sorry for calling so late," Shawn said. "I needed to talk to somebody."

"I went out with Gabrielle tonight,"

"Gabrielle," Tony said. "Gabrielle that goes to our church?"

"Yeah," Shawn replied.

"Oh no," Tony said. "I wish you would have told me you were going out with her, I would have warned you."

"What do you know about her," Shawn asked?

"I went out with her about three years ago," Tony said. "We went bowling and then she invited me back to her place to watch a movie. The next thing I knew she dimmed the lights and turned on some slow jams. I had to get out of there fast. I should have known better because she was only 22 at the time. I was 29 and I should have been dating somebody closer to my age. I thought by now she would have changed."

"She really fooled me," Shawn said. "I watched her in church always shouting and dancing and I thought she was all about living right."

"Let me tell you something Shawn," Tony said. "Acts of worship like shouting, dancing, and speaking in tongues don't mean a person is living holy. Holiness is a lifestyle that we have to live inside and outside of church. Unfortunately everybody doesn't live the life 24/7."

"I was just shocked." Shawn said. "I thought women at church were different."

Tony laughed.

"They are different," Tony said. "You still have to be very careful in choosing someone to have a relationship with. Some people still have issues that they are working out even though they are in church. We have to pray for them. You should be proud of yourself. You handled the situation like a true Christian man."

"Thanks," Shawn said. "I still have a ways to go. "I still have some issues. Some things I just don't feel comfortable talking about but I know I need to get them out. Last week I started getting counseling from Brother Jones."

"That's a good thing." Tony said. "I've talked to him on many occasions and he always gave me excellent advice. Don't be afraid to share your most personal feelings with him. I promise it won't leave that room."

"Okay," Shawn said. "I'll keep that in mind. "It's getting late so I guess I'll holla at you at church Sunday."

"Alright man," Tony said. "God bless."

"Talk to you later," Shawn replied.

Shawn's night had been so crazy that as soon as he got in to the bed, he was sleep within minutes.

The next morning Shawn went to the church for his second session with Brother Jones. He saw Anita's smiling face sitting behind her desk.

"Hi Shawn," Anita said.

"Hi Anita," Shawn said. "How are you doing this morning?"

"Good," Anita answered. "I'll let Brother Jones know you are here."

Before Shawn could sit down he heard Brother Jones's booming voice.

"Come on in Brother William," he said.

Shawn walked into the office, shook Brother Jones' hand, and sat down.

"It's good to see you," Brother Jones said. "How have you been?"

"I've been good," Shawn said. "I had an interesting night last night. I went on a date with someone from the church. We went back to her place and she got kind of aggressive. I had to roll out. I just don't understand women."

"I'm 48 years old and I still don't fully understand everything about women," Brother Jones said. "We have to get to the root of your problem. We have to take a closer look at your childhood to understand the issues that you are dealing with as an adult. Talk to me more about your Mom and what is was like growing up."

"I think I told you everything last time," Shawn said. "My mom worked a lot. I went to school, work, and home. That's about it."

"Last time you said she wasn't there for you when you needed her," Brother Jones said. "Do you mean to help you with your homework, give you advice, or what?

"Some things a little boy should not go through," Shawn said. "His Mom or his Dad should protect him from certain things."

"I'm not sure I know what you are talking about," Brother Jones said.

Tears welled up in Shawn's eyes. He knew if he was ever going to move forward in his life that he would have to eventually address his childhood pain. He couldn't hold it in any longer.

"When I was about four years old my Aunt Sarah started molesting me," Shawn said with tears running down his cheeks. "My mom would be at work. Aunt Sarah was supposed to be talking care of me instead she was abusing me. I told my mom about five times and she didn't believe me. By the sixth time she finally confronted my aunt. Aunt Sarah got really mad, packed her things, and left a couple days later. My mom and I never talked about it since then. I was mad at my mom for not being there for me. I was mad at my aunt for abusing me and I was mad at God for allowing it to happen.

Shawn buried his face in his hands and sobbed deeply. Brother Jones got up, walked around his desk, sat beside Shawn, and rubbed his back.

"It's going to be alright Brother, just let it all out," Brother Jones said.

Shawn cried for almost an hour while Brother Jones sat quietly. He also told what happened in more detail. Shawn finally wiped his tears and took a deep breath.

"We need to have a lot more sessions," Brother Jones said. "I've dealt with sexually abused people before and it can be a long road to full deliverance but with the help of God you can overcome. Can we meet again next Saturday at the same time?"

"Sure," Shawn said. "Thanks for listening and allowing me to release what I've been carrying for so long."

"Anytime," Brother Jones said. "This is what God called me to do."

They ended with the usual prayer. Shawn walked out feeling like he just took a giant leap forward. He knew he needed to completely forgive his mom and his aunt but he had taken the first step in the right direction. There was one thing he couldn't understand. Why would God allow this to happen in the first place? He couldn't wait for church tomorrow.

The next day Shawn was on the front row at church having a great time. The praise and worship team done an amazing job and Pastor Johnson was deep in to his sermon. Shawn still couldn't believe what happened Friday night but he didn't have any bad feelings toward Gabrielle. He daydreamed for a minute and then tuned back in to the pastor's sermon.

Pastor Johnson preaching:

"*Everybody has been through something. Sometimes we want to ask God Why. Why did you let this happen to me? I'm here to tell you that the devil meant it for evil but God is going to turn it around for your good. Every trial and every hardship didn't come to kill you, but so God could get the glory. He wants you to know that if it had not been for Him on your side you would have never survived. The greater your struggle the greater the glory God will get out of your life. Turn to your neighbor and say, "God is going to get some glory out of this." Somebody shout hallelujah."*

Before Shawn knew it he leaped out of his seat and shouted hallelujah as loud as he could. He started to realize that maybe something good could come out of even the worst situation. He was willing to do whatever is takes to keep moving forward in his life. He was even considering calling his Aunt Sarah. Shawn knew he wasn't finished dealing with his past yet, but he was going to keep on reaching forward.

VERBAL VACANCY

Clarence "Baba Simba" Mollock

"Chunk it - chunk it!" yelled my brother Sammy. So I chunked that ball as hard as I could against the side of the house. It bounced off the wall and hit the porch. You never knew which way the ball would bounce when it hit the wooden porch because some of the boards were uneven and warped. Sammy started back peddling. Then, he planted his right foot into the dirt and moved left. He caught that ball before it hit the ground. He was fast. And when it was my turn Sammy faked a hard chunk but let the ball out of his hand real slow. I ran forward and side stepped to the right. I dove to the ground and caught it. I was just as fast.

We lived in a two story shotgun house with a three-quarter wrap around porch. The first level of the house had a tin roof. Then, there was the side of the house which made up the second floor. Of course, there was the shingled roof at the top of the house. When Mommo wasn't looking we would race from the front porch right through the front room door, straight through the dining room, straight out the kitchen door, pass the smoke house and end up at the outhouse. And vice versa! And when Mommo stopped us from running through the house we would play catch the ball off the side of the house.

Sammy and I were five and four years old respectively. We were so young and too short to chunk the ball up to the side of the house which made up the second floor.

Sammy had a twin sister, but, he and I played together most of the time. We understood each other as brothers do. That next year the twins would be going to the first grade. I would be home by myself.

I talked to Mommo alot because we were the only ones home when the twins went to school and Daelay was at work on the farm. When I talked she would always say something like "uh huh" or she would just shake her head as if she understood every word I said. Sometimes I went with Daelay to help him on the farm where he worked. I listened to all those stories that he told. I listened to his stories so much that It got to a point that I could tell his stories to him. Sammy and Saundwo got home from school before Daelay got off work. The twins and I had specific chores to do before supper. We did not have to be told what to do. Sammy and I brought in the wood. We had to make sure that the wood box behind the front room stove, the dining room stove and the kitchen stove was full. Plus, we had to rake up a half basket of wood chips so that Daelay could use the kindling to make the morning fires. Of course there was the usual job of feeding the chickens and slopping the hawgs. Saundwo helped Mommo clean the house and make supper. She also had to make sure that the honey pot was in for the night.

Daelay always said, "Womens' work was inside and mens' work was outside, but, you better be ready to do either one if you have to." At the supper table everybody took turns telling about their day. Whether boring or not we all respected and understood each other.

My cousins all lived down the road. They would come over to our house because we had the biggest yard. We played dodge-ball a lot. When the game got boring one of them would say that the ball missed them, but we knew that it didn't. I think they did that just to hear me fuss. They would gather around me. Instead of fussing back they would be laughing the whole time I was fussing. Sometimes they would laugh so hard that everybody would be laughing but me! The dodge-ball game could not continue. Since I was the only one not laughing I figured out that they must have understood my argument..

Besides the twins I had a big brother named Chawls and a big sister named Calin. Chawls was always gone somewhere. But, he did find the time to teach me how to hunt for squirrels. During the hunt we never talked. I was not allowed to carry a gun, yet. I was there to help spot the squirrels. Chawls and I could gesture exactly where a squirrel was hiding. The only sound heard in the woods was that of a shotgun blast. Then, I would quietly run to get the squirrel while he would reload and stay focused on looking for other squirrels. We never said a word to each other until we were about twenty-five feet out of the woods. When we got back to the house I looked intently as he showed me how to skin the squirrels. Through the whiff of the smoke from the chimneys and the occasional smell from the chicken house the freshness of the skinned squirrel was a welcomed aroma. By the time we were finished and I put the squirrels in salt water Chawls was gone.

Now, Calin was always around. She liked to draw. I could rest my elbows on her knees and watch her draw as long as I kept my mouth shut. She would make an outline of a woman and commence to draw clothes on it. Once when I was home by myself I picked up a pouncil that I found laying around. I could see in my head the figure that Calin drew. So, before the image left my brain I began to draw what I could remember on the front room wall! Before I could draw clothes on it Mommo saw it and beat the tar out of me! When Daelay came home, she told him that I was drawing the upside down naked women on the wall and needless to say, I got another whooping. I tried to explain, but they didn't seem to understand.

Finally, I went to the first grade. My teacher, Miss Caldwell, said that I was quiet and shy. It was she who first noticed that I could really draw. She told my second grade teacher about my skills. I think that was one of the reasons I passed from grade to grade. I never said much, but I could decorate the bulletin boards.

I never made friends. During recess I would work on the bulletin boards. Sometimes when I did not want to do classroom drills I would ask the teacher if I could work on the bulletin boards. They usually said yes because they knew that I would still do real good on my class work. My classmates started calling me the teacher's pet. Whenever I tried to talk to someone they would just walk away shaking their head. I figured that being the teacher's pet was not a good way to make friends. I could not find one person willing to carry on a conversation with me. I thought that if I could get out of doing the bulletin boards, then I might make a friend to talk to. But those teachers made sure that I did those boards. So, I spent much of my time working on bulletin boards, doing my homework, drawing, and playing with Sammy.

By the time I got to the fifth grade there were six students in the one group that was supposed to be made up of the smartest students. I was the only boy in that particular group. The second group was the next smartest while the third group was, well, the third group was just the third group. In those days girls were said to be smarter than boys. My fifth grade teacher did not seem to like the fact that I was as smart as the girls. Mr. Goslee would do all kinds of things just to prove that I was not smart enough to be in the first group. After he thought he had sufficiently proved me to be inferior to my female counterparts, he would move me to the second group. I was too smart for the second group, so, he would move me back to the first group. He moved me back and forth so much that he reserved a seat just for me in the second group.

Everyone and their grandmother knew that Mr. Goslee had a short temper. Not only was he our fifth grade teacher, but he was also the Principal which gave him the right to beat—I mean—punish us. He did not tolerate students who did not study or who

did not do their homework. He definitely would not tolerate messy work or cheating. He saw everything that went on in his classroom. Someone once said that his eyes were so keen that he could tell you when you ran out of invisible ink. It was his way or the way of the left top drawer. Curled up in that drawer was that black leather strap. Rumor had it that it had notches on it for every kid that he beat. And those edges were frayed. I have seen that strap and the third group in action. That is why I never argued when he said that I was wrong about something and he put me in the second group. He once put me in the second group because I ran away from the class bully. I ran because she was bigger than me. But, I was too smart for the second group, so like I said, he had to move me back to the first group. One time the class was practicing the capital cursive alphabet on the board. After I wrote the letter "W" he asked me to name the type of letter I had written. I knew that it was the Zaner Bloser "W" but I just could not form my mouth to say it. As I stood there sweating and stammering he reached into that top left drawer and pulled out that leather strap. He wrapped that strap two times around his massive hand. About a foot of strap would be left dangling. You know, he beat me across my back all the way to my seat in the second group. While he was hitting me all I could think of was
why I could not say "Zaner Bloser".

How well I remember that first thing Tuesday morning. Chawls and I had been out hunting the night before. We were up late skinning squirrels. Early that morning when Daelay went to the chicken house to get eggs he found a hole in the wire fence. Some of the chickens had gotten out. He told Chawls to mend the fence and wake up Sammy, Saundwo, and I. We had to find and catch those chickens and put them back in the chicken yard before we went to school. By the time we did what we were told and got dressed for school the school bus was blowing it's horn. We grabbed our books and lunch boxes and ran down the lane to catch the bus. That was one heck of a morning. I barely got myself seated in the first group when he started.

Mr. Goslee must have decided to just pick on me! He talked about my red plaid shirt, my overalls, and my PF Flyers tennis shoes! I was not embarrassed, I WAS GETTING MAD! By the time he started talking about my hair and how it looked bushy my teeth were grinding, my eyes were squinting and my nose was flaring. He yelled at me while reaching for that leather strap and asked, "BOY! WHY DIDN'T YOU BRUSH YOUR HAIR BEFORE YOU CAME TO SCHOOL!?" I stood up abruptly and yelled back, **"IWAZENAWUSSHH!!!"**

There was dead quiet... He looked at me and said "Wh-h-hat?" I lowered my head and quietly repeated, "Iwazenawusshh." He got up and slowly walked over to me. I closed my eyes and was ready to flinch from the bite of that strap. I thought that I deserved that strap because I should not have yelled back at him. He leaned in close to me and said, "Boy, look at me." I opened one eye at a time looking for that strap. It was not in his hand? He told me to repeat, real slow, what I had just said. I slowly repeated, " I -waz-zen-ah- wusshh..." He stood straight up and said, "Boy, I didn't understand a word you said!" You know, the nicest thing he had ever done for me was to get me a speech therapist.

So, here I am, ten years old and learning how to talk. The speech therapist said that I had a lazy tongue—meaning that I was tongue tied. She once asked Mommo why I talked the way I did and why so fast? Mommo simply said that I got it from her husband's side of the family. She said that as a child I would sit and listen to Daelay and his brother Lil Waller telling tales. They would be talking so fast back and forth to each other that she just walked away. She said that it got to the point that not only could nobody get a word in edgewise, but, they were the only ones who understood each other. It was very clear that I was in dire need of help.

When I wasn't working on a bulletin board or doing my class work I was practicing my words. Once when I simply could not form a word the speech therapist got so disgusted with me that she put my finger *in her mouth* so that I could *feel* how her tongue moved when she said the word. And every time I mispronounced the word she would bite down on my finger! "Enunciate, ENUNCIATE!", she would say to me. She taught me to be aware when I got too excited when talking. That was my cue to take a deep breath and slo-o-o-o-ow do-o-own.

I was poised and ready to catch the ball off the bounce. All of a sudden Sammy started backing up. I knew that he was going to chunk the ball real hard against the wall, but he didn't. While I was looking at the porch he chunked the ball high against the second story wall! That ball bounced off the wall and hit the tin roof. The tin roof had ridges and grooves in it. I looked up just in time to see the ball hit one of those ridges. It bounced to the left and seemed to speed up. I planted my right foot to go to my left and slid in the dirt. When the dust cleared I had the ball in my hand! I asked Sammy why he chunked the ball up to the second story wall. He looked at me and said, "We're in middle school now."

Middle school. Girls. And I was too scared to talk to them. Not that I would say the wrong thing, but rather that I would probably say the wrong thing wrong. And now, I'm beginning to hate bulletin boards. Still, one good thing about doing the bulletin boards was that I got to look at her. Rosalie. If she only knew how much I liked her. My big chance to show her how much I cared was when we had the Spelling Contest. It was the boys against the girls. And who were the last two standing? Rosalie and I. She knew that she could not out spell me. You should have seen the look on her face when I misspelled my word and she won! Yeal, the girls won. If I did not have friends before I certainly did not have friends now! Later that day she came to me and asked why I had misspelled that word. I told her that it wasn't that I wanted her to win. I just wanted her to notice me. We were friends for about two days. Well, it was friends to her, but I was in love. I once told her that she smelt like a "fresh skint squirrel." She frowned and answered that I had a strange way with words. Then, she asked the question to end all questions. She realized that I had never called her by name. I started sweating. She all but insisted. Sweat was pouring out of my well combed head. My underarms were dripping wet! She threatened not to speak to me again if I did not call her by name. My breathing was labored! I took a deep breath, looked her in the eyes, opened my mouth and said as lovingly as I could, "WHOASSALEE...". To this day I do not know where she is. I told Sam what had happened as we chunked the ball against the second floor wall. I had a girlfriend for two whole days. I probably will never get married. Well, maybe if I just kept my mouth shut. Sam just laughed.

No matter how I tried I just seem to not be able to master the letter "R". Instead of reading more I began to write and draw more. I loved poetry. I found alliteration to be the most enlightening - She symbolized sweetness, surpassingly sublime, superbly soft, she sedately shines... I'm in high school now. My speaking is more deliberate because I think about what I am going to say before I say it. I do not do bulletin boards, but I continued to be the teacher's pet. The same year that I was inducted into the National Honor Society was the same year that I was called to the guidance office. It was explained to me that we were about to integrate schools. My counselor told me that I probably would not make it in "their" Honor Society because of my inability to speak up. He said that I lacked leadership quality. Now, if he had said leadership *ability* I might have given up right then and there.

Integration was my second biggest challenge - learning to speak well was the first. I fell in love... with my English class. I could work with a word. I learned to take a sentence apart like integration took me apart. I learned to diagram my life like I would diagram a sentence. And I learned to lead like an overworked prepositional phrase. I went from pump to faucet - from chunk to throw. As I stood with my graduation class, the only colored person with a Honor Society sash, I realized that I had conquered that verbal vacancy. That summer Sammy and I took turns throwing the ball off the roof of the house.

Being the number five child made me experience what it was like being the youngest. But, four years after I was born there came three more children. All of a sudden it seemed that I was the oldest. The pleasure of being cared for by my older brothers and sisters and then caring for my younger sisters and brother made me very responsible. It also made me realize that I had to leave home. And that was the hardest decision that I ever had to make.

You see, the more children in the family the more workers you had for the farm. My sisters were not immune to working on the farm. When Carolyn went to New York the rest of us had to work a little harder. Then, Charles went into the Air Force. Sammy and I had to work a little longer during the day. Sandra got married and left. Samuel went off to a Business School before he got drafted. That left me and my two sisters and brother. If I left, my father and the three younger ones would take on the burden of working on the farm. I could see that the work was taking its toll on my father and I did not want my younger sisters and my youngest brother trying to make his work lighter by making their work harder. Mom and dad told me that I could not go to college because they could not afford to send me. I tried to explain that before I graduated high school I knew enough to talk to the right people and filled out the right papers to get me into college. I would be in a work study program and I would be a Provisional Student for the first year. They looked at me as if they understood. I could see in their eyes that they did not. I did not let them see me cry when I left. I cried because I knew that I had sentenced my father to hard labor on the farm.

I was a freshman in college tutoring senior English. After that first year I went home and met up with my cousins. You know, my cousins had the nerve to tell me that I wasn't any fun any more. I was saying words like Mother and Daddy. It still was a great summer. Samuel, Sandra, Carolyn, and Charles came home for a visit. The first time I called to my sister Sandra she started looking around because she didn't know that I was talking to her. When Charles and Carolyn heard me talk they asked, "What happened?" Sammy and I had a talk. After a lengthy conversation he leaned in close to me and with all sincerity he whispered what I consider to be my very first compliment regarding my speech. He said, "Why are you *putting on airs?*" I was thinking: My speech is the culmination of years of aggravation and abasement, but I said, "This is how I learned to talk."

I may have loved English, but I graduated college as a Secondary Art teacher. There were five Afro-American teachers in that school of about sixty-five teachers. I was by far the youngest male. After thinking back about integration I concluded that the Lord works in mysterious ways! The first thing that I told my classes was that I hated to do bulletin boards. Therefore, since I did not want to think about decorating those boards, everybody had a chance to get their artwork placed on the boards. Then, I explained to my classes that I had a speech defect. I would give them a demonstration of how I might get
tongue tied if I got too excited. I told them to raise their hands and ask me to slow down if I started talking too fast. I did not mind them laughing at me, but I warned them not to make fun of me or anybody with a learning deficiency. They got used to the way that I talked to them. Sometimes, instead of giving verbal instructions, I would print the instructions on the chalk board:
Gitcherskeegbukannapouncil'n'dwawldasteelliefonertabul

(Get your sketchbook and a pencil and draw the still-life on the table.)

It was amazing to see how some of the students:

a. deciphered the instructions and went to work

b. tried to be the first to decipher the instructions and tell others what it read

c. refused to try to decipher the instructions and used that as an excuse not to work

One of the students got so upset that she banged the table and said, "Why don't you just write in English like all the other teachers do?" I explained that it was English and I was not like all the other teachers. It just looked different just as I did. The trick was to either accept the difference and deal with it or reject the difference because everything is supposed to be the same way. Then, I asked her if her boyfriend was like her brother? She surprised herself by replying, "HELL, NO!" The class got quiet. I leaned toward her and said," But, they're both boys. Aren't you glad that they are different?" I think that she was not the only one beginning to understand that being different does not mean being denied. And, no, I was not making fun of the English, I was having fun with it. I told my students how important it was to know how to do something well enough so that you could have fun doing it and maybe have fun making fun of it. Those who understood what I was trying to explain to them became better students in all of their classes.

Eventually, I did get married. Sharon helped me to speak better by simply having the patience to let me finish whatever I was s-s-sh-saying when I got stuck on a word. Sometimes I would have trouble just saying "Sharon". One of the best things about our marriage is that we made each other laugh. I still do not understand why she laughed more than I did. One day she joked that when we were ready to have a baby she wanted a son. I told her that I'd see what I could do. Well, we had two sons. After our second son I told Sharon that I was glad that we had two boys. When asked me why. I replied, "So that they will always have someone to play with."

Not too long after we got married all of my brothers and sisters and I got together. It was then that I realized that I was not the only one who felt bad about leaving home. It was then that we decided to do something for our parents. Each of us had a part in purchasing land, building a house and furnishing it. This was the early part of the seventies and I was proud to say that both of my parents finally lived in a house with running water! I was so overwhelmed with happiness that I looked at my new wife and said, "Shearn, thanks for understanding." "SHEARN!", she exclaimed. Suddenly I realized what I had said. I slapped both hands over my mouth and waited for her reaction. She started laughing. Then, we both laughed. She understood me.

It was a Saturday evening when Sharon asked me to go with her and the boys to the public library to hear a woman called Mary Carter Smith. She was a storyteller. I told Sharon that I was not going to go to some library to listen to some woman tell stories. Since I was outnumbered three to one I went. I was awe-struck after listening to Mother Mary, as she was called. When she finished telling stories she mentioned that she and other storytellers were going to start a storytelling group. Mother Mary invited all of us to join them. Sharon had the bright idea that I should join the group because I was always telling her and my boys stories that I had heard my father tell. I started looking around the room. Sharon wanted to know what or who I was looking for. I told her that I was looking for my wife because *she* knew that I would get tongue tied if I talked in public. She assured me that *my wife* understood and that she would probably sign me up whether I liked it or not. I was out numbered one to nothing.

I joined the group. We called ourselves the Griots' Circle of Maryland. We would tell stories about Bre'r Rabbit or adorn ourselves in African attire and tell stories about Anansi the Spider and other folklore. I designed the group's logo which is still being used today. Once when I had finished telling stories with the group someone in the audience asked me what part of Africa did I come from. I asked them why they thought that I came from Africa. They said that they could detect an accent when I spoke. I told them that I was a farm boy from Maryland who happens to have a speech impediment. They did not want to believe me like I did not want to believe that my fifth grade teacher used to be a barber!

I made up for all the times I was quiet. I became the third president of the Griots' Circle of Maryland. Many know me now as "Baba Simba" Mollock. I have been telling stories across the United States of America and up and down its East Coast. Mom

and Dad and my big sister Carolyn have since passed on to the level of the ancestors. I often wished that they were still alive to hear their tongue tied stammering son and brother speak in public.

Thirty-two years later I retired from teaching. I like to think that I had a lot of practice telling stories to my students. They could easily tell when I was getting excited about what ever I was teaching them. I would have to make a conscious effort to slow down. I can remember when I stood on stage in an auditorium filled with people. I was telling the story of the Signifying Monkey by Oscar Brown, Jr. I got so excited that I started listening to what I was saying. Big mistake! My mouth started running faster than my mind. Then, it happened. I started stammering. My face began to distort. I started perspiring profusely. I got stuck on a word that began with the letter "R"! I stood there and began to tear up. The audience was sympathetic and urged me to go on. I thought about the last time Sammy and I played ball. I took a deep breath and finished the story to a round of applause.

"Chunk it, CHUNK IT", yelled my brother Sammy. And I *threw* that ball - *over* the house.

ADAM, WHERE ART THOU?

Alvin C. Romer

This is a plea to get Black Men to stand up and be accountable to self, family, and community. Let's take an introspective look at Adam and his Garden of Eden dilemma as I want you to draw your own parallels for a moment. A disobedient soul, lack of initiative, coupled with shame truly did Adam in, and when our Lord came looking for him, he hid. Is it safe to say that Black men are still hiding, sans the fortitude needed to be accountable? It was once told to me that people of other persuasions fear the Black man most, and because of it, have systemically done more to keep him down and relegated to second class citizenry more than anything else. There's no doubt that Black men have had problems throughout the annals of time. We've known success, have been exalted, and have given to the world viable contribution…but, inasmuch as we've smiled and basked in our glorious euphoria, the pendulum swings in the other direction where frowns have become frequent and foreboding. All is not hunky dory in 'da hood', nowadays, and men of color have a lot to say. Our souls are bursting at the seams for pent up emotions to explode with a vociferous voice and I'm worried.

Something is amiss and definitely wrong in how Black men have been perceived, yesterday and today. Look no farther than historic content in the figures that have succumbed to selected genocide – Marcus Garvey, W.E.B. DuBois, Paul Robeson, Adam Clayton Powell, Harold Washington, Steve Biko, Max Robinson, Medgar Evers, Malcolm X, Nelson Mandela, et al -- all men of great standing that found the ire of white suppression and supremacy. Name me one of them that wasn't excommunicated, discredited, slandered, or even murdered, and perhaps you'd see the need to silence them, or keep a foot on their necks for submission. Adam, representing the first man that God ever made was tapped to be the prototype of the human image of His being, exemplifying the problems faced with us today. Is it no wonder that He had to go looking for him? How different is it in these times where many factions are asking the questions where are we? As a child coming up, my father always instilled in me to be a man and a respecter of women…and I marveled at the respect he commanded in the neighborhood. If one were to believe all that is made to support the perceived habitual treatment of Black men, it would, in my opinion feed into the syndrome that most people of color posit that it's the white man's fault…. or that slavery has kept us behind. True to a certain extent, but I beg to differ where better decisions were ours to be made.

I understand, and can sympathize concerning historical content, but I feel that brothers need to step up, exert themselves and demand respect on all levels of achieved reckoning. There's no mistake that all is not well, and I ask, where are the men? Where are you? I see too many of my sisters heading households where men should be firmly in place, I see far too many young boys idolizing the wrong images, without fathers to their children, and I'm definitely tired of taking the brunt of the angst women hurl at me because of the brothers before me who didn't treat them right. Ask me how I feel to see fine sisters walking hand in hand with others of another race because of a shortage of a few good men? I can imagine and understand how the sisters must feel.

There's no second guessing Christ. He asked for Adam because Adam wasn't in place. He defied orders, and succumbed to inequity. Just like Adam, we are hiding behind all of the 'self dysfunctions' that are prevalent – Self-denigration, Self-deprecation, Self-rejection and Self-hatred. We shouldn't take these maladies lightly for it bodes a continuous ill wind that has blown much too long for the same plight that defines us in the minds of many. Pertinent issues that permeate our communities are virtually ignored – and the brothers are mute! Too often the outcries are loud and wailing, especially from our sisters. Cry, the beloved Black man, fleeting and ever so elusive.... where are you? Too many people are looking, wondering and lamenting on whether we can still hold dominion over our brood, command our communities, and regain self-respect. It is so hard for me to close this article without first coming to closure with how can we reverse this trend. I can't do it alone, but this is what I can do within my stead:

-I will stand up on my own and proclaim to be a child of God, made in His own image with all the tools to for love and self-discipline

-I will come out of hiding, and accept responsibility for self, family, and community

-I will gather all the strengths that have always been mine – Spirituality, artistic fortitude, and physical prowess to know that I am part of a blessed race!

-I will uphold the storied legacy of my Black woman by giving her all the respect to rule by her side and not backslide; I will make my ancestors proud, by not allowing roadblocks (real or imagined) stop me.

-I will clean up, restructure, uplift, and fortify my community so that my schools, churches, and ethics are pointed toward Godly good

-I will work diligently and dutifully to repair my image by instilling integrity, a sense of ethical pride, and righteous resolve to stay one step ahead and above mediocrity to exceed far beyond status quo.

If all of my brothers follow these creeds, there will be no doubt that the whole world would rejoice and be a better place. Black men stand up, and be counted. We are not inferior; we will fight all the battles, and regain our rightful place in time. All of this is in the souls of men as we clamor for change. Adam where art thou?

THE CHOICE

K.L. Belvin

As they placed their bags down Elijah stopped to take in the cabin where they were going to spend the weekend. He wondered how he was going to make this final romantic getaway the best getaway ever for his lovely wife Marie. It had been a few years since they had had the chance to get some rest and share a moment without the children. They had been married over nine years and had twin daughters from Marie's previous relationship. They never had a honeymoon because they couldn't afford one or get the time away from their jobs to gone on one over the years. Married life couldn't have been better though; Marie was Elijah's life and there wasn't anything he wouldn't do for her.

"Hey Marie, did you bring the cooler bag from the truck?" Elijah yelled from the front door.

"Elijah, please, I just carried both our bags in."

Maria was trying to take in huge cabin. She walked over to the fireplace and ran her hand along the soot-filled bricks.

"Elijah it has a fire place, an outside and inside hot tub, and did you see the deck that over looks the wooded area in the back?" Marie looked out of the gigantic picture windows. Smiling she said, "I just love how the mountains peek over the trees and speak to you. This is going to be fun." She turned to her husband. "Elijah are you listening to me?"

Elijah hears her but his mind was racing with ideas on what they could get into this weekend. Part of him was sad and he wanted to lay everything on the table. He had never hidden anything from his wife, but the truth would come out soon enough, that particular moment was not that time. All the way up to the cabin he was trying not to let his mind drift.

"Hey Marie, are you hungry? I am going to put my stuff away and figure out what I am going pick up from the supermarket to make for dinner."

"You do your thing big daddy. I am going to read my Bible and thank the Lord for blessing us with this time away from home. I am going to enjoy this. I have a feeling things will never be the same for us after this weekend."

"You're right love, this weekend is going to change our lives more than you know," Elijah whispered lowering his head.

"What did you say honey? You know I hate when you whisper. Open your mouth, man," she joked. "You have been zoning out all the way up here. If I didn't know better I would have thought you were sipping wine or something."

"Marie you need to stop, you I know I don't drink. How would a man of God look hitting the sauce?" Elijah laughed at the idea , but admitted to himself that he did favor a little taste with dinner. Hey, even Jesus had a little wine with his meals.

Elijah began to take inventory so he that he could decide what he is going to make for dinner; and that was where he planned to start this marvelous trip. "I am going to make this as much about Marie as much as I possibly can," he thought to himself. Elijah was about to get his Chef G. Garvin thing going. He knew secretly Marie had a crush on Garvin. Marie had an attraction to big men.

Elijah called it a big man thing. His size was what attracted Marie to Elijah. Being a football player Elijah always on the larger side. She always loved his great big bear hugs. Elijah laughed as he reminisced on it.

"Are you still here? Marie asked, "And who are you talking to? Man, don't let me have to check you into one of those hospitals. You know what they do to crazy brothers. You are going to mess around and some old nurse named Helga is going to get my stuff as she keeps you drugged up".

"Marie, that's nasty. Hey listen, I am going to head out to the store, I'll be back. Love you baby."

"Okay baby, I love you too, please drive safe, these roads are horrible. Keep your mind on the road; remember that truck we saw flipped over. SUV or not please take it easy. I know you don't want me to go home looking for another chef and Bible study partner." Elijah loved Marie's sarcasm, she kept him laughing.

"Very funny, girl I'll be okay. I'm going to take my time. Plus, I can listen to the Bible CDs and talk with the Lord." Elijah closing the door slowly behind him whispered, "He knows I have much to say to him."

"What was that Elijah? I didn't hear the last part. What did you say about the Lord?"

"Nothing, just rambling."

As he drove he took in the beautiful scenery. The pond at the side of their cabin, the skyscraper trees, wild rabbits scurrying along the side of the road all spoke to his senses.

Elijah was a city kid at heart so all this country side was a blessing for him. He truly believed the Lord was speaking to him., The sun had just met the horizon as he turned a bend. The leaves seemed to sway and bend in the direction he was driving as if to tell him he is heading in the right direction. Elijah slowed the car down to take in all of God's creations. He had been rushing through life so much that he felt like he took it for granted sometimes.

The air is so fresh it had been one of the first things he noticed when he left the city.

Elijah enjoyed the ride so much he didn't realize he reached the store. He almost drove past it. He made his way down each aisle. This was the first time that he took a moment to enjoy grocery shopping. He used to see it as a chore and wished he could pay someone else to do it. "Funny the things you take for granted," he thought to himself. After spending almost an hour shopping, Elijah headed for the cashier and finally to his car. It was time to get back to the woman he loved with all his heart.

"Guess I'll listen to the word," he said to himself. Marie was the best. Elijah had begged her to buy the new CD set, *The Bible Experience*, but he had never gotten a chance to listen to it. It was one of the best gifts she had ever given him. "God you know I love that woman," he said aloud as the CD played.

It seemed like every time he was in the car with his own daughters, they'd want him to listen to that trash they listened to. Which was not scripturally correct, but despite their taste in music, they were growing into fine young ladies. "First chance I get I am going to add some O'Jays and Whispers to their IPOD's," he thought to himself.

"See if J. Holiday can top those brothers."

Elijah enjoyed listening to all the different black entertainers tell the stories of the bible. Listening to Phil Morris brought a smile to his face. One of Elijah's favorite topics for a good sermon was 1 Corinthians, which is what he had decided to listen to on during his ride back to the cabin. He loved how the letter from Paul spoke the heart of the people of Corinth. They were so much like the people nowadays. As Phil Morris got to the thirteenth, verse Elijah's ears tune in closely. He believed that too many people failed to understand the definition of the word love. He had said, many times in and out of church, if people tried to live up to the true definition of what God said love was, as defined by him in the Bible, the world would be such a better place. He has heard Pastor Watkins at church say, "How can you argue about what love is when God himself gave you the true definition to live by?" Elijah always got choked up by the thirteenth verse. It epitomized what he found in his wife and their wonderful kids. In his wedding vows he had included it because he wanted to show Marie where his heart was. As a very active man in the church, Elijah tried to live his life as close to the scriptures as he could. Even when they argued they used the Word to settle the fights. The few moments of heated conversations didn't seem so bad when they thought of that verse and the others that might reflect some part of the Lord was trying to say about love.

Elijah and Marie had sworn their love to the Lord many years ago through his son, Jesus Christ. They believed that they have been blessed since becoming born again. Because of that they had been able to do well enough to make each other happy and make a loving home for themselves.

Elijah was jolted from his daydreaming when the jeep veers to the side of the road.

"Whoa! Where is my head? Let me get my mind on the road. I'm about to have an accident and mess the weekend up before it starts. Its going to be hard enough with what I have to do."

"Well Father, you'll give me the words and strength when its time. I'll leave that in your hands. Well its time to get back to see if I can make this woman happy."

Upon entering the cabin, Elijah smiled at the scent of burning candles which was very much to his liking. Peach was Marie's favorite scent and he knows what that meant. There was something about peach scented candles that brought a room to life.

"So Marie, are we skipping dinner honey? I see you jumped ahead and have the scented candles going, sooo what do you say I cook later?

"No way," she said coyly. "I just wanted to make the cabin more about us in here. Plus, I want you to eat so you will have your strength for later."

"Marie you know how you are with the way things smell. You're the same way about my cologne. You'll smell one thing and demand I wear it over and over," Elijah chuckled.

"You know I just love the smell of candles. Keep talking junk and it will be a lonely night for you mister. I can't help if I like what I like. This month it's Calvin Klein's CK One. I really like that one right now. So don't complain. You know if mommy is happy then daddy is going to be happy. You hear me?"

"No doubt sugar, you have never steered me wrong in that area."

"So mister man, you're not getting out of cooking for me. We made a deal before we left and you're sticking to it. Now if you're a good husband maybe we can skip dessert." Marie winks seductively to drive her point home.

"Marie, you better stop playing, Is that any way for a woman of God to be talking?"

"Please boy, we are married. In church we talk about things like this all the time."

"You do?" Elijah asked with a raised eyebrow.

"Yes silly, people forget when you're married you can do anything you want with your husband or wife as long as you are not crossing any scriptural lines. God wants us to be happy with each other. This is why he smiles on marriage."

"I remember pastor talked about that one Sunday in the men's meeting?" Elijah recalled.

"So there, you are my husband and I am your wife and we are alone with no kids. So quiet up and cook for your Queen," she giggled. "Man of God!"

After dinner Marie decided to turn up the heat on the romance part of the evening. They had been looking forward to this trip for months when Elijah came in one day and told her he had a dream that they'd get some time

off and go on a trip. He assured her that it would be a blessing for the both of them. Marie was a human resource manager and he was a painter. Their schedules always clashed, however this time everything worked out completely. Even the girls' father, Dan, had decided to keep them for the weekend while they were away.
Dan had stopped being supportive when Marie and Elijah got married. One Sunday, right out of the blue he was he showed up to church, and after that things changed. He had become a father to his children for the first time in their lives. In the twin's eyes Elijah was their father figure. In their eyes he is the only father they have ever known. With plenty of prayers and one on one discussions, Elijah was trying to help Dan make up for not being around for over ten years. The girls really wanted to know their father and he never stepped up to the plate. The twins were tough but they were learning to be forgiving as it is written in the bible. Elijah remarked often that he wouldn't trade them for anything.

Standing in the mirror inside the bathroom, Elijah was deep in internal conversation. How am I going to make it through this evening? I have to keep my mind focused on Marie. She is going to sense something. *Holy Spirit, please work with me. Get me to the point where I can tell her what is going on. I didn't get any work done the last few days just thinking of this night. Either way, it is going to happen. I just have to be strong for the both of us. I am not going to think about anything except Marie's happiness.*

"Hey what are you doing in the bathroom, man? Why do you have your wife in here all alone? You better not be on your cell phone sneaking calls to another woman on our honeymoon!"

Hearing her laugh always brings a smile to his face and warms his heart. Marie was the type of thick country woman Elijah loved. He grew up with country women and Marie was picture perfect. With her light skin, she got tired of him calling her Red or Redbone.

"OK Red, just wait, big daddy is on the way."

Once nestled in they took their time and share a moment that has taken too long to come. Elijah with a big smile slid close to Marie so she could hear him say,

"You know I love you. Red?"

"You better, don't make me leave you and marry G. Garvin."

"Listen if I ever were to leave here; don't hesitate to find someone who makes you happy," Elijah added changing their playful mood to serious.

"Elijah what are you talking about? Shut up, you are all the man I need and will ever want. I am not marrying nor do I plan to ever find someone else. Did you forget that after you read 1Corinthians 13 about love, we both swore till death do us part?"

"I know darling, I am just saying that you never know what the future holds and we aren't promised tomorrow."

"Elijah, I know and understand that too well. Now listen, I didn't come all this way to talk about not being with you when I have you right here in this big ole bed. I got my favorite candles burning, and you have me feeling like I am twenty-one all over again! Now get on your job and make this girl feel like she is still the sexiest girl in the room."

With that said they made passionate love. It was what being married is truly all about. Two connected souls in the way the Lord intended. They are truly in a state of bliss.

Later that evening Elijah rose and sat on the side of the bed. While Marie was sleeping he gathered himself and moved to sit at the desk in the corner of the bedroom. He reminded himself that that night was unlike any other night they had ever shared or would share again. Looking back over at his partner, lover, and best friend, tears come to his eyes. He had only heard of women crying after lovemaking. Marie noticed that Elijah was no longer in bed and came over to him, placing her arms around him tightly.

"Baby? What's the matter?"

"Nothing Love, I am just happy and I love you so much."

"Here, let me get those tears." Marie bent over to wipe his face with her hands.

"Elijah, look at me, this is why I married you. In my heart I know there is nothing you wouldn't do for me. I have shared this love for you for so long that I don't know what I would do without you. I thank the Lord for you and what you have brought to my life and the girls' lives."

Marie walked around to face Elijah and sat on his lap. "How many men would have stepped in and took on the responsibility of raising another man's children, and raised them as his own knowing they don't have his blood? You're also a mighty man of God. I have seen the things you do around church and when you take time to preach a sermon, I know you make pastor nervous about his job. Don't tell him I said that," she giggled.

"You are my equal, truly a blessing from the Lord. I know he sent you to me for a reason and I am happy that you're here. Now come to bed."

"I got you girl, go hop in, I want to take care of a few things and I'll climb in next to you in a sec."

"Hurry, you know I can't sleep when you're not cuddled up next to me," she warned in a playful tone.

"Please Red, you could sleep through a hurricane. You just like the heat my big body brings you."

"OK you got me. Just hurry up back to bed OK?"

It was at that moment that Elijah realized that it would be the last time they would ever be together. That was why all the moons and plancts had aligned to grant them that magical moment. There will be no other after tonight. His tears fell from the knowledge he had of what was going to happen. Elijah pulled a sheet of paper and pen from desk drawer and begins to write. Once he was done he collapsed next to Marie. He was speechless, except for the soft "I love you with all my being" that slid from his lips on to her forehead. She responded back with "I love you more. I am the happiest woman in the world."

As the night rolled forward, Elijah was awakened by a voice in his dream. It's time Elijah. Your time has come, please come with me now. As he walked out the door he placed the letter where he knew Marie will find it. As the morning crept into the cabin Marie awoke to find she was alone. She looked around for Elijah. She called out to him. "Elijah."

As she got up she saw the letter, her heart raced. She tried to catch her breath, but the tears came before she read the first word.

Marie, as you sleep I am writing you this letter trying to explain what has happened and will happen. Well baby here is the whole thing. Some time ago, an angel came to me in a dream and explained that something bad was going to happen to the girls. I asked why are you bringing this to me. The angel said, I was told, because of the life Dan led it was decided that a price must be paid. However, since I called upon the Lord often and serve him as best I can, I could change the outcome if I chose to. Baby, the angel told me, I could pick someone else to take the girls place. The angel even suggested I could choose Dan if I wanted to... I was offered a chance to remove him from the picture as payment for his sins. I couldn't do it honey, I just couldn't take another man's life no matter what he did in the past. I know Dan is trying to make things right with the girls. After seeing him come to church, I know there is still a chance for him. So, you see love on this night I traded my life for our children. I couldn't see myself randomly picking a person's life to be taken. It didn't seem fair or right. I felt I was being tested. It turns out I was, darling. Marie after making my choice and deciding to lay down my life, I was given a reward. The reward the Lord granted me was one wish before I left this earth. I chose this trip! This wonderful evening we shared was that wish. I thought since we had been blessed with so much, even though it wasn't that much in money or status, it was still a blessing. I wanted to give you the honeymoon night I couldn't all those years ago because we couldn't afford. I did this for you Marie. Baby, there is one more thing, the angel felt sad at the fact that I was leaving someone I truly loved and who truly loved me, so they requested one more wish for me. It was granted. When you get back home go to our doctor and you will see you are pregnant with a boy. Yes my love! God granted us a son. The son you said you always wanted, but were so sad about losing when we lost him three years ago and the doctor said there was no way you would ever have children again. Your prayers were answered too Marie. Baby, love him as you would me. Raise him to be a Godly man the way I was. His name is to be the same as mine, so when you see him grow into the same type of man I was, you will remember me. Stop crying baby, I am in a good place. When the time is right you'll see me. We will share forever together. Marie listen to me, stay strong and trust in the Lord with all your heart. This was the Lord's plan for me and he has plans for you too. Stay in the word and keep the children close and in the word also. The love of God and love we had will protect and guide you. Like I said, when the time comes we will see each other again. I LOVE YOU Marie! You'll always be my sexy redbone gal!! I have to go now they are calling me. Don't feel bad I am going to a great place. One more thing, I know I said we couldn't afford it, the only lie I have ever told you: when I said I needed money to eat lunch every day, I was using money from my savings for insurance. Yes love, I said we couldn't afford it because I didn't want you to worry about the payments. When you get home the insurance policies are in my metal box under the bed we have shared for so many years. The key is under the girl's bed in a key box. I made sure you'll want for nothing. I wanted to make sure you and the children were taken cared of. You'll see there is one for you, one for the children, my family, and of course for the church. They better put my name up there with the elders. Make sure they use my wedding picture too. I was sexy in that one. You have to agree, right? Well baby, this is it. Take great car Marie. I LOVE YOU WITH ALL MY HEART, GOOD-BYE BABY!"

At that moment the phone rang;

"Hello, Mrs. Jackson?"

"Yes?"

"This is Sheriff Thompson. It is my unfortunate duty to report there was an accident out on the highway a little while ago. I am very sorry to bring you this news, Mrs. Jackson. Your husband was out walking along the highway this morning and he was involved in an accident. He didn't make it. He passed away en route to the hospital. Mrs. Jackson, I am so sorry Mrs. Jackson, but there was one odd thing about the situation?"

"What is that officer?"

"Mrs. Jackson, he passed with a smile on his face. He seemed so at peace. I have never seen anything like it. He also had a piece of paper in his hand. All it had written on it was *Remember, 1st Corinthians 13, Love."*

A Hoop and A Holler

Tyrell DeVon Floyd

I feel genuinely lifted!

A jolt of energy, like none other, has rushed through my veins! A fiery feeling, meshed with a whirlwind of the most emotional love, has overtaken every sane bone in my body. I am a true representation of God's yearning desire to have a relationship with all his children. My hands are moist beyond belief and beads of sweat trickle down my forehead as I unleash a divine word from the Lord.

The degree of my intensity can be compared to that of a professional athlete who's playing in the 4th quarter of a highly contested game. The only difference is I've replaced a football field or basketball court with a pulpit and podium.

My beautiful hand crafted royal blue suit, complimented by silk pin stripes is flashy enough to compete with suits donned by Steve Harvey, but classy enough to be worn in any corporate boardroom meeting. Someone sure loves me for them to keep me looking as good as I do!

I attribute my sharpness to my wife, Cynthia "First Lady C" or "Cool C" Lawson; yeah that's what they call her. Cynthia is an exquisite woman who can do no wrong in my eyes.

Her beauty is always on display, and that's saying a lot when you're as modest and as conservative as she. Nothing too dramatic from my counterpart; just a precious woman who's filled with love and an undying commitment to maintain the promise she made to God on our Wedding day 10yrs ago. She's the only woman I know who's been to Hades and back, but has maintained a cool temperament the entire time.

I try not to look directly into Cynthia's eyes as I'm preaching. I'm fearful of one day being convicted to the point where I'll have to give the supreme testimony that I've attempted to rid myself of time and time again.

Now, just as my mind begins to think about everything else, besides being a vessel for God's Word, I hear Mother Mitchell begin to praise God with a spirit of Triumph! About 4 or 5 rows behind my wife, I see Mother Hatti-Faye Mitchell. Mother Mitchell has been a great source of encouragement for the entire congregation. but especially for my wife. You see, Mother Mitchell lost Deacon Kirby- her husband of fifty years-to complications brought on by pneumonia about two years ago, but her joy has never been subdued. She is a certified woman of God; anyone can learn how to be strong during tough times if they stay around her for a few minutes. She's that profound.

"Thank you Jesus! Thank you Lord God for keeping me!" I can hear Mother Mitchell clear as day from the pulpit. Now as the Spirit of the Lord begins to move all the more, I realize I'm one of the many people in this Church who seemingly looses their mind when the name of Jesus is lifted up. My bones quiver, my knees shake, and my spine feels as if it becomes a single twine of spaghetti. And before I know it, I'm hooping and hollering as flawlessly as Moon Pies and cold bottles of Coca-Cola go together in the south. Everything stops when I'm in mid hoop. I don't hear anything except for my soul chanting harmonious words of joy while my heart shouts "Thank you, God!"

Wow, it seems like I just started preaching, but out of the corner of my eye I see Minister Donnavan approaching the podium so I know that I must have been up here for sometime now. It's too late, though; I can't stop now. I'm on a roll; so Minister Donnavan and anyone short of the Lord is gonna have to sit this one through. I'm known to preach with vigor & passion and often times I'm unaware of what I'm saying or who I'm saying it to; I just preach.

Today my sermon came from the oh-so-popular John 3:16. However, the message wasn't the conventional sermon often times connected to this particular chapter and verse of the Bible.

It's easy to direct your attention on the enormous sacrifice God made in wanting to save his children, but there is also a very simple principle found within the powerful John 3:16: God so loved the World that he gave... The fact that God would be willing to give his son for the sake of our inequities is more than profound. But God loving us to the point that he would give in the first place is where our blessing truly begins. Everything we have is a result of God's gracious giving. It's no secret why I'm up here hooping & hollering, and that's because of God's grace and mercy!

In minutes, I find myself in my seat listening to Minister Donnavan rave about what a wonderful word from the Lord he received via my preaching. I'm in awe How is that? A person who's so inadequate, such as myself, being able to play a part in something that could potentially change a person's life for the good.

I smile at the congregation and give Minister Donnavan a wink. He's a good young brother who reminds me a lot of myself when I was his age; with the exception of his intelligence being channeled in the right direction. He's a quick thinker, and a young man who's more than willing to pay homage to those he has no idea he's better than. He's only 24yrs old, and already he's had great impact on our Youth Ministry and beyond. While Minister Donnavan proceeds with the benediction as well as with some final words of his own, I feel myself- my mind and my heart- completely detached. If only people knew me as I know myself, just what would they say? Here I am posed as a man that every young man should strive and aspire to become, but on the inside I'm ill and searching for a spiritual pain killer. Minister Donnavan wraps up the service, and for just a moment I feel relieved as I step down from the pulpit.

I feel a great deal of jubilation on one hand, but on the other hand I'm convicted beyond means. Paul's words in the book of Romans 7:15 echo throughout my soul. I wanna get better, I wanna do better, but why is it that I never can get better? "Pastor Lawson", I hear a voice say to me I turn around to find the indirect answer to my inner question.

"Pastor Lawson can you pray for me" Sister Shayla says with a painful stare.

If only she knew what I was going through, I doubt she'd ask me for anything; in fact she'd probably wanna pray for me. The life of a pastor means continuously being bombarded with questions & requests and hardly ever being granted the opportunity to say things such as "no" or "I don't know".

"Sure, Sister Shayla what's the problem?", I ask without giving any hint of my own difficulties I'm enduring in my walk of faith.

"Pastor I need you to intercede for me," Sister Shayla says

"Pastor the power in your voice is anointed and I know you can get through to the Lord on my behalf", Sister Shayla goes on

I try not to let on that I'm curiously pondering where people get this thought from. I'm just a mere mortal and I don't have the ability to do anything that any other Christian can't do. Sister Shayla and anyone else who places me in some kind of elite regal fraternity, only occupied by the "true" saints of the Lord, better think again.

I'm just a man. In fact, if my voice is so anointed then how is it that this same voice also has spewed negative insults toward his w…?

Before I even have time to conclude my inner thought Sister Shayla is having a spiritual conniption; what makes it worse is that most of those left in the sanctuary probably think it's because of my "power" that she's carrying on with these theatrics. It's not my intention to be negatively judgmental toward Sister Shayla or anyone else's style of worship, but in my opinion some folks are much *too* emotional. Often times I greet the congregation with a simple "good morning church", and some folks are ready to do back flips, somersaults, and cartwheels just based on that; and if you ask me that's being just a little over the top. But, eerily enough, some ol skool conservative pastors would probably say my charismatic preaching was a little too “much” also.

By now some of the women of the church, led by Mother Hatti-Faye, take notice of Sister Shayla's condition and promptly come over to assist.

It's not uncommon for us here at the Greater House of Praise to have a lil church even after the actual church service has been concluded. One of the most taxing things about being in leadership is the feeling of always having to be on call. I often feel as though my job/responsibility as a Pastor never stops. I suppose anyone in leadership, whether its church affiliated or not, feels subjected to this harsh reality. But it's different when you're a leader of "The People of God". You see, a Pastor doesn't have any margin for error. The Good Book says "all have fallen short of the glory of God", and it doesn't go on to say that pastors are exempt from that portion of scripture. Lord knows I'm no where near perfection, but at the same time; I don't get joy out of pretending that I am. My question is, just how much joy does a flaw riddled human being get when he or she assigns another fellow human being the task of being perfect? I guess I'll never
know.

After shaking hands and partaking in some small talk with those who stay a while after church, I leave the Sanctuary. As I'm walking down the church corridor headed to my office, I see Brother Greg Jennings. Before I even have a chance to say hello, Greg beats me to it.

"How you doing Pastor?" Without hesitation I quickly forget about the turmoil that RJ Lawson, the man is

enduring, and find myself conforming into the happy-go-lucky Pastor who appears to not have a worry in the world.
"I'm blessed by the best," I say with great zeal.
"Pastor I wanna thank you for all that you've done for Elaine and me," Greg speaks with seriousness and joy all rolled into one.
"What cha mean," I ask with a slight smile. Greg's eyes begin to tear up while he unveils his best attempt to answer my question, "I'm not sure where to start Pastor, you've done so much. Had it not been for your continuous prayers, as well as counseling sessions, I doubt that Elaine and I would have made it". Greg slows down his speech as he looks directly in my eyes. "Pastor you're the man I wanna one day become. You're strong in your faith, and you have an answer for everything,"
You see it's times like this that I begin to feel sick. While I appreciate the words of encouragement and admiration, I feel myself becoming overwhelmed.

Everyone knows me as "Pastor", but they don't know my story. They don't know the untold tales of Raymond Jermaine Lawson. People see me as being nothing more than an upright preacher with credentials from one of the best seminaries in the country. They don't know that my upbringing was filled with street-crimes.

Sure, they've heard me share the pg-13 version of my testimony; but what they don't know is that it was often times my index finger squeezing the trigger, and often times my backhand making contact with the faces of women on the streets! They don't know that good ol Pastor Lawson had a mean, uncontrollable temper back in the day; that same temper can sometimes resurface, just like it did a few months ago when I violently raised my voice at my w…

Greg interrupts my flashback session as he continues to talk about how great I am.

"You also taught me and Elaine how to communicate better."

"All I did was direct a fallen brother back to the God who saved him, " I say to Greg in hopes of shunning his compliments.

"I know Pastor, but you also welcome me to the church when I got out of jail. I would have never thought a man like yourself would've been so welcoming to a former street hustler like me," Greg speaks boldly. I can't help but be at a loss for words when people say things such as Greg is saying now.

Greg means well, but even in his thirties he's an infant in his walk of faith. The petty unpaid traffic tickets and small time marijuana movement he was associated with, during his so-called street life up here in Portland, all pale in comparison to my life as one of the coldest pimps and cocaine distributors on the Southside of Chi Town.

"Your Pastor hasn't always been saved; even after salvation I'm still dealing with some things," I speak in hopes of lightening the mood.

Greg gets the point and jokingly says," I know Pastor, I'm sure you've plucked a few grapes from the vine while in the produce section".

"Believe me my brother, you have no idea", I say with a smirk on my face.

"Great sermon today", Sister Elaine says as she and my wife approach us;

"Thank you sistah," I reply.

"Alright Pastor, well I guess Elaine and I should get out of out here. We've got some Pot Roast at home that's calling my name!" Greg says with much humor. "Greg you are a mess, Elaine I'ma pray for your husband," Cynthia echoes Greg's humor.

"Please do Cool C, because I'm positive that Pastor RJ don't put you through half of what Greg puts me through"; Elaine innocently says. I notice a half- hearted smile as it creeps upon my wife's precious face.

But luckily for me, this particular image of a woman in despair can only be witnessed through the eyes of a convicted soul; so I'm sure the others don't pick up on it. My wife's hurting inside, and that makes me hurt all the more knowing she's suffering behind my wrongful acts.

Surely there's not a soul outside of the Lord himself who knows, or could even imagine for that matter what's going on in her head. But the point is, I know that she deserves to be happy, and unfortunately I've went back to my old ways of not properly assisting in that process.

She stands there bright eyed and receives a dagger to the heart of her emotions, but she doesn't come close to breaking down. In fact, it's almost as if God gives her a divine strength as she begins to speak.

"My Husband is amazing; Satan tries to tempt all of us, but my husband is a man of God, so y'all better send the Devil a memo!" All four of us began laughing hysterically. I stood back and watched as Cynthia covered for me once again.

My prayer is to one day become the husband that her faith declares I'll be.

"First Lady C, you are too much," Greg says while still laughing.

"Alright you guys we're outta here", Elaine says as she and Greg begin to walk away.

"Drive safe" Cynthia and I both shout.

Once Greg and Elaine leave, it's immediately awkward. The last few months have been hell for me to be alone with my wife. It's not that I don't want to be around her; it's really more of a feeling of not wanting to be around myself and being alone with her is a reminder of that. I cherish my beautiful wife beyond means. But I have sinned in the worst way, and I'm not ready to forgive myself. I could wave good bye to Greg and Elaine forever if it meant that I wouldn't have to confront the guilt I'm carrying right now.

"Alright Baby let me just grab my jacket and keys and I'll be ready to go," I said as if everything is perfectly fine.

Without saying a word she slowly nods her head in approval. The laughter, jokes, and steady flow of sarcasm have all been replaced with an abrupt tone of sadness. Dear God, if Hell is as bad as your Word says it is then I'm a prime candidate to go. My spirit is in jeopardy of being drowned by the tears that fall from my heart and I feel helpless when it comes to being able to do something to

prevent the inevitable. Maybe I deserve this , Lord. Maybe all my close calls while have finally caught up with me. After all, I should be dead or in prison for all I've done and witnessed in my life. And yes, I do fine when it comes to being
able to mentor others; but who's the doctor's doctor when he gets sick? I'm seen as such a soldier for Christ that even the elders of the church feel as if they can confide in me about personal problems, and right now I wish I could go to them for advice. How did I even get here? Why is it that I'm a forty year old man with a feeling of the weight of the world being on my shoulders? I'm from the streets of Chicago, but for the last 5yrs I've been Pastoring a Church in Portland Oregon? Was the churches pastoral invitation too much for a young man like me to accept?

Thinking back, I remember when I first came to the Greater House of Praise exactly 7yrs ago. I was a guest speaker for an annual youth conference, but I never would have imagined the thought of one day being the pastor. At the time, I was simply a young man excited about where God had brought me from and where he was taking me. I was in seminary studying; trying my best to finally do right by Cynthia. Damn I've went astray! Lord you've blessed me with 3 kids, but I've never seen the faces of even one of them, and I doubt I ever will.

Lord please forgive me! I'm so sorry! You touched my heart as a twenty five year old man and I haven't been the same since; now I'm starting to question why you would even save a man like me. You blessed me with a beautiful wife whom I did so wrong before you showed me the way. Cynthia knew what I was all about, and all the dirt I did in the streets. She knew that she wasn't the only woman when we were dating; yet she stayed with me. I was a liar and a cheat, and even when I'd get caught I always knew my tongue was sharp enough to right my wrongs with fast talk. When I got another woman pregnant and forced her to have an abortion, I know that shattered Cynthia's world; but it was almost as if she loved me to a higher power after that incident. She went above and beyond to demonstrate to me that she was all the woman I needed. I told her that I would never cheat again, but that was another lie to add to my already established resume.

Lord please help me! I'm going through it, and I don't know what to do. I feel as if my 180 degree turn from sin has become a 360. I'm right back where I started from in so many ways. I don't want a brotha like Donnavan to feel as if he's infallible or a product of perfection just because others deem him with such characteristics. And if I don't speak up then the blood will partially be on my hands if he does. At one point I fell for the lie that "because I'm a pastor means I'm special". And now that it's clear to me that I'm not special; it's difficult to get those around me to come to that same conclusion.

"Raymond watch out for that car!" Cynthia screamed My private prayer is interrupted as I slam my foot on the brake, causing the car to shriek.

"I'm sorry baby," I respond in somewhat of a panic.

My Lord! My mind is so gone that I had no idea that I was even driving! The last I remember, I was in my office and on my way to follow Cynthia to the car.

I need to get my feelings off my chest before it's too late. If nothing else, I've learned in my Christian walk that when God continuously tugs at your heart you need to submit to that conviction. I've ducked and dodged God's way for the last few months and now I'm tired. When we arrived home and pull into the driveway, I know it's time for me to tell Cynthia what's been on my mind.

I rationalize that if Job could stand the test of his wife then so can I. After all, I'm partly responsible for my wife's passive reactions to my shortcomings. Had I treated her better throughout the years she'd expect nothing less than that. "Cynthia from the bottom of my heart I'm sorry," I tell her as I gently turn her face towards mine.

Cynthia looks deeply into my eyes for about five seconds without saying a word. She then places her left hand on the top of my right leg and says, "Baby I know you are," This time her tone, her spirit and her body language is different than the many other times I've said I'm sorry and she's forgiven me. There have been times in the past where I've brutally insulted her intelligence, and have even called her names that I can't even stomach to repeat. But never once have I went off as bad as I did a few months ago. Before he passed, Deacon Kirby use to call me an old soul, and say that my hooping & hollering was a gift. But now I'm starting to wonder whether or not all gifts are from God. Take for instance a world class athlete who can run very fast and jump very high. Is it fair to make him a role model simply based on his athleticism? After all, how do we know he didn't fine tune his abilities by running from the police and jumping fences to escape the bite of a canine?

The same hoop that has attracted sinners to come to God has also been the same holler that has abused my wife for years; I can't live like this. I can't continuously be viewed as the world's greatest pastor while being an abusive husband to my wife. Our last altercation consisted of more than just insults hurdled, and tears dropped. Cynthia miscarried our twin girls. And while there's no direct evidence that says our fight was the reason we lost our girls, I know the stress of the incident played a part in it at the least. It was the worse torment in the world to have had an entire church service dedicated to the loss of our babies. My legend of being an unfazed warrior for Christ and a husband who does nothing wrong, grew even more.

Ever since then I've had mixed emotions whenever I'm in church. I feel terrible, and though my natural mind says I'd be a fool to air my dirty laundry. The conviction of The Holy Spirit has made it more than clear that this is a cross I must bare. My question, though, is, what would you say on any given Sunday your pastor, who you admired, put on a pedestal and basically worshipped, gave a testimony such as mine?

Especially now that you know a hoop and a holler can sometimes be one in the same.

A SENSE OF FAITH AND COMMUNITY

Brian Ganges

"Those who educate children well are more to be honored than parents, for these only gave life, those the art of living well."
~Aristotle

Reaching out, lending a helping hand and doing good deeds are some of the most selfless things that we can do for one another. There are people who are less fortunate than us; and God blesses us to be a blessing. But what does it mean to be a blessing to others in the community? How can each one of us make a lasting impression in the lives of those around us? I, like many people, would be satisfied with just caring for my family, and living a peaceable life. But something (actually, it's an unction from God) constrains me to care for and to reach out to others outside of my immediate family. I have a heart for people, whether I know them personally or not. If no one ever takes an interest in or is appreciative of the efforts that I make to inform and prepare people for a better tomorrow, that will never discourage me from reaching out. I don't do what I do to receive the approval of the people; I do what I do for God and the establishment of His Kingdom in the earth.

I am a servant, and that is not synonymous with being a slave. Many people are just "fair weather friends," and we can't treat people the way that some people treat us. God will never leave us nor forsake us; and nor should we forsake our brothers and sisters who may not see things exactly as we see them. If I were to grow cold and heartless towards humanity, I don't believe that I would be able to sleep comfortably at night, and have peace in my life. But God has a love for humanity like no other, and He has the ability to transfer His love into the hearts of His people for His people. I am one of those people who love God's people very much. I don't know them all by name, and I possibly may never know all of them, but God does; and He has a great plan to supply all of our needs. Some of His people might not know or appreciate the plan; they might be in the club right now; they maybe on drugs or doing whatever. But God is putting people in position to bring humanity hope and the expectation of a great future. We are called to be God's hands, feet and mouthpieces in the earth. We are supposed to act as a conduit in the earth to channel God's love, blessings, and the manifestation of His presence for all to see. This is my story.

The year is 2050 and the United States has truly fallen from God's grace, as I can tell from reading history. Although some things about the history of this country were immoral, the U.S. was originally established as a sovereign country that attracted immigrants from all over the world; hence the moniker was given to this country: "the melting pot." They even elected an African American President in the early part of this century, but the ideologies and the mindset of Americans have changed too dramatically to continue along the same vein of generations past. By the way, my name is Brian, but everyone calls me "Trey." I was named after my dad, and his father (my grandfather), Brian Ganges; but you may have heard of him referred to as "BG," but I just call him "G" for short. Although, he's pushing 80 years of age, he's still passionate about informing people and taking a stand on issues that matter. He's been known to get under people's skin, but people always know where he stands. He's consistent and you have to respect that.

I love "G" he's a good man that helps a lot of people, and he has taught me a lot. I figured that it would be special to honor him as one of my heroes in an upcoming college essay. Sure, I could have used the usual icons of the civil rights movement; but they have indirectly influenced my life because I never had the opportunity to meet with them. But my Grandpop raised me along with my own parents; he was there and always tried to include my cousins and me in whatever he could. Whether it was television or radio interviews, lectures, symposiums, debates or book signings, one of us was always his little sidekick. He said that he wanted to directly demonstrate to us, what love of community, reaching out and giving back was all about. I didn't understand it then, but I do now.

My Civics class is pretty cool. We're supposed to speak about black history and an inspirational figure that has affected us most. I figured that the best thing for me to do was to speak about someone who is dear to my heart, that way it would be real and filled with all of the emotion and the connection associated with it. So I chose to speak about my grandfather. It would impress my professor, because my grandfather is one of our University's alumni, and it would make "G" very proud of me. I'm a third generation student of North Carolina Central University, in Durham, North Carolina, the home of the "Mighty Eagles." I have the opportunity and the desire to carry on the work that "G" is doing. I don't know if you want to call him an activist or not, but he sure does make you think and want to question things. But I know his heart and he always advocates thought, analysis and scrutiny when dealing with matters of importance.

I'm really excited about my speech; it's kind of "make me or break me," as far as getting an "A" for the semester is concerned. As I'm walking from the cafeteria with my boys through campus, either I start to get a bad case of butterflies or those nasty powdered eggs aren't agreeing with me. It's a terrible feeling but I just brush it off the best I can, because nothing is going to stop me from getting an "A" this morning. This speech took me about three weeks to prepare and everyone keeps asking me about the topic I have selected for my essay. I guess it's because the students whose last names begin with the letters G-L are scheduled to speak this week.

We finally arrived at the Education Building and my friends smacked me on the head and yelled as I went into the building. Classmates started to show me love as I walked down the hall, "What's up, Trey?" As I walked into the lecture hall, the professor conveniently insisted that I start the class with my highly anticipated speech. I sarcastically ask myself, "Why am I so fortunate this morning?" I'm nervous and my hands start shaking. I put my book bag down and slowly move towards the podium. Suddenly, I am reminded of something that "G" always told me when he does his public speaking: "Take your place, you are in charge." As I visualized him telling me that, I began to look around the room and smile. This is my essay. "Thank You, Jesus," I said under my breath. "Yeah," as my confidence level rises, I step forward with my noted index cards and calmly greet the class, "Good morning." I instantly felt as though I was in charge of the situation, and as I continued my speech, I became even more comfortable. "My name is Trey and my speech is about one of my heroes, fellow Eagle, and my Grandfather, BG."

"*Service to others is the payment you*
make for your space here on earth."
~Muhammed Ali

My speech is the chronological life of someone who has graced the halls of this great university and the lives of everyone in this room, directly or indirectly. The story begins in the 1970's when "G" was a little guy. We've all heard about those massive Angela Davis afros that made hat wearing an impossible wardrobe accessory; those bell-bottom pants that hid your shoes from plain view; and those polyester clothes that felt like plastic and became shiny if you ironed them too much. I saw hilarious pictures of "G" and his dad wearing those afros with a big fisted comb sticking out of it. Those were definitely the old days.

From what I know about "G's" earlier days, he was always a pretty knowledgeable and articulate guy. I heard that he gets that from his father, my Great Grandfather

Kelly. It seems as though I come from a long line of political activists/strategists/thinkers who have strived to give back to the community and inform the people about the world in which we live. Although this story started back in the 1970's, the inspiration to follow this path came from God's inspiration and the achievements and the examples of many figures of the Bible and African American history. For many of these heroes, activism stemmed from a genuine sense community involvement, reaching out, and survival; and many times, there was no pay involved. They did things like this because of a love for God and His people.

I studied African History last semester, and the professor was teaching us about our tribal and communal ancestry. Although there may have been different tribes, customs, locales, etc., there was still a familial bond that caused everyone to look after everyone else's property and family. If someone within the tribe wronged another tribe member, tribal/communal punishment usually would act as a deterrent against future incidents. The key is commitment to the community. As a people, we have lost that part of our culture and have erroneously adopted the crab complex. Instead of everybody supporting the goals of others and ensuring their success so that they can lift others up, many of us try to tear folks down because they get a bit of momentum behind them. "G" would always tell me "that was just insecurity and a lack of vision in the community. We have lost our way, but we can't give up on people. We are obligated to stand up for truth, even if the whole world is against us."

It's in our nature to look out for one another, and when we don't, we act out of character. I thank God that "G" followed his heart and decided to give back. Often times, we don't understand or appreciate the sacrifice and the preparation of those who are laboring among us. Have you ever stopped to think about how much time is actually spent in order to prepare physically and mentally for speeches, writing books, and staying informed in order to be fresh and current on one's perspective? It's a sacrifice; but when the people only see the person in the spotlight, but not all of the toil, research and preparation that goes into making that public appearance; then we fail to appreciate the commitment of some of those who are truly looking out for our best interests.

When "G" was in college, his dad would have him go back to New Jersey from North Carolina to work as a summer intern for the Governor of the State. He did that for two summers and learned about the political process and law. As "G" continued to develop as a principled young man, he became more familiar with the process of governance; and unbeknownst to him, that experience would give him some of the insight necessary to affect great change.

"*Take the attitude of a student, never be too big to ask questions, never know too much to learn something new.*"
~Og Mandino

A few years after his internships, "G" became a Christian and began to be a student of the Word of God. His Christian quest began nearly 60 years ago, and after all of these years the passion and the zeal seems to still get stronger daily. One of the main things that "G" learned was that the same Words that God spoke in the beginning to frame the world are the same Words that should frame our individual worlds (our lives). Living in a secular world isn't without challenges, but living by the Word of God taught "G" that no matter what everyone else is doing, the Word of God is still the standard of truth. "G" has never subscribed to the idea that we should just go to church, and wear crosses around our necks without affecting substantive change. He always taught me that "the cross" is fabulous because it demonstrates the picture of God's love towards humanity. Certainly Jesus isn't on the cross anymore, but we can always be reminded of how much God loves us and how we should sacrificially love one another. We must always keep this in mind: "We should act out of a heart for God towards His people."

"G" was an English major in college and his ability to read, comprehend and analyze information well gave him an insatiable appetite for learning more about history and politics. Two of his favorite historical quotes are from British statesman and philosopher Edmund Burke:

"*Those who don't know history are destined to repeat it.*"

and

"*All that's necessary for the forces of evil to win in the world is for enough good men to do nothing.*"

These two quotes made "G" think about his accountability to God and humanity: the actions that we do and don't do; and things that we allow or disallow. These quotes lit a fire in him to find out what was really happening in the world, and how he could truly make a difference. It also caused him to question everything and to put things into perspective: how the law, politics, finance and history all tied together; how the makers of history tell you what they want you to know, instead of what they know. This allowed "G" to become a savvier Christian by expanding his knowledge and understanding of our secular world in light of the Scriptures.

"G" began to see himself as a trailblazer, in some respects. He could see himself doing many wonderful things with all of this new information. But the knowledge and the insight that he possessed were only being increased and nurtured during his own study time. Many times, he wondered if he was the only Christian or American that thought that things were wrong; wrong with the church; wrong in the government; wrong with corporate interests. So "G" began to employ a Christian worldview as his way of thinking. A Christian way to run the government? To run a business? Christians involved in politics? Jesus did say that we were the salt and the light of the world, and that everywhere the soles of our feet trod is our's. "G" felt that Christians and Christian thought needed to be in the local, state and federal government. It sounded good, and there were examples of strong Christians earlier in the history of this country, but in "G's" generation the Church seemed to become a bit more compromised. Earlier in life, "G" always waited for someone else to stand up and make a difference. But then he learned to follow the motivation for something that is within each one of us. He became a doer and started challenging the status quo that was so prevalent in his day.

"A teacher affects eternity: he can never tell where his influence stops."

~Henry Adams

Steadily growing and maturing in his Christian walk with an arsenal of history, knowledge and spiritual insights, "G" became sharper and more in tuned with a vision and a calling to serve God with these gifts. He began following a path that seemed to not pay big dividends in the short term, but it was his dream, desire and passion to be an advocate for the Kingdom of God and the people. Money wasn't his master, but it was his passion that he followed. "G" told me many times that "you have to follow your heart. Your family and your friends might not understand you; in fact, you might not understand yourself, but your heart will never fail you." That is another one of those powerful lessons that I learned from "G" and he always spent quality time with me sharing these priceless nuggets of wisdom and perspective.

Some time later, he finally decided to test out his insight on the public. He ran for public office a few times, but he never won. However, he did claim victory in that he did inject real issues into the debates and choked out the status quo in the political process. His will and tenacity against mediocrity sparked a fire in others to rise up and not settle for anything less than God's best. He challenged the politicians in his city to be servants of the people. He also challenged the people to take back their communities, the seats of political power, the police departments, and businesses. He encouraged the community to love, to support and to stand up for one another. He never won the popular vote in those elections, but he won in the hearts of the people who wanted to know truth.

These successes led to a constituency of great people who desired more. They weren't looking for a leader, per se, but they were hungry for the truth. They obviously saw something in "G" and he answered the call. He began to do a lot of public speaking, as well as writing books, articles and newspaper columns. His message began to get popular, and so did the criticism. "G" always told me "if you mess up the hustler's hustle, then the hustler will eventually get mad and lash out at you." That was so true. I never thought that a message to free people and get them off of dependency would ever be a threat to anyone. But it did. Preachers and other Christians, politicians and other secular people tried to shut down "G" and his message of love, hope, responsibility and action. These messages were a threat to the people who wanted to keep our people bound spiritually, mentally and financially. I was amazed and saddened to hear about how some of our leaders were complicit in the destruction of our communities, that they were hired to strengthen.

What began to happen was a great awakening; kind of like the black Renaissance in Harlem of the 1920's and 1930's. Our people started to wake up and see the world and the system for what it was. It was a crippling system of defeat, clothed in smiles and handouts. "G" helped to put things into perspective and exposed the corruption of the system in terms that everyday people could understand. Instead of people just going to church, shouting, and not remembering what the preacher talked about, "G" made the Word of God as plain and simple as the morning newspaper. People began to get tired of the same nonsense from their ministers and politicians. The people finally started to rise up and demand something real. The gravy train was over for the community leaders, but the empty promise of change that we've heard too many times continued to resonate in the ears of the hopeful. "G" told me that "you can't wait for things to happen, you got to make it happen." Many people were just waiting for things to happen, and that quieted the crowd and lulled many of them back into complacency.

Unfortunately, significant and substantive change never happened. Many people bought the lie and others were bought off to promote the lie. The so-called leaders promised people a paradise that they never intended to deliver; and the community leaders were hopeful that people would ride the wave until the next church service and/or election cycle. Unfortunately, many of them did. But "G" says we're on another wave and we can't stop unless Jesus stops (and He won't). Jesus asked us when He returns will He find faith in the earth; and we all know that faith is an action word. Will we be busy doing our Father's business? "G" calls this second wave of his ministry, the wave that he wants to pass to a new generation of soldiers; I guess that he means my generation.

"G" really did help to show people the way things were. The white man wasn't the problem, and the devil wasn't a guy with a red asbestos suit. He told people that the enemy was a spirit that operated in people and situations where lying, stealing, killing, destruction and all that is contrary to the Word of God was taking place; no matter how subtle. He started to show people about their liberty and identity in Christ, and taking a stand for truth in the midst of adversity. He began to show people the Word of God isn't just a bunch of legalistic rules to follow. But it is God's mind and principles that can be employed at anytime, in any area of life to produce the kind of results that God desires for us to have. When "G" started to inspire people with this type of information, they were ecstatic, and his ministry ascended to another level.

"*If I have seen further, it is by standing on the shoulders of giants.*"
~Isaac Newton

The legacy of reaching out and giving back is what has been instilled in me. Passing on your faith to your children and grandchildren is a principle that we see in the Word of God from the Patriarchs, i.e., the God of Abraham, Isaac and Jacob (three generations). For my family, and me we will serve the Lord (**Joshua 24:15**), and I have received the torch from my patriarchs. "G" isn't just walking as an example for me, but he is an example for all of us, to reach those that he never will. Friends, you and I have a sphere of influence that is unique, and God wants to use each one of us to reach them. But we have to stop being passive, afraid, and full of excuses. Simply put, if we don't reach them, then they won't be reached. God has invested a lot into equipping us and informing us so that we can go forth in His name and do the work that we are called to do.

"G's" vision is inspirational. I am fortunate to have him in my life, because of all of the love and the valuable lessons he has shared with me. I didn't know what I wanted to be when I was younger. Like most kids, I wanted to be a doctor or some other profession to help people. But as I began to grow up with "G," he showed me how to love people unconventionally and unconditionally. The rewards that "G" gets from fulfilling this mission can't be quantified with a dollar amount. Does he make money? Certainly, he wouldn't be able to travel; to self-publish his material; to start radio stations; to build churches; to daily teach the Word of God and inspirational messages to every continent on the planet; to feed, clothe and house 50,000,000 people worldwide daily; and to provide job training and internships at all levels without it. So the money is a means to a Godly end; it isn't the driving force and the motivation for the effort that he exerts. I hope that we all can glean something positive from my hero. He has truly done a remarkable job giving back and winning many people over for God's Kingdom. Let's all get motivated and do our part to establish God's Kingdom in the earth. "Thank you."

When I finished the speech, I received a tremendous applause and a standing ovation from an overwhelming majority of the people in the lecture hall. For the first time in my life, I was experiencing such a powerful sign of approval from my contemporaries. I was speechless. As the applause started to cease, a few of the people who were sitting during the standing ovation stood up. Just then my professor came over and patted me on the shoulder and said, "Good job!" He smiled and looked behind me. As I turned around, the people who were sitting down during the standing ovation came down and were walking towards the professor and me. It was my dad and "G;" and with tears in their eyes, they hugged me and "G" looked at me and said "Thank you, son." I asked him why he was thanking me. He said, "Just like God likes to loved, appreciated and thanked, so does everyone else. I know that my labor hasn't been in vain."

I explained to "G" that this standing ovation wasn't because of me, but it was because of his efforts and labor of love towards humanity. He, and other great leaders have laid the groundwork to make things better off for us today. We may not always show our love and appreciation for those who directly or indirectly labor for our benefit, but this speech certainly touched "G" in a very special way that he will never forget. How can we repay the debt of someone sacrificing their time and their life for us? You do so by being sacrificial and helping someone else. The sacrifices that were made on our behalf were actually done after the model of our Lord and Savior Jesus Christ. Today, we should all be grateful because God loved us so much that He sent us His Son; and subsequently, He continually sends us more sons and daughters to demonstrate His love for us through various means. I can't imagine not being able to vote, or not being able to eat in the restaurant of my choice. The efforts of those brave men and women during the civil rights movement and other points in history have made it possible for us to never experience those bad days. I thank God for "G" and all of those great men and women that have inspired you to do all that you do. Through you, they inspire me; and I only hope that I can touch half the amount of lives that you have touched, are touching and will touch. God Bless.

The Soul of a Man

Joe Thomas

I was a kid, only ten, when I saw two lovers kiss. I still recall their soulful sighs. Heard him say to her; "You've got stars in your eyes."
I wondered about that. Heard some older guys talk about the things they liked to do. Later, I asked my Daddy please, "What do they mean about the birds and the bees?" then I became a young man. All grown up, you see. No longer did I need those things explained to me. After all, I'm smart, "Chilly" too. So I thought. Then I fell in love. Love's a crazy game. Sometimes you win, sometimes you lose. Better keep your fingers crossed each and every time you choose. But in spite of it all, love is still a ball. A game I love to play. Like a child would, may it always be that way.

What you just read was a song I wrote while in my "young" fifties. To better understand what it was all about, I'll walk you through my life.

It's May 31, 1933. Hey world! I'm here! Everything's gonna be all right. Although I didn't know it, a depression was well on its way. We were about to get a new deal, compliments of President Franklin S.

Roosevelt. I'll stop there, historians are better at reciting history than I am.

My First Love…

"Listen, Mel D., I'll be coming back down the street. I've got to go home now and see if there's anything my parents want me to do. Don't matter what they want, I'll have to get this 4th grade homework done first. Mel D., don't you think we get too much homework? Will it really make us smarter?"

"I'm sure it will. They wouldn't have us do it if it wasn't gonna make us smarter."

I went home and completed everything I had to so that I could get back with Mel D.

"Mel D. I told you I'd be back. It's getting dark and Momma told me not to be out too late. Hey, here comes Smarty. Maybe we can get some answers to some of the things we've talked about, especially the girls."

Smarty must have been reading our minds because he walked up just as we were talking.

"Hello Joe. Hello Mel. D. You guys just chillin' on the porch?"

"Yeah, Smarty. It's a good warm night just made for "guy talk," I replied.

"You said you'd tell us the best way to get our point across with the girls. No better time than now," Mel D. added.

"I'll tell you a little something, but there's only so much you nine year olds need to know. First, you most likely won't understand it and you'll just fantasize about it. Truth is, you end up believing you know what it's all about but you won't really be ready for at least seven more years to have that experience. I can tell by your reaction that what I've told you has registered deeply into your minds."

Smarty went on to tell us some things that blew our minds.

"Mel D., Smarty is really somethin'. He told us so much.

"That thing with girls is definitely something to look forward to," Mel D. remarked.

"Yeah man, but my Daddy told me, "You can get involved if you want to, but if things get out of hand, there will be a wedding, even if it is a shotgun wedding." He said, "There will be no children born without a last name."

Although we didn't fully comprehend it at the time, I knew that what my Daddy was saying was serious.

"You know, Mel D., there's that girl that lives next to you, her name is, uhm, let me think, oh yes, Princess. That's my own private name for her. "

"Yea Joe, but word is she has designs on being a doctor or lawyer's wife. She feels like anything less than that is not likely to be of interest to her."

I'm tickled to this day about how we'd talk to one another, even back then, and even at the tender age of nine.

The years went by and Mel D. and I were still the best of friends. Still on the same porch in Newark, New Jersey

"Its nice spring night Mel D. and you know it is the type of night when you get the urge to be with someone you love. Remember what I told you about Princess? I want her to know how I feel."

"Okay, Joe, let's go around the corner, sit under her balcony and you tell me how you feel about her," Mel D. suggested.

"Really? Do you think she'll be impressed?

It was some years later, around four, but I knew that I was in love with Princess and had dreamed about being with her.

"Well, Joe tell it all. I'm rootin' for ya."

And so I poured my heart out. I went on and on about my feelings for my Princess. Didn't talk about intimate things, just about how much I loved her.

Princess did approach me shortly thereafter and told me about all the things I didn't have. She made a point of it. Of course, she could have been more tactful, she could have just told me that she wasn't interested. I guess this was my first heartache – the first time my heart would be broken.

Family…

My family was a large one. Seven children, inclusive of three boys, and four girls. Mom and Dad were priceless. They kept us well-disciplined. Mom would designate what was to be done. Dad was the enforcer, when needed, which was very, very seldom. He had a "strap" made from barber's blade sharpener. He would cut it down from being an eight of an inch piece to seven one-eighth of an inch straps. Needless to say, we never forgot how it felt. One time was more than enough. The girls were for the most part not likely to receive the strap as a form of discipline.

It was bad enough that you got whupped, but Daddy would have the strap hanging on a nail in plain sight all the time. When you fouled up, he'd say, "Got get the strap." It was like walking the plank. When you would walk really slow, in an attempt to prevent the inevitable, Daddy would say, "You're gonna get whupped the same time it took you to get the strap.

Talk about mixed emotions. Hurry and get the strap so the dreaded pain about to be inflicted upon you would last a shorter period of time. You know what? He *never* had to go to the police station to get any one of us.

Dad would invite all of us to listen to him read the Bible and to participate in the discussion later. He'd also lead us in songs of praise. He never told us we had to take part in any of the aforementioned. He had a tremendous amount of strength and wisdom. As the son of a slave, there were many opportunities that were denied him. Born in Savannah, Georgia in the 1800's, my Dad experienced much abuse, racially, and because he was a smart man, he moved to New Jersey and met his soon to be wife, Sarah, my mother. Their marriage lasted decades, ending only with the passing of Dad in the 1950's.

Returning to Dad's mother wit. This man was very gifted. He didn't have a long background in formal education, yet, he read extremely well. He wrote with confidence. Dad would make our shoes. And, before I speak of the many other great attributes of this man, what is most outstanding was his integrity and veracity. He said what he meant and meant exactly what he said. He was a highly-principled man. His word was always his bond. All of us children patterned ourselves after him.

We had some pot-bellied stoves that we cooked all of our meals on and in, in the large one in the kitchen. WE used the smaller one to help heat one of the bedrooms upstairs. What I recall with crystal clarity is the time, unknown to me, that the top of to the stove in the bedroom had been removed so that more coal could be put into it. It was dark in the room and I had no shoes on. I immediately received both a severe shock and a smell of something cooking. What was cooking was me!

In order to keep the stoves going, we needed wood. Dad would say early on Saturday morning, "Joe, get up. It's time to go get wood." We'd walk about three to four miles to the railroad tracks near the city dump, and get some discarded cross-ties. These are pieces of wood used to hold firm railroad tracks. The way they were shaped lent themselves to be quite favorable to fitting in the large oven of our kitchen stove.

The one time I remember that was not so good for me was the time when Dad decided to get that wood during the week when I should have been in school, High school. Being out was one thing, but the route Dad chose to return home went right by the school I was attending. I was quite dirty from the charred wood and my face was almost unrecognizable. I looked like I was a commando about to go on a night raid against some enemy base. But the real problem was that it was lunchtime and, you guessed it, all of my classmates were having lunch outside the school. They thought it was quite amusing to see me like that, however, a great turnabout was about to begin.

The Music…

The sound I heard seemed as though it came from my house. It was. It was my older brother, Frank teaching himself how tot play the saxophone. "Squeak, squeak, honk," half notes sang an awful tune. The melody went on over a period of days. But to Frank's credit, he didn't give up. In not so long a period of time, he began to shape-up on the born. He got to be rather good at it. That was Dad's mother wit coming through.

As for me. I had this fascination for war stories. Even though I was in my early teens, I followed the progress of the allies in Europe and the Pacific by looking at the maps in the local newspapers while other guys my age were playing sports. I found fun in drawing guns on a thin plank of wood, using a coping saw; I cut them out and gave them to some other kids in the neighborhood. We played war games.

Back to Frank, who, by the way, had a self-placed nickname, Demosthenes, after the Greek philosopher of the same name.

"Joe, why don't you learn how to play the sax? I can teach you if you're interested."

I soliloquized, "One of us making those horrid sounds while learning is more than enough. I don't think I should be bothered."

Frank persisted. "I think you'll learn faster than I did."

I thought, "Maybe so," but why should I be interested. One of us playing the sax in the family should be more than enough. But Frank, he kept persisting. He would come back time and time again insisting that I learn how to play the saxophone. His persistence worked. After an extended period of "squeakin' and squawkin', things began to happen – it began to happen. Wow, a melody, then two, then more, then I could solo some. Did I play the right chords? They applauded. Was it because I was only fifteen years old?

It was a moonlight evening at Oliver Street School. There was nice crowd waiting to hear us play. "Oh my God," I said out loud. My mother was there. She stood out in the crowd. She was so proud. Proud that two of her sons were playing in the Swing band. The elder taught the other. The show went well. I knew then that I would always see my mother's face in the crowd.

There was a "gig" in Asbury Park, New Jersey at a place called "The Palm Garden." Frank asked me if I wanted to go. "Wanna go, Joe?"

"I thought you would never ask." I figured, I'd get to go to a place I've never been, play for some new faces and get paid. We were going to stay the entire weekend, so the idea was fabulous.

"Who's the "Chippi?" Back in those days, a chippi was a young man. The person questioning was the waitress talking to another waitress.

"He's that young saxophone player we were told about. I heard he's pretty good, we'll see."

"Flyin' Home" was the song all tenor-Sax players had to know. It was a hit song for a tenor sax player named Illinois Jacquet. What you would do was play his solo while either walking the bar or walking from table to table, when you walked the bar. Yes, you walked *on* the bar, carefully avoiding any drinks that would be on it. When you were coming close to somebody who loved to be seen (you could usually tell from a distance. The folks were loud, waved money around, and they would scream "set up the bar.") When you got to them, you'd dip the horn in which they could toss a bill. Mostly $1 or $5 and rarely $10. Others would throw in change. When the song ended, there would be a nice piece of money in the bell of the horn. This was quite rewarding, except for when there was just a small amount of change. The horn would be weighted down, however, on the other hand, should there be paper bills in there, they could block the flow of air and distort the sound of the horn.

This gig in particular was nice, and was so new to me, and didn't take too long to get used to. Being away from home on the weekends while making a nice piece of money was a big deal for a black kid in the 1940's.

Millie was the waitress who asked who the Chippi was. We got to be good friends and our friendship grew stronger and stronger over time. Millie was in her late twenties, compared to me being in my teens, so she felt much of our thoughts and intentions should be kept private. It was undoubtedly the right thing to do. All she had to hear were things that outlined where I hoped it would ultimately lead to that long-awaited experience, so I didn't say a word.

Princess…

"Hi Joe!"

"Hi Princess."
"Another nice summer evening. It reminds me of the day when you and Mel D. were sitting on the steps under my balcony. Things were so quiet with the exception of an occasional car going by. Everything rang loud and clear, especially when you told Mel D. how you felt about me. You were so precise, describing my shape, the size of my rear end, the longness of my hair, the lips you would love to kiss, while your hands explored those areas that were bound to make me very, very interested."
I thought to myself, "Wow, I didn't expect this kind of response." She's really interested. Will I be too nervous? I have no experience. Suppose I didn't get it all right. Will she push me away and say, "You don't know anything about anything. You are a disappointment, matter of fact, you are a drag." That's what I was thinking. Turns out it was big build up for a big let down.

"Joe," Princess said. "What makes you think that I would really come anywhere close to considering you as someone I would become involved with? It is well known that when the time comes, I'm gonna marry a wealthy man, or better than that, a richer than rich man. Nothing short of that bears no interest to me. I don't intend to ever have to do anything more than bear children, be a good loving wife and a "somebody" in the higher society group. What can you offer me? You're poor, and you don't even have any nice clothes to wear.

When she first started to put me down, I was crushed, devastated. Then suddenly, my Ego came up to the plate. It told me, "You know, she ain't all that fine when you really look closely as stuck up as she is. She'd probably not be much fun during an intimate moment of intimacy, she'd be too busy saying, "Ain't I real fine?" Don't you just love looking at me?" She'd take all the thrill out of anything because of her huge ego and love of herself.

My Ego continued, "You probably didn't miss anything. Besides, that was only the first time you tried approaching any girl. Your day will come, Joe." My ego was my dearest friend that day. I learned later what it really was called, "sour grapes." You'll learn a little more about Princess later on.

The Music…

I, along with another saxophone player and a trumpet player were incorporated into a trio. Piano, bass and drums. The owner of the night club wanted to take us on the road as a sextet. We went to Portsmouth, Virginia. It was our headquarters. We branched out from there to North Carolina as well as other parts of Virginia.

"Big Boy," a nickname given to our trumpet player, struck gold. He met a woman who had her own "still." She loved her some Big Boy. He lived like a king. She made some real good corn liquor. Smooth as silk. That's exactly what caused me to almost kill myself. I guzzled it down, ignoring those who knew better, who told me, "take it easy, man. That stuff will sneak up on you." But I was trying to impress a young lady. I said, "I can handle it. They all looked at each other, smiled and shrugged their shoulders and said, "Okay, Joe."

Oh how I wished they'd been more persuasive. Before I knew it, I had no real understanding of anything. Questions like, "Where am I?" and "Who are you?" surfaced. I had never before been nor have I ever since then been so terribly out of it. I was passed drunk. For days, every time I'd drink anything, including water, I'd get drunk again. Misery was my middle name. About four days later, I finally came back to normal. It was wonderful.

Returning to the gig and the band for some reason, I can't recall exactly, there was a problem that developed between the rhythm section and the horns. It boiled over. The producers, who favored the rhythm section, packed them up and left the rest of us stranded. No income. No gigs pending. I ended up working as a dishwasher in Norfolk. I ate well. As a matter of fact, I brought food home to my buddy, the other saxophone player.

Big Boy didn't need any help. After a few months, my Uncle Clee came to Portsmouth. He had been visiting relatives nearby and stopped in to see me. Clee was an imposing figure. Standing at a solid 6'2", not fat, just big, with a deep roaring voice. He said, "Your Momma's worrying about you, Boy. You gotta go home." Needless to say, I went home.

It was good to be home, actually. I realized that after a while. But there was no work at home. No gigs. I wasn't even sure I wanted to gig anymore after the horrendous experience I had being stranded. One thing I knew for sure – Music was in my blood, in my heart and soul and it would be something that I'd never be able to let go.

Family…

Dad would make our shoes, ***really.*** Including the soles, heels of course, but thank God he couldn't make the strings. He had some clippers to cut the boys hair. I remember one of my sisters saying to the other, "Look at Joe frownin' while getting his hair cut."

I mused, "Oh yeah. Just wait until Momma starts braiding your hair. It will take longer and she'll pull it too tight from time to time and hopefully someone will come by to see her without prior notice and you'll just have to sit there until the torture continues. Ha."

Speaking of my Momma. She was quiet – a strong, silent type of woman. She was quiet until she had to be otherwise. She would rather have done the whuppin' as she knew she would not be as severe as Dad would be. The idea to her was not to inflict any lasting, scaring type of injury, but to vividly show us that there was a price to be paid for doing the wrong thing. She would tell us, "You don't do things that are wrong anywhere. In the house or outside the house. The family name is not to be disgraced."

It never was.

Momma would tell us, "Here's some cookies. I'm only going to give you a couple because I don't want you to spoil your appetite. I don't know how many are left in the jar. I'm gonna leave the room but don't take any more. I won't see you, but God will."

After she left, we would look around the room, wide-eyed, trying to see God even though we knew we couldn't. But what she'd told us was more than enough to prevent us from taking any more cookies. On a particular day, I wish the above-mentioned testimony was true.

We had gangs, but don't think of them in any small way as one of the gangs of today. For the most part we'd limit our activities to harmless mischief. I was pretty much a loner, and gangs did not appeal to me. One day, I decided I'd see what it would be like to run with a gang. What we had in mind was to take some fruit from an outside produce market. We grabbed whatever food we could and ran. The fruit stand owner saw us and shouted, "Stop! I'll call the police. You'll go to jail." No one stopped. I had a few oranges and apples and I became separated from the rest of the gang because I took short-cut. Down an ally I went and jumped over a fence. Much to my horror, on the way down, I saw a huge German shepherd dog waiting. His mouth was wide open and I swore he had a dinner jacket on, and I was to be his main course. Don't ask me how I did it, but I reversed course in mid-air. That was my first and last experience with a gang.

The War...

There was a war going on in Korea. People were being drafted and I was almost of age to be affected by the draft so I decided to volunteer. This way, I chose when I went in, I figured.

I was asked which branch of the service I wanted to be in. I decided to join the Marines. I loved that outfit. They were unique. Their uniforms were sharp. Everybody loved them. I was off – to join the Marines. Alas, during my physical examination, it was determined I had "flat-feet." I was told that I'd never make it down there in Parris Island, the place where the Marines took basic training. This was in the state of South Carolina. I asked, "So you mean I can't join the Corp?"

"Try the Army. You may succeed there."

I found success. I was in the Army. My brother-in-law told me to choose the Infantry. I had so many questions. "Will I have my own gun?"

"Sure, you will."

The question itself showed how terribly naïve I was. Eventually, I began to like the Army.

One day, a draftee and I were goofing off from basic training. We left the training area, went to the main post. There, no one would question anyone was doing. While sitting on the grass, a soldier came out of a billet. He had "jump boots" on – only paratroopers were allowed to wear them. His "Ike" jacket and pants had the creases sewn into them. Therefore making them look pressed at all times. He had zippers on the inside of his boots and laces in the front. The purpose of the zippers was to allow him to take off his boots without untying them. I said to my buddy, "I'm gonna join the outfit." He replied, "So am I." After some time, I emerged from the billet and saw my buddy again and told him that I had become a trooper. He thought it was very interesting, but expressed his displeasure in being there. He told me, "See that's your problem. You volunteered and I got drafted. I don't want to be here, but you do, so you'll probably do anything."

"Welcome to Fort Benning, Georgia. You're here to take training to become paratroopers. Airborne. One of the United States' elite units. Now gentlemen, the fun will begin. There will be P.T. (physical training) and P.T. and more P.T. You will double-time (jog) everywhere you go. No matter what the reason is. The only time you will not have to double-time will be when you're inside the guidon. Oops there is another time, once you're in the john. If you're caught walking, you'll have to give me ten. (push-ups). Matter of fact, anything that you do that you shouldn't be doing, well, you'll have to give me ten. No exceptions."

We didn't know why that was the case. It seemed odd. Later, during our training, we found out why. There were 600 of us in the class. We would all be lumped together, therefore, we'd be in alphabetical order. What differentiated us was our tower number. My number was 585. So this was the deal. There were quite a number of Thomas', Johnsons, Williams' and when it came to Smiths, forget about it! So when a Thomas would do something wrong, the D.I. (Drill Sergeant) would say out the corner of his mouth, along with a sideward glance, "Thomas, you're not at attention, give me ten." Okay, but which Thomas. It was a "Catch 22." If you were guilty and didn't get ten, you had to get twenty. If you were not guilty and got ten, the D.I. would say, "I wasn't talking to you but since you feel like gettin' push-ups get me twenty. And you (pointing at the culprit) since you caused those guys grief, you get me twenty. We were double-timing in formation.

Due to attrition, I was first in my column. The D.I. said, "Thomas, slow down. Your legs are longer than some of the guys behind you. They can't keep up." I did it again. D.I. said, "Alright, Thomas, I told you before, you didn't do what I said. Get out, give me ten. I fell out of the formation, went to the side of the road, on the dead run, hit the turf to get ten. You can't stop; find a spot where there are no pebbles, then gently lower yourself and start. On top of that, you've got to shout, "One, two," and so on. Meanwhile, the group continued to double-time. When I got to ten, they all looked about three feet tall.

"Now, up on your feet, Joe."

Determined not to be defeated, I succeeded in catching up with them, only to be told by the D.I., "I only heard you count to eight. You owe two more." That was only part of P.T.

The 34-foot tower was the biggest challenge in the first of three weeks of jump school. It was a tower that you jump out of to learn how to position yourself when you exit the plane. You never hit the ground. You're in a harness that jolts you after you've fallen about 15-feet.

You count, hup thousand, two thousand, three thousand. Your counting would be cut off as you've fallen the maximum number of feet you can before you get the "opening shock." You're told to look, when you have a parachute on, and if you don't see an open canopy, you must pull the "D" ring that's in the palm of your right hand. It's attached to your reserve chute. Yank it and your reserve chute will open. If it doesn't, you turn those chutes in and get another two. That would be come accomplishment since you'll have fallen about 1,200 feet. It was a standard joke in jump school as well as in the Airborne unites. You're required to make a three day and one night jump to qualify. When you finished the three week course, you got to the parade grounds to get your wings, pinned on the breast of the jacket you were wearing. Needless to say, it's a very proud moment.

"So, graduate Thomas, what's next?"

"Some Airborne unit, of course."

I want to rewind for a moment. I do this because I want to share with you one of those times when a decision you've made comes back to bite you. Before that fateful day, when I joined the paratroopers, I had tried out for the army band. I did that because when I first came into the army as an infantry man, some guys knew from the outside world and civilian life asked me, "Joe, what are you doing in this outfit? Join the band. We don't have very much. We may or may not have to play reveille." In the service, that was a call, usually by music, to get up.

"We can have the creases sewn into our uniforms. We can get off the base during the week. No K.P., kitchen police, cooking, washing dishes, pots."

I was thinking, seriously at that point.

"We have an emblem on our caps and it is sometimes mistaken as an officer's emblem. We get saluted once in a while too. It's fun, so man, get out of that infantry mess. Come over here with us."

"Great," I said. "What do I have to do?"

"Take the exam. If you pass, you'll be here with us in no time."

I took the test and passed it. I was told that I had to complete six weeks of basic training because that was the minimum amount of time you had to do before you were able to go into special group. Well, six weeks passed. No call. Eight weeks passed, and still no call. I decided to get in touch with the higher ups, and no one had any explanations as to what happened.

I went to Lieutenant Jackson and inquired.

"I was told I would be transferred after six weeks. It's been nine weeks and I've heard nothing."

"I'll look into it, Private Thomas."

About a month later we were in touch again and Lieutenant asked me if had joined the paratroopers. I told him I did. He informed me that the paratroopers had a band too, that there was a war going on and they were a special unit. "They have priority," he told me. He told me I needed to decide which way to go. He did inform me that because I finished jump school that it wouldn't affect my record no matter what I decided.

Eventually the orders came down and I had to go overseas. "You got the 187th Regimental Combat Team of the 11th Airborne." Only thing I could say was "Oh my God."

They had jumped in Korea two times already, and it didn't seem like there were any bands there to join. I hoped for it though.

It took two weeks to cross the Pacific Ocean from Seattle, Washington. Uneventful, really, except when we entered a storm that produced twenty plus feet swells. The ocean tossed the ship around as if it were a matchbox. At times the bow of the vessel would dip so far under the surface that the screws – rear propellers would lift clean out of the water. When the props hit the surface, it would shake the entire ship. It was very scary, and that's putting it mildly, but that was to everyone else. But no, not if you're seventeen years old and don't fully realize what real fear is. We paratroopers had to play it tough.

We laughed, opened some of the port holes and watched the sea waters come in while the "straight-legs" were in and out of their bunks bringing up all they'd had to eat.

We made it to Japan, and assignments were being called out.

"Private Thomas, you're going to the 34th Regiment of the 24th Division."

I thought, "That has to be a mistake. That a "leg" unit."

Turns out, it was no mistake. The aforementioned unit had borne the full impact of the North Koreans who were supported by almost a million Chinese soldiers. They were overrun and slaughtered. There were so many men killed, wounded, missing or captured that the unit came back to Japan on "paper."

Had the enemy been aware of that, it would have been a propaganda bonanza, that's why, no matter what you had done before, it really didn't matter. This unit had to be replaced, and fast.

"You men will be training here in Japan until we can shape you up into a fighting unit. You will listen to and learn from "the vets." If you don't, you're more likely to be a casualty. Obviously, in ware there will be some, but the more you know, the more likely you'll survive."

For the most part Japan was swell. We trained hard and partied hard. Then it was time to get into some very serious business, combat.

"Get off the trucks, guys. We're going to relieve the 24th Infantry regiment. They've had their hands full for quite some time now. They're also the last all Black unit in Korea."

President Truman had ordered all military united to desegregate. When those guys came out the trenches, we were going North, they – South. We knew there were many our age, but they looked so much older. It wasn't just because they were unshaved with mud-crusted clothes. It was what was behind their eyes. It didn't fully register at that time, but it certainly did after only a few days and nights of combat.

"Give me your grenades, give me your spare ammo."

We all replied, "You can have it all except its not up to us."

We had to dig our foxholes five feet or more according to our height. We had to put up barbed wire, stones in tin cans and if anyone touched the barbed wire, the stones in the can would rattle. We had watched shells explode on the enemy hills.

Some veterans within ear shots of our planning and conversations simply smiled.

Night number one fell and everything around us changed. That enemy held hill, so much higher than ours, looked like it was moving toward us. There was no talking and if you heard something, don't fire your weapon. It would give the position away. We threw a grenade instead.

All night, Private Hart and I would raise our heads slowly above the edge of our foxhole. Peering into the darkness was pointless. We couldn't even see our hands in front of our eyes. A rat or some other animal would rustle through the bushes or make some noise, and we couldn't panic, we had to remain calm.

You have a better chance in your foxhole that the enemy does on the other side of the barbed wire. A can rattled. Sweat on your brow suddenly seemed to pour down your face but we had to remain as cool as possible.

"Charlie" – the nickname given to the enemy would attach a string on the wire, stretch it out for 10 – 15 feet, then tug on it. Should you fire at the sound, he wouldn't be there. We always had to keep our guard up.

The remainder of the first night on the front line was quiet. Speaking of grenades, it was one of Charlie's grenades that earned me a Purple medal.

I won't continue with these war stories, but honestly, they're very difficult and uncomfortable to recall.

There is something that I believe is most worthy of mention. We were an integrated unit. As I said before, we had a lot of folks from beneath the Mason-Dixon line. Let me tell you this, to this day, some 58 years later, I had never before been around anyone who would do what they were set to do, no matter what.

In combat, they were your comrades. You weren't Black, they weren't White. You were American soldiers who looked out for each other. I've had many, many friends as well as musician friends, but I can tell you from the bottom of my heart, even reaching down in my soul – I've never seen this comradery equaled anywhere.

There was a time when Charlie dropped some leaflets on us. One the leaflet was the picture of a Black man who had been lynched in the South. The leaflet read, "Black G.I.'s, is this what you risk your lives for? Do you think it will make any difference when you return home? It won't. Come over to us. Get out of a war that is not yours and will benefit you nothing."

Now prepare yourself. The problem at that time with what the Koreans said, was that they referred to us as "Black." At that time, it was considered insulting to be called or referred to as "Black." Oh no, we were "colored," or "tan," or even "Negro," but not "Black." This was 1951. We were so profoundly ignorant that this truly was deemed as insulting.

If any of us had any sense of history, we would have known that in World War I, we were called "Black" in Europe. Of course, no one defected.

There was a humorous thing that developed later that day. Word came down from Regiment that if anyone was caught with "commie" propaganda on him, he'll be in big trouble. We laughed, we laughed real hard. We concluded it this way. We were on the front lines, in an infantry unit, shells exploding on enemy held hills, and at any minute they could fire on us. An enemy sniper could have infiltrated our lines during the night, and have our heads in the crosshairs of his telescope. We may have to go out on a night ambush but get ambushed instead. We may be ordered to take one of his hills or may decide to take ours. How much more trouble could we be in?

I had received a box of goodies and was just about ready to share them when orders came through that I was on my way home. Home on emergency leave. I was ordered to pack up my gear. I told them how much I loved them, and told them to share the goodies that had just arrived. I never saw any of them ever again.

The plane trip home was long. Five hours from Seoul, Korea to Japan. Nine hours from Japan to Wake Island, and twelve hours from Wake Island, Hawaii to California. We flew through some Pacific Ocean storms. It was on a propeller driven airplane with a jet assist. I've never ridden on anything like that since then and that is just fine with me.

For me and the other men coming home on emergency leave, all we thought about was the inevitable. Most emergency leaves meant that you were coming home to bury someone or to see them in their last days on Earth, so the turbulence of the plane ride failed in comparison to what was on our hearts and the anxiety that lied beneath.

When I returned home, my family informed me that Momma was gravely ill and that she was in the hospital. The doctors weren't sure how long she had left. Well, Momma did make it, and as a matter of fact, she lived many, many years after that.

The Church…

This startling revelation lead me to what could very well be the core of this book, the core of our lives, that defining moment in our lives where we gain a sense of purpose, that moment where we realize our soul, we feel it, we know its there – I joined the church.

As I walked down the aisle toward the pulpit in my military uniform, someone shouted, "Praise Jesus!" After being received as a new member of the church, I asked Reverend Wilder, "Would you please ask the choir to sing, *Sing to the Power of the Lord Come Down*," one of my favorite hymns.

When the choir began to sing, tears of joy poured down my cheeks. I wept unashamedly. I felt guilt. I felt guilty about being safe at home, safe in a church, safe with my God, our God, while my buddies were facing death, every minute of the day and night.

The Holy Spirit took hold of me and didn't let me go. I was baptized a short time later.

I remembered being in Korea, and being on the line, they would ask us if we wanted to go to service. Church service was on the hill. Frankly, there was a limited amount of interest one time, any given time, to go to service.

Word had come down that we were going to make a big push against the Chinese and North Koreans. It was gonna be pretty bad, very severe. Planes were to bomb their positions for two days, and artillery will also pound there continually before we were to jump off. They were supposedly "dug-in" pretty well and it was going to be tough. And because of this, there were so many people at the next service you would have thought that Billy Graham or someone that large was there.

This is the power of God, this represents the almighty belief in God, how we run to Him for protection, how we need Him, always.

The big push never happened. The negotiators on both sides saw there was no real reason to keep stalling, so a cease-fire agreement was reached and signed.

Eventually, I rejoined the army. The lieutenants referred to this as "esprit de corps." Why would I go back? It seemed that the army had forgotten about me. I missed my buddies, the comradery, but what I didn't realize was that I'd been gone nine months. When I did get back to my unit, I discovered that all of them who made it had rotated, done their tours of duty and returned home. There were other major things that happened, like me being hit, and almost killed, I still have shrapnel in my body to this day, even near my heart. I was awarded the Purple Heart and honorably discharged from the army.

The Music...

I had a vastly different experience as a civilian than I did being in the army. I didn't want to go back to the music because of the experiences I had early on with the music, I felt like, been there, done that.

I ended up with a job in a paper box company, as a bailer. The guys were all friendly and as time went by, I told them that I played the saxophone. They thought I was joking. It is something the way God works in our lives.

"You play music and you're in here slavin'? Either you're jivin' or b.s.ing."

The day came when I got the chance to show them. A guy named Dahlie came into the factory. He was a "number writer" who took bets. There was no legal lottery at the time in the state of New Jersey. The guys told him I played and he told me, "There's a place called "The Brass Rail" that needs a band. My friend ragged, "Why don't you get "Big Time Joe Thomas" to bring a band in there?" Laughter ensued. But Dahlie asked me, "Do you play music?"

"Well, here's what you do, go there and tell them Dahlie sent you."

I did and got the gig. It went very well and another gig followed and then another. I eventually got so much work playing the horn that I was able to leave my day job and make a decent living playing on the weekends. As a matter of fact, I made as much in three nights, four hours a night, as I made in five days on the day job including working up to twelve hours a day.

My music career blossomed. Specks Williams gave me a place in his quartet. I met a beautiful young lady nicknamed "Mike." Mike was bright and worked in the music industry. She was a promotions person for a well-known record company. We became close friends and ended up pledging ourselves to one another. We would go on to have three children, three beautiful daughters, Monique, Jodi, and Elissa.

I formed my own group. Joe Thomas and the Nightlifers, a Rock & Roll group. We played a lot in Canada. In Montreal, Canada, I met Bill Elliott, who would end up being the greatest friend I had in my life. He was a drummer with another band. Billy loved my band and soon became part of it. Billy, what I used to call him, and I left Canada and became part of the Dee Dee Ford Trio. Then we were part of the Rhoda Scott Trio. We were a cooperative band and we all shared equal publicity and money.

The famous Key Club in New Jersey was our home base. We were very, very well received and was approached by a guy named Ozzie. He wanted to produce us and have us record an album.

We got the studio, and outside there were three beautiful women. We learned they were to be background singers on our record. Billy spotted one and said, "Joe, go tell that woman, "she's got legs!"

I looked at Billy and said, "What are you talking about? All women have legs."
I told her what Billy said, and she accepted the compliment. All of the women were blood relatives. Eventually Billy and the beautiful woman became good friends, and then were married, she became a great singing sensation – Dionne Warwick.

Over time, Rhoda moved on the Europe, and at the time we thought she was crazy, but it turned out to be a great decision. She became a huge star over there. Billy and I made one album together, then Billy moved to California, and appeared in a move with Elvis Pressley and another with Peter Sellers. He eventually was given the lead role in a movie called "Hang Up" which received modest success.

I went on to record nine albums of my own, and some have been reduxed and are now CDs. They may be found on the internet. For the last two decades, I've been playing the saxophone in my church, taking on an occasional gig here and there. I love especially the jazz gig cruises where I performed; they were great gigs featuring some o the world's greatest jazz artists.

Among the many engagements, one stands out for a special reason. I was performing at a gig in honor of professional black women. It was a gala affair. And guess who was one of the women in attendance? Princess Lang.

Princess had remained true to her goal of meeting and marrying up, and she had married well, a very prominent and success politician. We exchanged greetings. Here I was, a successful musician, a jazz recording artist – it was a very fitting reunion since we had seen so little of each other most of our young adult life. On second thought, I don't know if she was there due to personal achievement or because she was the wife of a prominent man. Doesn't really matter.

Talk about the power of God. I didn't want to return to music, yet He knew music was in my heart and soul and was my life's calling.

I've experienced life's ups and downs and while looking back over my life, I can honestly say that I would have done things differently given the chance, but I'm content and comforted in knowing that God knows exactly what He is doing, All the time.

Today, I'm happily married to my wife, Ruth, and I have two surviving daughters, Monique and Elissa and I am deeply honored that she would invite me to share in her journey, and allow me to share my life's journey, by baring my soul, in *The Soul of a Man.*

As I complete my story, I take a moment to look up to the Heavens and say, "Love you Much," to my middle daughter Jodi, who passed away January 18, 2009. I dedicate this story to her loving memory.

ACKNOWLEDGEMENTS

I would like to thank all of the contributors to *The Soul of a Man* for making this great work possible. Had it not been for the dedication and effort on the part of these brilliant contributors, this book would not exist.

MEET THE CONTRIBUTORS TO *THE SOUL OF A MAN* ONLINE AT WWW.THESOULOFAMAN.NET

JOE THOMAS

Joe Thomas' musical career spans over four decades; during that time he has performed throughout the world.
He began to play professionally at age fifteen (with his older brother's guidance) in small clubs. He met the fabulous James Moody, who was then playing with the Dizzy Gillespie Big Band. Moody told Joe to pursue his craft and Joe did just that, including a short southern tour. A three year stint in the United States Army interrupted his career, but after he was honorably discharged he continued to play his horn, touring Canada for three years.

He returned to the United States and helped to form a group call "The Rhoda Scott Trio". Featured in that group along with Rhoda and Joe was drummer Bill Elliott. The group stayed together for three years. They made two albums together.
Joe then formed his own group and made nine albums. He was featured on the flute and saxophone. He also appears on several other albums including a couple of Jimmy McGriff's. Two of his albums have been re-issued as CD's "Platos Retreat" and Masada."

Joe has performed at the Blue Note, Birdland, Carlos One, The Cave, Count Basies, La Détente and Smalls Paradise. All of these places are/were in New York.

Joe was one of the "All-Stars" invited to play at the Pythodd Club (Rochester, N.Y.) and Pine Grill (Buffalo, N.Y.) reunions. Notables performing at these jazz festivals were: Charles Erland, Hank Crawford, Jimmy McGriff, Nat Adderly, Houston Person, Etta Jones, and many others. Joe has performed with the legendary Carrie Smith blues/gospel singer on three jazz festival cruises.

Joe has received the Key to the City of Newark from Mayor Gibson and the Whaler's Emblem which is tantamount the "The Key to the City" from Mayor Edward Harrington of New Bedford, Mass, for his musical accomplishments. He has also performed for the former President of Haiti, Jean Claude Duvalier.

JIHAD

Jihad was an intelligent child who was raised by a single mother in Atlanta, GA by way of Indianapolis, IN. By the age of 16 he was selling drugs and embarking on a criminal career that six years later would lead him to prison, but not before his lifestyle would cause him to be stabbed, shot on three different occasions, and left paralyzed from a car accident. Although over time he miraculously regained the use of his legs he still served over seven years in six different federal prisons up and down the east coast. While serving time, Jihad gravitated towards a group of older, socio-political, self-taught prisoners who raised his awareness about himself and his past. He discovered a love of books, mostly by black authors and historians, which was something that had never grasped his interest while in school. Jihad started researching and writing about subjects that he was sure many misunderstood. Subjects like history, religion, hood-psyche and society in general. His focus and discipline prepared him to write his first book, an autobiographical novel entitled Street Life. Since penning his first title from prison back in August of 1998, Jihad has gone on to write four other thought provoking, enthralling novels, Baby Girl, Riding Rhythm, MVP, and his latest Preacherman Blues. Jihad is highly energetic, provocative and compassionate about youth issues. He's a highly sought after inspirational speaker who always avails himself for interviews. For more on Jihad, log onto www.jihadwrites.com.

WILLIAM FREDRICK COOPER

William Fredrick Cooper. An Assistant Managing Clerk at a midtown law firm, a member of First Corinthians Baptist Church in Harlem, New York and a proud father of a lovely daughter named Maranda, Mr. Cooper is the active secretary of Brother 2 Brother Symposium, Inc, a non-for-profit literacy program that encourages black men and young adults to read fiction literature. An ordinary guy trying to make a difference, Mr. Cooper is the author of the critically acclaimed novel Six Days In January as well as the African-American Literary Award-Nominated, National Bestseller There's Always A Reason. Described by writing peers as a message-delivering, emotional masterpiece within the African-American Community, There's Always A Reason was a Master's List Finalist for a 2008 NAACP Image Award Nomination in the Outstanding Literary Work Fiction Category. Touching minds when giving thought-provoking radio interviews or in the alternative, moderating or facilitating panel discussions throughout North America, capturing hearts when writing enlightening, uplifting fiction, and arousing female bodies when composing white-hot erotica tales, he has contributed articles to national periodicals such as EBONY MAGAZINE and many Bestselling anthologies and novels such as Zane's Dear G-Spot: Straight Talk About Sex and Love, Twilight Moods: African-American Erotica, Zane's Caramel Flava, Sistergirls.com, Morning, Noon and Night: Can't Get Enough and Erogenous Zone: A Sexual Voyage. He can be reached at his e-mail address: areason006@yahoo.com

ALVIN C. ROMER

Alvin C. Romer, is a Freelance Writer, Journalist and Essayist calling Miami, Florida home, and is the father of 5. He is the Founder and Editor of a popular online African-American literature site, THE ROMER REVIEW and devotes quite a bit of time as an Editor, Literary Publicist, and as an Independent Book Reviewer in the African-American publishing Diaspora. He frequently hires himself out as a Demographer and as a Technical Writer in the corporate world. A successful businessman, Romer currently is self-employed as the CEO/President of ACR Data Research, Inc., a Deacon in his church working with the Children of the Kingdom, and a successful grant writer and motivational speaker. All things literary and a supporter of the humanities, he strives to keep the muse as directives in his quest for legitimacy. Teaching creative writing and giving workshops on the publishing industry are also a part of his legacy. Much of his literary acumen can be found on his website which houses the subsidiary Write On! Literary Services, an organization that helps aspiring writers, edits manuscripts, plan events; generate marketing & publicity, along with book reviewing. His non-profit organization, The South Florida Literary & Education Foundation (SFLEF) is committed to making life and attaining educational goals a priority for needy and risky kids. Mr. Romer aspires to one day join the ranks of published novelists, and is currently producing a two-volume set of essays, short stories, and poems.

MARC LACY

Huntsville's own Marc Lacy, a graduate of Alabama A&M University is a nationally renown, award-winning poet/author and spoken word artist. He has performed all of over the country for many national literary events and spoken word venues. Marc is the author of Rock & Fire - Love Poetry from The Core, and The Looking Heart - Poetic Expressions from Within. He is also the producer of REFlux and RTIQLation spoken word CDs. Marc is the contributor to many anthologies such as: The Soul of a Man, Step up to The Mic, and Witness the Truth. He is the co-host of Essence Best Selling Author Donna Hill's...The Donna Hill Blogtalkradio show which airs weekly.

Marc is due to release during the summer of 2009: Wretched Saints - Spiritual Fiction Short Stories, LyriCode 256, and LickOrice spoken word cds. Marc is a member of ArtNSoul Society of Expression, Alpha Phi Alpha Fraternity, Inc., Church Street CPCA, Huntsville Literary Association, and National Society of Black Engineers. He credits his faith in God and love of family for providing energy to succeed. Checkout marclacy.com, myspace.com/mlacy, and Facebook (Marc Lacy).

CLARENCE "BABA SIMBA" MOLLOCK

Clarence B. Mollock, a native of Maryland's Eastern Shore, is number five of eight children who grew up on a farm. He was diagnosed with a speech disorder while in the fifth grade. After speech therapy and years of practice he began to master the English language. Before and after integration in 1966, he developed a love for reading. That love enabled him to be the only minority to graduate in the National Honor Society. Pursuing his number one love - Pottery - he graduated from Bowie State University with a degree to teach Art. Shortly after receiving a Masters Degree in Art Education from Towson State University, he meant Mother Mary Carter Smith, a storyteller. She was later proclaimed Maryland's Official Griot. With her guidance he, too, became a storyteller. She inspired him to write his stories of accomplishments and failures - of pain and pleasures. In 2005, Clarence retired after teaching Art for thirty-two years. He is a member of the National Association of Black Storytellers, Inc. and a past President of the Griots' Circle of Maryland, Inc., the local affiliate in Baltimore, Maryland where he resides. Today, many know him as Baba Simba Mollock.

BRIAN GANGES

Brian Ganges is a native New Jerseyan who resides in Houston, Texas. He has written many articles that are very thought provoking, principled, informative and insightful. His topics (including secular) of interest are: current events, politics, health related topics, economics, relationships, and principles for daily living; which are always from a Christian worldview. Brian is currently working on his debut book entitled "The World According to BG: Real Perspective for Real Issues," to be released in the near future. He communicates with his growing audience via his website www.insightfortoday.blogspot.com regarding his new articles, speaking engagements, radio interviews and upcoming events. Brian has also worked with and/or met some prominent politicians in the past, which includes radio interviews that he did with 2008 US Presidential candidates Former UN Ambassador Alan Keyes and US Congressman Ron Paul. Brian can be reached at bgnjtx@yahoo.com for more information.

Jarold Imes

Jarold Imes is the author of the Hold On Be Strong Teen Series, a collection of books that focuses on young black men and their issues. He is a contributor to OurTeenVoices.com and TheUrbanBookSource.com. He lives in Winston-Salem, North Carolina with his family, where he is working on his first Street Christian Lit title. The Journey to Create Fiction for Young Black Men Continues... SUPPORT THE MOVEMENT!

K.L. BELVIN

I was born and still reside in South Jamaica, Queens, New York. At 40 years of age I am a Christian, a father of four, a teacher for the New York City Department of Education over ten years, and recently married. My lovely supportive wife is my strength, best friend, and 1st editor of most of my work. I obtained my A.S. in Business from Kingsborough Community College, B.S. in Education from York College, and holds a Master's Degree in Education from Walden University.

I anticipate beginning my PhD. studies in late 2008. A writer of fictional stories and poetry I have completed my first book titled "A Man in Transition". A mixture of poems, stories and my observations of the world. Over the years I changed my writing focus from erotic based content to romance and spiritual inspirations due to my religious choices. I hope to offer the world focused insight of a man who has completely changed his life. I believe my writing expresses my growth as a man who now attempts to offer counsel, entertainment, and guidance to all I meet.

JOEY PINKNEY

Joey Pinkney's love for books and reading naturally turned into book reviewing. His book reviews have been featured on the websites of The Urban Book Source, C&B Books Distribution, RapWars, Glover Publishing as well as his own JoeyPinkney.com, and on Myspace, myspace.com/joeyreviews. He also produces the "5 Minutes, 5 Questions With..." series where he interviews authors of various genres. The closet novelist, Pinkney is honored to be a part of The Soul of a Man anthology. "Like Father, Like Son" is his first published short story. He wants to continue being a book reviewer/interviewer and add author as a regular part of his repertoire.

THOMAS ASHBURN, JR.

Thomas Ashburn, Jr. has had a passion for writing since high school. He is the author of God's Greater Glory: Why We Experience Hardship. Thomas graduated from Norfolk State University with a bachelor's of arts in journalism. He has written several articles for daily newspapers on topics like religion, race, and entertainment. Thomas is a member of St. Mary's Holiness Church in Chesapeake, Virginia where his father, Thomas Ashburn, Sr. is pastor. He is a deacon and financial trustee at St. Mary's. Thomas's purpose for writing is to glorify God and to inspire others to overcome every obstacle. He can be reached at ashburn_thomas@hotmail.com.

Tyrell DeVon Floyd

Tyrell DeVon Floyd. This twenty-something innovative poet, writer, and radio personality hails from the Great Northwest. Although Seattle, WA is chiefly known for its beautiful scenery and memorable rain falls, it can also stake claim as being home to one of the up-and-coming minds of story and poetry.

Invoking passion and emotion through deep story lines and raw subject matters, the words of Tyrell DeVon Floyd are sure to resonate with readers. Whether it be a love poem such as Butterflies Arrive as Beauty Flies Away, or a romantic poem of intimacy such as Into Her of Course, this young writer seamlessly connects his words with the interests of those who read them.

MAURICE M. GRAY, JR.

Maurice M. Gray, Jr. is an author (of two novels), an editor, a speaker and a comedian. He currently serves on the faculties of the Sandy Cove and the Greater Philadelphia Christian Writers Conferences, where he evaluates manuscripts for conferees and teaches workshops. Along with Lacricia A'ngelle, Dr. Linda Beed, and Wanda Campbell, he is a member of the Damascus Road Authors. As a Christian comedian, Maurice has worked with the likes of James "The Storyteller" Ford and Pat "Sister Betty" G'orge-Walker. Maurice is a member of Bethel AME Church in Wilmington, DE, where he is active in many ministries (including the Singles Ministry and the Men's Chorus). He is also a member of Kappa Alpha Psi Fraternity, Inc and of the Greater Newark Area Toastmasters club. He lives in New Castle, DE with his family. Please visit Maurice online at www.MauriceMGrayJr.com.

EDDRICK DEJUAN

Eddrick Dejuan currently lives in St. Louis, Mo. He is a veteran having served a stint in the U.S. Air Force. He is the author of the entertaining book Madam Eve and the owner of Atonement Publishing. He is also building his publishing company into a brand, all the books released by the imprint will feature the theme of revenge and forgiveness. Every book that he writes will have the main character go on a journey from wanting to getting even to forgiving. Eddrick Dejuan can be reached at ed@eddrickdejuan.com. Please visit his website at www.eddrickdejuan.com

ELISSA GABRIELLE

Author, Publisher, Poet, & Visionary is the author of two poetry books and three novels. We first met this incredible talent with her debut collection of strong and moving verse, Stand and Be Counted. Focusing on themes of love, race, religion, inspiration and society, Elissa Gabrielle has put together a collection of inspirational poetry geared toward positive change that is both moving and entertaining. Through insightful visions and strong declarations, Gabrielle instills confidence in readers as she illuminates the path to a more self-rewarding and gratifying life.

Utilizing the resurgence of her desire to write and "a God given talent that wouldn't go away," Elissa Gabrielle was inspired to pen Peace In The Storm, which has testimonials from some of the entertainment industry's finest. Peace In The Storm came to Gabrielle while reflecting real life experiences, both her own and from the lives of others. Elissa is the Creator and CEO of Greetings From the Soul: The Elissa Gabrielle Collection which is a greeting card line that features poignant messages and heartfelt poetry and themes. Find out more at www.greetingsfromthesoul.com. A contributor to several outstanding literary works, Elissa has graced the covers of Disilgold Soul Magazine, Big Time Publishing Magazine and Conversations Magazine. Gabrielle is a graduate of the Connecticut School of Broadcasting. She also holds a degree in Communications. Elissa has a certificate in Business from Tulane University's A.B. Freeman School of Business which she earned March 2004. Gabrielle is a member of NABFEME, the National Association of Black Female Executives in Music and Entertainment, a professional empowerment, networking and support base for African American women in radio, recorded music, the media, and related entertainment industry fields. Elissa is the creator of The Triumph Series, and the first book in the series, The Triumph of My Soul was nominated for several literary awards. The Soul of a Man and The

Breakthrough are the second and third in the Triumph series, respectively.

Elissa is the Founder and CEO of Peace In The Storm Publishing, LLC, which will release incredible titles from gifted authors beginning in January 2009, www.PeaceintheStormPublishing.com.

Elissa Gabrielle is the Media Consultant for both First Bethel Baptist Church and the Baptist Ministers Conference of Newark & Vicinity in Newark, New Jersey. Find out more at www.PeaceintheStormPublishing.com.

THE SOUL OF A MAN
Ordering Information

Yes! Please send me _______ copies of
The Soul of a Man.

Please include $15.00 plus $4.00 shipping/handling for the first book and $1.00 for each additional book.

Send my book(s) to:

Name:______________________________________
Address:____________________________________
City, State, Zip:_____________________________
Telephone:__________________________________
Email:______________________________________

Would you like to receive emails from
Peace In The Storm Publishing?
____Yes _____No

Peace In The Storm Publishing, LLC.
Attn: Book Orders
P.O. Box 1152
Pocono Summit, PA 18346

VISIT US ON THE WEB
www.PeaceInTheStormPublishing.com

Printed in the United States
146470LV00002B/2/P

9 780981 963136